Praise

MW00989428

"Who hasn't longed to be someone richer, more glamorous, more famous, more fashionable, more powerful and alluring? Who hasn't wanted to slip out of their own skin? Kirthana Ramisetti explores these ideas through a zany protagonist who makes the highly questionable, yet hilarious choice to assume a wealthy Mumbai socialite's identity. Yet, for all *The Other Lata*'s humor, hijinks, and memorable party scenes, Ramisetti also tackles deeper themes of identity, belonging, class, and money in her third novel. While ultimately posing the question: How radical would it be, in fact, to love our true selves?"

—Daphne Palasi Andreades, author of *Brown Girls*

"*The Other Lata* is an energetic romp through New York City's high society, following our eponymous heroine, Lata, as she navigates the dizzying transformation from outsider into bona fide insider. This cat-and-mouse game of mistaken identity and deception will delight fans of both rom-coms and suspense."

—Caitlin Barasch, author of *A Novel Obsession*

"As lively and refreshing as a chilled glass of champagne, *The Other Lata* is a sharp, surprising exploration of identity, class, and what it means to truly belong. Kirthana Ramisetti has done it again!"

—Kirstin Chen, *New York Times* bestselling author of *Counterfeit*

"Identity thief Lata Murthy is all heart, an endearing underdog with a penchant for lying and stealing. She bounces around high society scenes in New York City and the Hamptons, but I would have followed Lata's antics anywhere. The hot dog juggling scene (yes, you read that correctly) in particular had me cackling. Thanks to Ramisetti's assured prose, *The Other Lata* manages to be both a delicious romp and a profound examination of what it means to belong. Move over, Anna Delvey."

—Stephanie Wrobel, internationally and *USA Today*
bestselling author of *The Hitchcock Hotel*

"Kirthana Ramisetti's latest novel is both irresistible and impossible to put down! If you received an email invitation for a more exciting life, wouldn't you consider accepting it? Readers everywhere will be surprised and satisfied with Lata's journey with identity, power dynamics, and New York City. I know this will be a story that so many readers will love to return to. *The Other Lata* is my favorite type of novel: juicy, clever, and full of heart."

—Saumya Dave, author of *The Guilt Pill*

"*The Other Lata* is a page-turning examination of class, wealth, and privilege, and just how fully you can erase yourself in a desperate attempt to be seen. Ramisetti is a master at creating the kinds of complex and nuanced female protagonists you can't help rooting for even when they're at their most exasperating. Fans of *Inventing Anna* will be taken in by this compulsive mistaken identity romcom that's as insightful as it is satisfying."

—Bianca Marais, internationally bestselling author
of *The Witches of Moonshyne Manor*

"Energizing, riveting, and often very funny, *The Other Lata* features a scammer you won't be able to stop rooting for. When Lata receives an invite to a fancy affair meant for another Lata Murthy, she decides to RSVP yes—setting off a whirlwind chain of events that includes romance, mystery, and even crime. With subtle but effective nods to classism and racism, Kirthana Ramisetti's newest is thought-provoking while also unendingly fun."

—Julia Bartz, *New York Times* bestselling
author of *The Writing Retreat*

Praise for *Advika and the Hollywood Wives*

"Kirthana Ramisetti is a gifted storyteller, and *Advika and the Hollywood Wives* is such a gift. The glitz and underlying darkness of Hollywood make for a setting as complex and compelling as Ramisetti's characters, and every page of this smart, sharply observed novel rings with insight—and with heart."

—Meena Harris, #1 *New York Times* bestselling author

"I could not put this book down. Advika is the kind of heroine we've all been waiting for: readers will laugh with her and cheer her on as she opens our eyes to the truths of grief and sisterhood, of friendship and love, of ambition and fame. Kirthana Ramisetti has a rare gift for penning page-turners full of wisdom, nuance, and depth, and I know I am not alone in saying that I will read any book she writes."

—Qian Julie Wang, *New York Times* bestselling author of *Beautiful Country*

"Pure delight! With Advika, Kirthana Ramisetti has gifted us the boldest of heroines—one who will fight to discover her own worth, and learn to love what she finds."

—Mira Jacob, author of *Good Talk*

"A Cinderella tale with a dark twist. Beneath the glamorous exterior of this page-turner is a thoughtful story about female empowerment and what happens when promises of happily ever after don't quite meet fairy tale expectations."

—Margarita Montimore, *USA Today* bestselling author

"Kirthana Ramisetti is quickly becoming the go-to author for nuanced stories about fame, family, and love. *Advika and the Hollywood Wives* is an insightful and moving portrayal of a woman fighting for what she deserves. Told with equal parts humor and heart, this delightful novel is sure to be a favorite for book clubs!"

—Saumya Dave, author of *What a Happy Family*

"*Advika and the Hollywood Wives* is my favorite kind of novel: smart yet unassuming, entertaining, and deeply compassionate. With sharp characters and complex insight on fame, ambition, love, and loss, Kirthana Ramisetti has given us a page-turner for movie buffs and book worms alike."

—Liv Stratman, author of *Cheat Day*

"*Advika and the Hollywood Wives* is my favorite kind of page-turner: packed with juice, humor, intrigue, and a complex heroine on a quest to discover what's real beyond the mirage of all that glitters. Kirthana Ramisetti's knowledge of celebrity culture shines through in every scene, and I couldn't help but binge!"

—Dawnie Walton, author of *The Final Revival of Opal & Nev*

"Kirthana Ramisetti has a knack for the intriguing, propulsive kind of writing that had us sneaking our mother's paperbacks as teens. Like *Dava Shastri*, *Advika* is a good old-fashioned page-turner, centered around a character we've never seen in fiction, but sorely needed to meet."

—Priyanka Mattoo, writer and filmmaker

"This delicious book is for all of us who love romantic comedies—and yet also mistrust the ways Hollywood romantic tropes can stifle our individuality and creativity in real life. Ramisetti's zippy, nuanced take on the Bluebeard tale is especially insightful about who gets to be a professional storyteller, and about the pressure to squeeze our lives and stories into the boxes prescribed by popular culture."

—Kate Reed Petty, author of *True Story*

"This book is deliciously suspenseful. I raced through the pages and found not just a delightful intrigue but also a thoughtful exploration of manipulation, power, and the legacy of sisterhood."

—Marie Rutkoski, author of *Real Easy*

"Suspenseful and cinematic, *Advika and the Hollywood Wives* will have you on the edge of your seat from the very first page through the nail-biting grand finale. Kirthana Ramisetti is a novelist in the tradition of Jane Austen, masterfully blending complex human psychology and sharp comedy to bring her finely drawn characters to vivid life. This book is both a cautionary tale about power imbalance in a relationship (trust your instincts, ladies!) and a valentine to friends who are like family."

—Erin Carlson, author of *I'll Have What She's Having: How Nora Ephron's Three Iconic Films Saved the Romantic Comedy*

"A page-turner packed with mystery, drama, and romance."

—Associated Press

"Nails the Hollywood milieu and offers an incisive portrait of Julian, a powerful man who feels compelled to control the women in his life. This is a winner."

—*Publishers Weekly*

"Looks at Hollywood from a unique and unflinching lens, but also allows for themes of grief, friendship, and love to bloom in unexpecting ways."

—*Cosmopolitan*

"Part love story, part thriller, this novel will appeal to fans of Hollywood and May-December romance."

—*Kirkus Reviews*

"A vivid, engrossing drama…Ramisetti juxtaposes the glitz and glamour of Hollywood against its underbelly of power imbalances, racism, and the consumption of young hopefuls, especially women. Deep, thoughtful characterization of Advika and the former wives brings extra heft to a complex story of wish fulfillment gone wrong."

—*Shelf Awareness*

"Ramisetti excels at holding back just enough to keep you furiously turning the pages looking for answers in this mystery-meets-romance."

—*BuzzFeed*

"A compelling portrait of a young woman fighting erasure, learning to accept help from her friends, and coming into her own."

—*Booklist*

"A disturbing twist on the classic Cinderella tale…Juicy, propulsive and insightful."

—*Parade*

Praise for *Dava Shastri's Last Day*

"A rich portrait of a family facing their powerful matriarch's death, *Dava Shastri's Last Day* is full of music, magnetism, and familial obligation. If *Succession* were about a multicultural family who actually loved each other, it might look like this."

—Emma Straub, author of *All Adults Here*

"Ramisetti beautifully weaves keen analysis of celebrity culture and a deep love of music into this perceptive, intergenerational story of resentment, trauma, love, and redemption. A page-turner with humor, heart, and lots of pop music."

—Jennifer Keishin Armstrong, *New York Times* bestselling author of *Seinfeldia*

"Kirthana Ramisetti has written a sweeping saga and also a poignant story about sacrifice and the exacting price of secrecy. Cinematic and intimate, *Dava Shastri's Last Day* is an intricate story about family and love."

—Devi S. Laskar, author of *The Atlas of Reds and Blues*

"*Dava Shastri's Last Day* is a story about ambition and greatness, wealth and family, full of secrets, love, and music, and those eternal pop song complements: heartbreak and hope. It's a gripping, deeply satisfying story about one woman's tremendous life—and the infinitely complicated ways we create our own legacies."

—Kate Racculia, author of *Tuesday Mooney Talks to Ghosts* and *Bellweather Rhapsody*

"Ramisetti draws nuanced characters who are introspective and entertaining."

—*Kirkus Reviews*

THE
OTHER
LATA

KIRTHANA RAMISETTI

THE OTHER LATA

GRAND
CENTRAL

New York Boston

Copyright © 2025 by Kirthana Ramisetti
Cover art & design by Sarah Congdon. Cover copyright
© 2025 by Hachette Book Group, Inc.

Grand Central Publishing
Hachette Book Group
1290 Avenue of the Americas, New York, NY 10104
grandcentralpublishing.com
@grandcentralpub

First Edition: April 2025

Grand Central Publishing is a division of Hachette Book Group, Inc. The Grand Central Publishing name and logo is a registered trademark of Hachette Book Group, Inc.

The publisher is not responsible for websites (or their content) that are not owned by the publisher.

The Hachette Speakers Bureau provides a wide range of authors for speaking events. To find out more, go to hachettespeakersbureau.com or email HachetteSpeakers@hbgusa.com.

Grand Central Publishing books may be purchased in bulk for business, educational, or promotional use. For information, please contact your local bookseller or the Hachette Book Group Special Markets Department at special.markets@hbgusa.com.

Library of Congress Cataloging-in-Publication Data

Names: Ramisetti, Kirthana, author.
Title: The other Lata / Kirthana Ramisetti.
Description: First edition. | New York ; Boston : GCP, 2025.
Identifiers: LCCN 2024047916 | ISBN 9781538770993
(trade paperback) | ISBN 9781538771006 (ebook)
Subjects: LCSH: New York (N.Y.)—Fiction. | LCGFT: Romance fiction. | Novels.
Classification: LCC PS3618.A4656 O84 2025 | DDC 813/.6—dc23/eng/20241021
LC record available at https://lccn.loc.gov/2024047916

ISBNs: 9781538770993 (trade paperback), 9781538771006 (ebook)

Printed in the United States of America

LSC-C

Printing 1, 2025

For Corey

THE
OTHER
LATA

1

Zara

I SHOULD HAVE NEVER OPENED the email. If I needed to pinpoint the exact moment my life went from forgettable to flaming disaster, it would be clicking "Invite! Elephantine Presents Galaxy Unknown," even though it wasn't intended for me. It was meant for her, of course. But the invitation had landed in my inbox—latamurthy@gmail.com—and didn't that make it officially my property?

Also, I was bored.

I blame August in New York. The dullest month of the year, and the hottest and most miserable. Anyone who could afford to flee the city's swampiness had already done so, and the people who remained behind were too poor to do anything but await the arrival of that most blessed month of possibility and beautiful weather, September.

On the first Saturday night of August, I was in my fifth-floor walk-up in Hell's Kitchen, sitting between two fans, wearing only a blue bralette and boxer shorts, and fanning myself with an IKEA catalog. With $630 in my checking account, I was playing shopping roulette on Zara.com. I would go click, click, click on everything I coveted, then close my eyes and unclick as many items in my basket as possible before moving my cursor to "Purchase." (I had done this so many times that I had memorized exactly where I needed to position my mouse.) In this instance, all I ended up with was a gold-studded leather belt that cost $52. I hadn't overspent, but I hadn't bought anything exciting either.

When my email pinged to notify me of the purchase, I went to Gmail to move the Zara.com notification to my "Shopping Roulette" folder, which was my way of pretending I was in control of my impulse spending. The IKEA catalog slipped out of my hand when my phone rang.

"What are you up to?" said Mimi between slurps of what sounded like a Popsicle.

"Getting ready for my date with Leo—we're taking his yacht to Saint-Tropez." I leaned over the side of my bed to retrieve the catalog, but my hand only swept over dust balls and a sandal.

"And any second I'm going to walk down the aisle to marry Antonio Banderas. I told him he needs to wear the Zorro mask on our wedding night." More noisy slurping and biting. "*The Great Food Truck Race* is on in a couple minutes. The third season, with the twin grannies. Wanna watch?"

"Okay." Usually we'd be hanging out together on a Saturday night, with me making the trek to Mimi's because she had a studio in Williamsburg and I had roommates. But neither of us were willing to take the subway to each other's borough on sweltering nights like this one. So we made do by watching TV while gossiping on the phone.

During a commercial break three episodes later, Mimi was in the bathroom and I was trying to stay awake. *Food Truck Race* was Mimi's show, while I preferred *Chopped*. I went back to my Gmail to take a look at the leather belt. I could see myself wearing it with my black J.Crew dress while getting drinks at Tao or the Electric Room. But fifty dollars could also go toward groceries or my portion of the cable bill. My practical side won out, and I clicked the link to cancel the order.

Food Truck Race had returned, but Mimi hadn't resumed her running commentary. "Meems?" I called out. "Are you there?"

Disinterested in *Food Truck Race* without her, I scrolled through the various folders of my inbox: "Work (Ugh)," "Shopping Roulette," "Bills Bills Bills," "Writing Projects," "Promotions," "Spam." And in that last category was where I saw the email for Lata Murthy.

I had no idea what an Elephantine was, let alone a Galaxy Unknown. But the invitation was so minimal—just a date (August 10, 2013), location (Iron23), and dress code (black or white attire only)—that I couldn't help but be intrigued. Since moving to New York ten years ago, I had attended a lot of parties that were so tryhard that they made me feel pathetic to be there. Think cheap-ass wine in cracked plastic cups, DJ Stupidhead playing some blippy musical nonsense with the occasional Robyn track thrown in.

"Hey, what did I miss?" Mimi was in my ear, slightly breathless.

"Sorry, wasn't paying attention. Actually, can I call you back in a few?" My fingers were already typing "Elephantine" into Google.

"Yeah, sure. But wait to call me during a commercial." Mimi's passion for *Food Truck Race* was inexplicable, but we were friends because we respected each other's weird obsessions.

Elephantine was a jewelry line that specialized in what they called "conversation pieces," which was just a fancy way to say "impractical and odd." Silver necklaces that featured pendants that spelled out random words like "beeswax" and "golly," neon-pink earrings in the shape of fishes and snails, arm bracelets fashioned out of twisted nails that seemed painful to wear. And rather than prices, each piece was given a colored dot. The five colors represented different price ranges, the cheapest at $300 and the most expensive at $12,000. I clicked through every single item, noting that all the jewelry was assigned to collections with inscrutable names like Manic Elixir and Serpentine Arise. Whatever Galaxy Unknown was, there was no trace of it on Elephantine's website.

I was still clicking through the site when Mimi called me back.

"You're missing the whole episode."

"Oh, sorry! I was just looking at something online." I set my laptop aside, as it was starting to overheat on my lap. "I might be done with TV for the night."

"It's only nine thirty." A pause. "Lata, don't invite Simon over. I don't care if he lives across the street. You can't treat dating like ordering takeout. It can't just be about convenience."

I hadn't slept with Simon in two weeks. I'd like to ascribe it to my restraint, but he'd gone to hike a mountain in Chile or Peru, somewhere exotic and, more importantly, far away.

"Are you kidding me?" I got up and headed to the kitchen to grab a Vitaminwater. As I'd expected, the living room could double as a sauna. "This has nothing to do with him, or any guys. I was just doing...research." I wasn't normally so cagey with Mimi. But I hadn't told anyone about the Lata Murthy emails yet, not even Mimi, who I'd known since our freshman year at Seton Hall.

"Well, just making sure. For your sanity as well as mine." She yawned. "Good night, then, early bird. I'm waiting up for Evan, he should be home by two."

Evan was Mimi's occasional fling turned official boyfriend as of one week ago. She met him at Cake Shop when he was playing guitar with his band, Misfit Slime. Yes, that was the real name of his band. And no, they weren't very good.

"Oh, wait, did I tell you he invited me to go when they play Craterfest?"

No, Mimi had not. "That's great!" I said too brightly. "When is that?"

"They're taking off Monday for Milwaukee to do some gigs in the area. I'm actually flying out Friday so I can see them at the festival. And then I'm using up the rest of my vacation days to join them on tour." She said this with some caginess too, as if this trip had been planned for weeks, but she was only telling me now.

"Wow, Mimi, sounds like fun." Had Mimi and Evan been serious for longer than she let on?

"I'm so excited. Sixteen days on the road, it won't be glamorous," she said with a nervous laugh. "But it's going to be a blast, I know it."

After hanging up with Mimi, I dug through the back of the refrigerator, where I hid my dragonfruit Vitaminwaters from Eleanor and Mallory, my two roommates, who were away that weekend. In fact, I really only hid my Vitaminwaters from Eleanor, even though she could afford a metric ton of Vitaminwaters if she wanted, yet always plucked away at my stash without a word. I kept wanting to tell Eleanor that none of our food and drink was communal, but then that would mean I couldn't snack on the cheese plates she brought back from her event-planning job. But it wasn't like she spent money on the cheese plates, whereas I allocated twenty dollars of my salary to buy one twelve-pack of Vitaminwaters per month.

Back in my bedroom, I sipped my drink, spent a little more time perusing the Elephantine website, and learned that the jewelry line had been started by Aqua (no last name), the only daughter of a former child star best known for the hit sitcom *Blondes Just Want to Have Fun*. Aqua had dropped everything that could make her immediately identifiable with her mother, from her name to her Farrah Fawcett–esque hair. She sported a shaved head, a septum piercing, and lavender-colored eyes, and the photo on her website showed her with a piece of masking tape over her mouth stamped with the word UGLY and crossed out with a red slash.

Everything about Aqua and her jewelry screamed "try-hard." And yet I still wanted to go to her event.

My thoughts went back to Mimi. I liked to tease her about

her taste in what I called grubbies: twenty-something men with ripped jeans and holey T-shirts, greasy hair, and dirt under their fingernails. Artist types who spent more time talking about art than they did creating anything. Maybe that was why she hadn't shared a lot about Evan. Mimi would know I could never understand how she could be excited about the prospect of traveling to Milwaukee with a bunch of grubbies to a sweaty music festival. I hadn't left the tristate area in over fifteen years, but I imagined that once I did, it would be to visit a place that was exclusively made up of white sands and palm trees. And even then, I'd still feel a bit wistful for the city.

As someone who was born and raised in Connecticut, attended college in New Jersey, and resided in New York, I defined myself by my tristateness. I even had the outlines of the three states as a tattoo, which I had gotten one month after moving to the city. It wasn't that I adored my hometown, nor could I say that four years at Seton Hall had been an incredible experience. But they had made me into the person who wanted to make it—and stay, hopefully forever—in New York City. I couldn't deny that the ambition that burned in me came from growing up in a suburb with my parents, who worked so hard that most of my childhood was marked by their absence. I couldn't deny that this ambition only doubled during my time at Seton Hall. No matter how many wonderful friends or fun memories I'd made, my time there had an asterisk next to it because I'd really wanted to go to Columbia, but I'd never made it off the wait list. The tristate tattoo could have been a literal chip on my shoulder, except that I opted to have it hidden away just above my bikini line. My tristateness was my origin story, my simultaneous kryptonite and superpower, and too personal to share with anyone else.

At that very moment, though, my tristateness couldn't abate my malaise. I thought of the next few weeks without Mimi, without Simon, weekends spent in my tiny bedroom with the noisy fans and cable television to keep me company, too broke to do anything fun or interesting. In that moment, I could envision myself running on this same tired treadmill of cheap Chinese takeout and *Chopped* reruns and shopping roulette with no end in sight.

"Argh," I yelled toward the ceiling. And then of course that was when I received a text from my mother. **Still coming tomorrow?** A simple question that nevertheless stung like an accusation.

Yes, Mom. I'll take the eleven a.m. train to New Canaan so I can sit on the sofa between you and Dad while you ask me "How are your friends?" (a.k.a. *Have you met someone yet?*) and "How is your website job?" (a.k.a. *When will you find a better one?*). It's a biweekly ritual we feel that we must do, even though Dad just wants to watch his cricket game, you want to watch your Shah Rukh Khan movies, and I pretend not to notice that the two of you barely speak to each other. That I suspect Dad moved into my bedroom as soon as I left for college, and you are still together because divorce is simply not an option. We will gather around the dining table and eat rotis in silence, while I wonder whether there is anything I can say to break the pall that has settled over your worn face and Dad's slumping shoulders. The word "family" barely applies to us, but we all cling to it out of habit and shared DNA, and I will take the train to see you two because it is the one thing I can do that will not fully disappoint you.

I texted back, **Yep, see you then**.

Outside, rowdy chatter from the Irish bar on my building's first floor floated five stories up, loud enough to be heard over my still-whirring fans. Hell's Kitchen was not an ideal neighborhood to live in on a Saturday night when everyone in the city was out and you could only afford to stay in. Even so, living in Manhattan was victory enough. At least, that was what I had always consoled myself with any time I felt pangs of distress over my paltry salary, or jealousy over college friends climbing the ladder from engagement and marriage to home ownership in Hoboken or Jersey City.

I picked up my laptop just as the screen saver went off, and the dark screen revealed my reflection. My untended eyebrows, my watery, downturned eyes, my thin lips pursed together. Even my high cheekbones, indisputably my best feature, were sprinkled with acne. With Simon out of the country, I guess I hadn't been as strident with my beauty routine. But beyond my bedraggled state, what disturbed me the most was how much I looked like my mother. Her light had already gone out. But mine was fading, and fading fast.

A bleak reality crystallized for me. At age thirty-three, with one dead-end job, two roommates, three credit cards nearing their limits, and four years since my last relationship, it was hard to see how living here could still be seen as any kind of victory.

So I was indeed bored when I clicked "yes" on the other

Lata's invitation. But let me clarify that I was bored with *myself*. Bored with my mediocrity. Because somewhere in New York City, the place that was supposed to change my life, and instead had only put me in debt, there was another Lata Murthy having a more dazzling time than me. And just for one night, I would step into her glass slippers and turn myself into Cinderella and see what it was like to be her.

———

Who was this other Lata Murthy? At the time, I had no idea. The emails had begun in January, trickling in about once a month. At first I thought I got added to some high-end mailing list by mistake, but the fourth one I opened was addressed to the other Lata directly.

Darling Lata, you must come! said the personalized message sent from melodie@bonvivant.com, followed by an invitation to a silent auction held at an Upper East Side manor. Not only that, but it had been sent to two email addresses: mine and thelatamurthy@gmail.com. I understood how it was easy to get us mixed up, but I also took umbrage at this Lata declaring herself "the" Lata, as if she had already determined she was superior to the rest of us. Even so, I sent the other Lata a quick message to let her know that I had received a few of her emails, and offered to forward them to her. But I received no reply.

Nevertheless, Darling Lata continued to be asked to attend art exhibits and cocktail parties and museum fundraisers, and starting in June, the invitations began arriving in my Gmail on a twice-weekly basis. By that point I greedily opened each one, curious to see where my glamorous name doppelgänger was being asked to next. When an email with the subject heading "Midsummer's Night at Soho Grand" arrived in my inbox, sandwiched between my cable bill and a *BuzzFeed* job application rejection, my curiosity mutated into a jealous despair.

So on that first Saturday of August, I decided to reframe how to think of these emails: as a sign that whatever magic had once visited the other Lata had now been transferred to me.

2

Alice +
Olivia

ON THE SECOND SATURDAY OF August, I stood outside a nondescript building in the Flatiron District, wearing a white Alice + Olivia dress with puffy sleeves, purchased at 70 percent off from TJ Maxx. My full-price Amina Muaddi slingbacks pinched my big toes, which usually would irritate me, except I was too busy fanning myself with an *amNewYork* I had picked up in desperation to combat the sticky humidity of an eighty-one-degree evening. I had dedicated forty minutes to straightening my hair when I should have just thrown it into a ponytail, since a quick glance at my reflection in a window showed it frizzing at the ends, like a straight line abruptly bending into a comma. After a sluggish fifteen minutes, I was finally just steps away from entering the party. When the couple in front of me were allowed inside, I tossed the newspaper and stood tall while jutting out my chin, trying to evoke the insouciance I imagined the other Lata would feel attending this event. It would be just another night for her, after all.

"Name," said the doorman, who had a large headset attached to his ear and the insouciance I was desperately trying to muster.

"Lata Murthy." I looked him in the eye, as if to prove I wasn't lying. And I wasn't, not really. He checked his clipboard and looked me over from head to toe. Then he gave me a curt nod and stepped aside to let me in.

So simple! I gave him a curt nod in return, then shuffled past him in my four-inch heels before he could change his mind. I took an elevator along with two dudes in white suit jackets and one in a tuxedo shirt and shorts, and the collision of all their heavy aftershaves burned my olfactory senses. When the elevator doors opened, I burst out first, nearly running into an astronaut carrying a tray of champagne flutes.

"Excuse me," I sputtered. The astronaut, who wore silver lipstick and a haughty expression, did not respond, except to thrust the tray closer to my face.

I plucked a glass from the tray and backed away, then took a moment to stand in the corner to get my bearings. The party space was an airy loft with tables set up in a giant X formation at the center, showcasing the jewelry. Images of Jupiter, Saturn, and Mars were projected on the walls, the planets overlapping in a blurred fusion of orange, blues, greens, and golds. A dance remix of "Space Oddity" screamed from the overhead speakers, and several guests were inspecting the jewelry with their hands covering their ears.

Before arriving, I had decided to give myself one goal for the party: speak to someone else there. Maybe I could make a new friend, or at least an interesting connection. The music made that impossible, and the only thing the party seemed to be achieving was giving everyone a migraine. So instead I settled on simply catching a glimpse of Aqua. Based on what I'd seen online, she had such a strange, off-center beauty, and I wondered if she would be as striking in person. So, a new goal: treat Aqua like my own personal *Where's Waldo?* and spot her in the crowd. I set off to the top left of the X and studied the Galaxy Unknown collection as if I had an actual interest in spending $3,000 on a Moon Rock Ultra ring, which to my eyes resembled a chunk of concrete painted with black glitter in a platinum setting. I moved down the X, all the while searching the crowd for Aqua, which wasn't easy when a dance remix of "Rocket Man" was playing at an even louder volume. If there was a DJ Stupidhead responsible for this, he needed to be fired immediately.

"Is that mwahble?" a bald man shouted next to me when I reached the center. I turned to him and put my hand over my ear to indicate I couldn't hear him. Instead he took that as an invitation to shout in my ear. "Is that the Mars Marble?" He pointed at a shimmering necklace of rubies resting in velvet at the center of the table.

"I think so!" I yelled. There was no signage at all, so I wondered how the man, who was about five inches taller than I was and dressed in a navy-blue sports jacket and white pants, would know the name of the necklace, which to my eyes was the most impressive item in Elephantine's collection.

"I'll take it!" The man beamed with triumph, and I shrugged in response, since I was tired of yelling. More people were coming off the elevator, and the guests were starting to pack in close together to look at the jewelry and take photos of each other. The air was thick and perfumed and overwhelming, and I took a long sip of my lukewarm champagne to cope with the growing throng. The man tapped me on the shoulder.

"Hello! I said I'll take it?"

At that moment, the music stopped with an actual record scratch. Some guests whooped in relief, others booed. I would have been one of the whoopers, but the bald man was staring at me like I had served him a meal that he hadn't ordered.

"I don't work here," I told him, finding myself shouting even with the music off. "I'm looking to buy, same as you." Did I look like a person working at the event? Or did he see my brown skin and just assume?

"Oh." Bald Man didn't apologize for his mistake, only adding, "Where's Aqua?"

We both spotted her at the same time. Well, everyone in attendance did. The music had been turned off to herald her arrival, and her outfit would make her the easiest *Where's Waldo?* to solve of all time. She strode into the heart of the party, wearing a crystal blue tiara and a fur-lined cape embroidered with stars and moons. I could see a glimpse of a silver bra and leggings under the cape, and she wore Moon Boots that gave her the height of a Knicks point guard.

"Thank you for coming," she trilled to those who came by to say hello as she traveled to the center of the X. "Great to see you. Please take a look, I'm really proud of all of it." The loft, which had been reverberating with chatter and squealing dance tunes, had taken on a monastery's silence. Aqua was a bigger deal than I had realized. And she was headed straight for me.

"It's not for sale, dear, just for show. I crafted it out of my own heart, you see." Aqua fluttered her blue-gray eyelashes at me.

"Uh, okay." I assumed she meant the Mars Marble, which I actually did covet, but not nearly as much as Bald Man did. "It's beautiful. Like, luminous." And really, the rubies did give off an ethereal, glowing quality. Unlike the majority of what I had seen on the Elephantine website, or even the other Galaxy Unknown pieces, it wasn't kitschy or willfully ironic. The Mars Marble was a true work of art.

"Thank you," Aqua said. "My artistry is ever changing, and this piece represents my cocoon stage. My latest blossoming. My calling card." She gave me a *tut-tut* gesture. "And I won't part with it. But please feel free to peruse my other—"

Bald Man butted in between us, mopping his brow with a handkerchief. He pleadingly repeated her name, but she ignored him, striding like a queen through the sea of party-goers as the man trailed after her. The music began again, but this time at a fancy restaurant volume rather than that of a rave.

"What did she say about it?" said a woman next to me, a phone clutched to her ear.

"She said it's not for sale. It's part of her artistry, or blossoming... Well, she won't sell it."

"I think we'll have to ask to borrow it," she said into her phone, rolling her eyes. She was wearing all black: maxi dress, choker, combat boots, thick eyeliner, manicure. The only pop of color came from her hair, with the bangs of her sharp bob dyed red. "I can approach, but now is not the time. And there might have to be a trade-off. I'm thinking front row. No, really. Maybe..." Her voice trailed off as she walked away.

Just to be a completist, I thought about following the X to get a look at the rest of Galaxy Unknown. But by that time too many people had squeezed into the room, rattling their drinks and exchanging air kisses. Based on the cool, minimalist invitations, my expectation was for the party to have a similar vibe, but the whole scene was too frenetic for me. I cast one more glance around, not wanting to feel pathetic about leaving a party ten minutes after arriving, especially after taking two hours to get ready for it. When I spied the woman in black heading for the elevators, I took that as a sign that if someone as chic as her felt okay about leaving, then I could too.

"I'm so happy to be out of there," she said as the doors closed on the party. "Nepotism enterprises are not my scene."

"Yeah, me too," I agreed, too nervous to meet her eye.

The elevator doors opened again, and a laughing gaggle of stilettoed women in short, tight dresses catapulted toward us. We both immediately stabbed the "Close" button and exchanged smiles when the doors shut on them.

"I'm glad you felt the same as me." My relief was so immense that I eased out of my painful slingbacks.

"I couldn't bear being around any of them even a second

longer. I thought Aqua had more sense than to publicize this party on Facebook. No wonder so many randos came." She gave me an appraising look. "Is that Alice and Olivia? I have the same dress in black." She beamed at me. "I'm Keiko."

"Lata."

"As in Lata Murthy?" Keiko looked at me and seemed impressed. She didn't say my name correctly (LAH-TA instead of LU-THA, MER-THEE instead of MOOR-THE), but I didn't care.

"That's right." I quickly slipped my feet back into my shoes.

"Your name travels far. Nice to meet you."

It does? is how I wanted to respond. Instead, with all the insouciance I could muster, I replied, "Likewise."

"Are you going to the Summer Sayonara next weekend? It's such a last-minute thing, but I can't resist when Charmaine decides to have one of his parties."

I recognized the event and the party host from a new invite that had landed in my inbox the previous morning. I nodded.

"We must talk more then. Here's my card." The elevator doors opened, and we emerged into the summer night, the air even more suffocating than hours earlier. A black car pulled up in front of the building, and Keiko got in. As soon as she was gone, I headed off to the subway in the opposite direction and glanced at her card. In short blocky lettering it said, "Keiko Sasaki. Womenswear Accessories Buyer, Saint Laurent." I had never met anyone who worked in fashion before. I knew I needed to meet her again.

As soon as I got home, I made a beeline for my laptop and

opened my email. Right after I clicked the RSVP link for the Summer Sayonara, I finally noticed that the party wasn't in New York City, but the Hamptons.

I collapsed back on my bed and sighed. How could I possibly pull that off?

3

Dior

EXCEPT THAT ON THE THIRD Saturday of August, I did pull it off. Three hours on the Jitney and one exorbitant cab ride later, I had arrived at Sea Cove, Charmaine Von Bon's summer estate in East Hampton. The fact that I was standing on a grand lawn while an ocean breeze danced along my bare shoulders was a minor miracle. And I hoped no one could tell that everything I was wearing—sleeveless pale pink Chloé dress with a tiny stain on the backside, Tod's handbag, Tory Burch sandals—was from the "All Sales Final" rack at Century 21. The only reason I could pull off a breezy ensemble and the three-hour journey east was because I had just gotten my paycheck the day before. But I had also allotted a sizable part of my rent money to everything related to this excursion, and had to keep an eye on the clock to make sure not to miss the last Jitney back to New York. If I did, I'd be stranded in the Hamptons without a place to spend the night.

Just like the Elephantine party, it had been a breeze (pun intended) to enter the Summer Sayonara. It was as if uttering "Lata Murthy"—my own name!—was a key to unlocking a world that I had seen only glimpses of in *Page Six*, *Vogue*, and *The Real Housewives of New York City*. And if Aqua's jewelry party had been scattered, loud, and crowded, Charmaine's was chic and serene, an oasis for the sights and senses. Honestly, the home was not to my taste, as it basically looked like several white cubes of various sizes stacked together by a toddler, a haphazard structure of glass, cement, and steel. But the lawn was magnificent and everything I expected to see at an East Hampton estate, an expanse of grass that seemed to go on forever, with modernist sculptures dotting the perimeter and a kidney-shaped pool at the center. And since the house was situated on top of a small hill, Sea Cove had a glimmer of an ocean view too.

Everyone there seemed to have chosen light, beachy shades to wear, an unspoken dress code that luckily I had also absorbed, save for my red clutch. And like a dream, the klatch of guests parted like the Red Sea, and Keiko walked toward me, a white puppy in her arms.

"Lata, you came," she said, and we exchanged air kisses. Her black-and-red bob was now styled with beachy waves. And with her white tank top, feathery headband, and linen shorts, she looked miles different from the first time I saw her.

"I did, I did." My triumph at getting myself to the Summer Sayonara flashed into panic at realizing Keiko had expectations of me as the other Lata Murthy. At a loss for what to say,

I reached out to pet her dog, his adorable little tongue lolling out of his mouth like a strawberry. "What a cutie."

"Yes, Hanae knows it too. She's only three months old but already a massive flirt, just like me." For the first time I noticed Keiko had an interesting accent, sort of Japanese and British and French, which made her sound like someone who would describe themselves as a "world citizen." When we first met, I had assumed she was in her thirties too. But in the sunlight I now noticed her skin was smooth and poreless and, with a thud of envy, that she wore no makeup. Keiko had to be in her midtwenties. And already at that age, she had an effortlessness about her, plus a cool job and perfect skin. I desperately wanted her to like me.

A waiter came by, and we each took a glass of rosé. Keiko looked me over with such intensity that I had to steel myself to keep my whole body from trembling. Finally, I couldn't take it anymore.

"Is there something on my chin?" I said, trying a playful laugh that sounded brittle to my ears.

"Oh, sorry, no!" She set Hanae down on the ground. "You must think I'm mad. To be honest, I... Well, can I just say how happy I am you're here? I can't wait to know all about you."

I took a shaky sip of my wine. "Why? Am I really that interesting?" Keiko likely didn't realize I meant that literally.

An online search of "Lata Murthy + new york city" had turned up five Latas, one of them me. Google's record of my existence amounted to my Facebook page, a LinkedIn page with a résumé of one People.com internship and three digital content jobs, the Twitter account I had reluctantly started as content specialist for my current job at TriviaIQ, and embarrassingly, a quote nineteen-year-old me had given to the *New York Daily News* about my experience on a *Sex and the City* bus tour. ("I had such a fabulous time. I'd give it five out of five cosmopolitans!") But all the other Lata Murthys on record had even duller jobs than I did, like dentist or software engineer. None of them seemed, to quote my younger self, fabulous enough to earn the kind of intrigued gaze that Keiko bestowed on me.

"Ha, so humble," she laughed. "I wish we had a chance to meet last summer, but I spent most of the time going back and forth between London and New York. It was a whole mess." This last part was uttered like an apology. "But let's not get into my drama. Tell me everything."

"Everything, then," I said, hoping I sounded mysterious rather than befuddled.

Keiko clapped her hand to her forehead. "I'm being too much. I promise I do know how to have a conversation like a normal human being! Let's start again?"

I nodded demurely, trying to live up to Keiko's outsize expectations of me. Or whoever she thought I was that she seemed so awed by.

"How about this: Where did you spend your summer?"

My job entailed writing trivia questions for a variety of mobile game companies. Sports, politics, movies, world geography, religion: name a topic, and I'd written a trivia question about it. Maybe ten, or even one hundred. After working there three years, I'd absorbed an astounding amount of facts about things I didn't care about. And usually this came in handy only when I went to trivia nights with Mimi and other friends. But on occasion it could be useful for making small talk. Or in this case, making up a story about my fake self so I could hold on to my new friend.

When I thought about summer vacation destinations favored by the fashionably wealthy, my mind spun a wheel and came up with Palm Beach, Bora Bora, Santorini, Lake Como, Saint-Tropez, the Maldives. All places I had never been. So I went a different route.

"I spent a month at New Moon Farm on Prince Edward Island—have you heard of it?" Keiko shook her head. I was referring to the main setting of my favorite childhood book *Emily of New Moon* and hoped that it sounded like a posh spa hotel. "It gave me the refresh I needed."

"It sounds amazing! I was looking into Labor Day getaways, do you know—"

"Oh, sorry, they have a yearlong waiting list. But I'll put in a word for you." I waited for Keiko to call me out on my bullshit. But she only thanked me and clinked my glass. It was weird. As I said these words, they felt real. Like I had just come back from New Moon Farm and weeks of massages, seaweed wraps, and mud baths. But I also needed to change the subject from my fictional summer vacation, and from me entirely. Keiko had never met the other Lata, but surely other people at this party had. Weirdly, I needed Keiko to tell me more about "me." It would be hard to circulate without getting a sense of who everyone in attendance thought I was supposed to be.

What had I gotten myself into?

I didn't have time to think about it. With her hand on my elbow, Keiko guided me through the sea of partygoers, and I noticed that she and I were some of the only Asian people in attendance. We arrived at a deck area on the south side of the lawn that had a rainbow-colored umbrella flowering over it. Too late did I realize that Keiko was taking me to the party host, who had invited a Lata Murthy that certainly wasn't me.

"Keiko, darling!" Charmaine reminded me of Cary Grant crossed with Mr. Peanut. Tall, slender, and elegant, he wore khakis and a gray shirt as if they were bespoke evening wear, and emanated an intellectual vibe with his black rectangular-framed glasses. "Always standing out in a crowd."

After he exchanged air kisses with Keiko, Charmaine gave me a sweeping look. And then he did the worst thing he could possibly do.

"Kya aap asalee hain, ya main cheezon kee kalpana kar raha hoon?" He was speaking Hindi, a language I do not speak or understand. It was one of the many things my parents neglected to teach me, and among the top ten things I wish my parents had given a crap about on my behalf.

"I'm sorry?" I said, stalling for time. Charmaine had a trio of short, buff male friends standing beside him, and there's no sensation more unnerving than four sets of eyes pivoting toward you at the same time when you have no idea what to say next.

He continued squinting at me, and I noticed a thin blond-flecked mustache glisten above his upper lip. "Tum kaun ho, meree ghadee kahaan hai?"

I nodded and laughed, laughed and nodded. What else could I do?

"Ah, Lata." Charmaine leaned toward me, and we did the air kiss thing too, but in an awkward and perfunctory way. "How have you been? How is your family?"

That's right, Lata hasn't been around this summer.

"They are fine, thank you for asking. We've all been traveling, off in different directions." Nothing like using half-truths to help tell lies.

"Aha. And now you're here, finally reemerging like the glorious butterfly that you are." I had never encountered a person like Charmaine in all my life. His voice sounded sincere, but his face was a permanently arched eyebrow. I couldn't read him at all. "Tell me, what do you think of my home? I don't believe you've been here." Did that mean the other Lata and Charmaine hadn't met before?

"It's stunning." Also a half-truth. Luckily, there was so much else to talk about at Sea Cove, including an eight-foot sculpture in the southeast corner of the lawn that had caught my eye earlier. "By the way, the sculpture that looks like Betty Boop eyes. Is that a Louise Bardot? I once saw something similar at Storm King."

Now this was actually true. My major was communications, my minor was art history, and I had visited Storm King Art Center three times in the past five years.

"Well, well." Charmaine slapped his thigh. "That it is. Not many know of Louise Bardot's work."

I blushed, and Keiko looked in the direction of the sculpture, confused. "Who's that? Is she related to Brigitte?"

Charmaine explained that Bardot was a sculpture artist who specialized in creating oversized female body parts. I chimed in, noting that Bardot based the sculptures on herself, to reclaim her body after a car accident had broken her limbs and scarred her face. And that those pieces were now valued at over a half million dollars apiece. Charmaine gave me an appreciative nod, and while I had no idea how well he knew the other Lata, at least for the moment I had won him over.

Okay, so here is where I admit, if it wasn't clear already, that I had been so focused on the logistics of getting to the party and looking the part of a Summer Sayonara guest that I had done little to no research on Charmaine or even Keiko. (At least I had tried to dig into the identity of the other Lata, so I'm not completely boneheaded.) But initially, the whole point was just about seeing if I could get inside an exclusive event like this and blend in. The conversation with Charmaine had cut too close and confirmed that whoever the other Lata was, she was not someone who faded into the background.

Between sips of a gin and tonic while stationed away from the party, next to the Bardot sculpture, I did a quick online search for Charmaine. He was a visual artist, which explained all the sculptures and the oddball house, and he also came from money, so ditto. The Von Bon family dated back to the *Mayflower* days, and while I couldn't exactly tell where they derived their money from, they definitely had a lot of it. The fact that the other Lata had received an invitation to a party from someone as wealthy as Charmaine impressed me. And also freaked me out. I couldn't tell how well he knew the other Lata—maybe they were merely friendly acquaintances, and she and I looked somewhat similar. Either way, all I could think while sitting there, legs tightly crossed and heels slipping off my feet, was that there was no way I could keep this charade going. I wasn't capable of sustaining a facade of chicness and wealth. This was not just a Summer Sayonara, but a sayonara to my time as the other Lata Murthy.

And truly this whole experience would have been just a strange one-off blip in an otherwise unremarkable summer had I not overheard a conversation taking place on the opposite side of the enormous Betty Boop eyes.

"Lata's here?"

I nearly choked on my drink.

"I heard she spent the summer at some sort of spa. Now that she's back, I'm hoping she'll come to my school fundraiser."

"But does that mean she has moved here, or is she heading back to Mumbai?"

"Who knows. She's so mysterious about her comings and goings. But while she's here, I need her to come and throw some money around."

"I don't think a private-school fundraiser in Cobble Hill is her scene. She sticks to the Upper East Side and the Hamptons, mostly."

"How do you know? You haven't even met her!"

"I heard that from Charmaine. He said she likes blue bloods and patricians, because she's cut from the same cloth. Her family's wealth apparently goes back centuries. Maybe her family is Indian royalty? It's all fuzzy now. But I think the Mumbai Murthys are like the Rockefellers of India. So no, she's not going to Brooklyn for your little dinky fundraiser."

The voices faded away, and after counting down from twenty, I surreptitiously peeked past the statue to see the figures of two women retreating toward the house. I downed the rest of my gin and tonic, then stared up toward the sun, which had just started descending toward the horizon. After a few moments passed, I let out a guttural, relieved laugh. Coming to this party was like staring at the sun, risky and dumb and yet so alluring I couldn't help myself. And somehow I was pulling it off. And now I knew, if I wanted to, I still could. And even if the other Lata Murthy decided to reappear, our paths would never have to cross.

My phone buzzed. Without looking at it, I knew it was from Mimi. Since leaving to join Evan on the road, she had sent me daily texts around this time complaining of van life with four men who didn't know how to use deodorant and preferred peeing in jars. I had written her vaguely sympathetic messages in return, knowing that Mimi was trying to make it work because she didn't want her relationship with Evan to revert back to being a situationship. As it was, Mimi had already burned through all her vacation days to join him on the road. But she had to know that they were going to split once Labor Day arrived.

It occurred to me that Mimi was stuck in a smelly van while I was watching the sunset in East Hampton. Considering Mimi's parents were both lawyers who paid for her studio apartment and I lived paycheck to paycheck without family support, it was like we had switched lives à la *Freaky Friday*. It was hard not to be awed by where I found myself. And I have to admit that in thinking about Mimi, I was a bit smug too.

"There you are!" Keiko was approaching me at a rapid clip, Hanae bounding beside her. I waved, then abruptly yanked my arm down, not wanting to draw too much attention, especially from the two chatty ladies from earlier. "Hiding out, I see?"

"More like spending time with my favorite sculpture." Keiko sat down near me, and I noticed a faded yellow stain on her stomach. Keiko followed my gaze and sighed. "Hanae's not quite potty trained. I can't stay here sporting the latest in urine couture, so I'm going to jet. But I'm glad I saw you before I do. I wanted to ask you something."

"Okay." My underarms went damp, and I crossed my legs tighter at the ankles.

"How well do you know Aqua?"

Of all the questions she could ask me. At that moment, Hanae settled her fluffy rump on my foot and licked my ankle. To buy some time, I bent down and ruffled her fur.

"I wouldn't say we were close." Based on what I had overheard earlier, the other Lata was too much of an Upper East Side snob to deign to attend a jewelry launch in the Flatiron District. Which meant the odds of her knowing Aqua were slim to none.

Keiko sighed. "I need to find a way to persuade Aqua to let me borrow the ruby necklace."

"For Saint Laurent?"

"No, a friend of mine, Rajeev. He's presenting at New York Fashion Week for the first time. And for whatever reason, he has his heart set on that particular necklace for the final look."

An Indian designer showing at New York Fashion Week? How intriguing. When I said as much to Keiko, she took out her phone and scrolled through a photo album titled "NYFW" with the pride of a stage mother. Rajeev had incorporated a paisley pattern into each piece, a collection that included crop tops semi-reminiscent of sari blouses, along with pencil skirts, smart trousers, and a few maxi dresses. The final outfit was a slinky off-the-shoulder gown that resembled liquid gold, with a red paisley pattern sparkling along the neckline. As I marveled at the designs, Keiko explained that she had met Rajeev while she was interning at Ralph Lauren and he was starting out as assistant designer, and they had remained close friends since.

"I'm just so freaking proud of him, he has worked so hard to get to this point. He's working with a small budget, which is why I'm helping out with accessories. But he's stuck on this necklace for the gold dress. I should have never sent him a photo from Aqua's party." Keiko gingerly pinched at her top, then sniffed. "This is starting to stink."

She dug through her handbag and spritzed herself with Chanel No. 5, and I flashed back to my brief conversation with Aqua, and how she'd said the Mars Marble wasn't available to purchase and was only for show. And if there was anyone who existed just "for show," it was Aqua.

"What if you asked Aqua to walk in the show wearing the final look with her necklace? She wants to make a big name for herself. And I don't think a lot of jewelry designers get to walk Fashion Week wearing their own creations."

I snuck a nervous glance at Keiko as she tapped her finger

against her chin while mumbling to herself. Then her face exploded into a smile. She took out her phone, and to my surprise, she put it on speaker.

"Yes?" The male voice sounded frazzled and slightly out of breath.

"Dinner at Per Se."

"Keiko? Listen, I'm in the—"

"I might have solved the Mars Marble problem. If I have, you're going to take me and my new friend to dinner at Per Se." Keiko gave me a conspiratorial glance, and I tried my best to match it.

"Okay, shoot. I'm listening."

"Take it away, Lata." Keiko held the phone in front of my face, and honestly, I was annoyed by her presumptuousness. It had been an offhand idea, and now she wanted me to present it to the designer himself? Just as I was about to demur, Rajeev spoke again.

"Who's Lata?" he said as we heard a door slamming and the disgruntled rumbling of street traffic. For once, someone didn't hear the name Lata and immediately think of the other Lata Murthy. And to hear Rajeev say my first name was like striking a match on a moonless night, producing a beautiful flame where no light had existed for a long time.

"That would be me," I replied lightly. "Keiko told me that you want the Mars Marble for your runway show, and I think I know the only way you can make that happen." I repeated my idea for him and noticed that Keiko had Rajeev saved in her phone as "Halston Junior."

"You know, that could work." A long pause followed, the

silence filled by a bus driver pressing insistently on his horn. "Okay, let's try it. Nothing to lose. Keiko, can you—"

"Rajeev, you're forgetting something." *He's such a putz*, Keiko mouthed to me while shaking her head. "You need to—"

"Right, yes. Thank you, Lata. If this works, we can do dinner at Per Se or any Michelin-starred restaurant of your choice. Keiko coming is optional."

"Bastard," Keiko giggled. "And I'll reach out to Aqua's team and will keep you posted." She hung up and did a triumphant fist pump with her phone still in her hand. "I knew he'd go for it! He hates the idea, but he knows it will work, so eventually he'll love it." Keiko gave me a quick side hug, nearly stepping on her puppy, who scampered away in the direction of a waiter holding a tray of shrimp cocktails. "Hanae! Hanae! I have to go. But I'll let you know what happens!"

Keiko ran off to catch her dog, and I glanced at my phone to check the time. Mimi had sent a long text that included the words "ugh" and "Evan" several times. More importantly, I had an hour to catch the last Jitney back to Manhattan. But I gave myself a few minutes longer to soak up the moment, and the residual tingles from my brief exchange with Rajeev.

Icona Pop's "I Love It" blasted from a faraway speaker, and I quietly sang along as I watched Keiko weave through the crowd of guests, Hanae in hand, bidding goodbye to all she passed. When she reached Charmaine, they both momentarily looked in my direction. In my red clutch was something that I had been hesitant to wear all afternoon: my first-ever pair of Dior sunglasses, delicate cat-eye frames with light pink lenses. When I felt their eyes on me, I swept them out of my purse and put them on, then turned to face east, toward the ocean, so they would see me in profile. Who knows what I looked like to them. But in my mind, I radiated someone unknowable yet magnetic. Someone enigmatic but always chic. My definition of what it meant to be Lata Murthy began right then.

On the bus ride back to New York City, I leaned against the window despite the stop-and-go traffic causing my head to bump against the glass. I was too euphoric to care. Because I had made a decision that felt momentous at the time, with the blind, naive hope of a teenager who finally scores a driver's license and believes that at last her life will change for the better. I had decided to pledge a year of yes, accepting every invitation the other Lata Murthy received. Now that I had entered such a rarefied world, there was no way I could ever be satisfied going back to my old life. This Cinderella might have had to leave the party before midnight, but she was taking her glass slippers with her so she could return again.

There was a caveat, though. I would skip attending stuffy suit-and-tie auctions and fundraisers—basically, any kind of event that would have a guest list with people over the age of forty-five. (Charmaine seemed to be in his early forties, and since his connection to Lata remained a question mark, I would aim to avoid him too.) If the other Lata decided to return to the States, this would ensure we wouldn't overlap. New York City didn't have to belong just to her anymore. She could have uptown, I would take downtown.

My phone lit up. It was an email from Keiko.

I contacted Aqua's team, and it's a yes! Can't believe they got back to us so fast. Rajeev is thrilled. Angry and thrilled.

P.S. Got your email from Charmaine. He doesn't have your number, neither do I! Call me okay? Let's do dinner soon, Rajeev's treat.

I couldn't help it; I whooped out loud. I don't think anyone heard me, because the bus was only half-full anyway, and every other passenger seemed to be talking loudly on their phone. I sat up ramrod straight, electrified by the thought that Lata Murthy of the New Canaan Murthys had made an impact on a fashion designer's career. I took out my phone and looked up Rajeev's website, then went straight to the "About" page. His black-and-white portrait showed him wearing a suit jacket over a T-shirt, seemingly caught mid-chuckle. He was as handsome as I'd expected, but the softness of his eyes— as if he had just woken from a refreshing nap right before the camera's flash—was an intriguing contrast to the chiseled squareness of his jaw. I wasn't a fan of his goatee, but it didn't detract from his looks in the slightest. Rajeev actually reminded me of my first New York City boyfriend, Dinesh. Although Rajeev had a lot more hair than Dinesh: longish and luxuriously curly, reminiscent of Jon Snow.

I gazed out the window and let out a sigh while eyeing the traffic as evening deepened into night. From my front seat on the Jitney, I had an expansive view of the twinkling headlights and brake lights as cars flowed in both directions, reminding me of Rajeev's sequined dress and the Mars Marble. I pictured myself wearing both while walking the runway as the designer looked on approvingly. My imagination was scaling Icarus-level heights, and I allowed myself to indulge in this ridiculous daydream. Because I needed to quell my uneasiness over the one aspect marring this otherwise magical day.

I had shoplifted the Dior. I wish I could say that this had been my first time. But before then I had limited my sticky fingers to snatching makeup from Sephora. I had noticed the sunglasses had lacked a security tag, and if my fingers hadn't been trained so nimbly in the art of tucking lipsticks in my palms before hiding them in my pockets, then I would have never thought to attempt it. But I had. And the best and worst part of those terrifying twenty seconds spent picking the sunglasses up and sliding them into my handbag was that it had been so easy to do. And if I wanted to fit into the new version of Lata Murthy, a fashionista socialite of the downtown scene, then at some point I would have no choice but to do it again.

What I didn't know was that a photograph had been taken of me while I was seated next to the Louise Bardot sculpture, wearing my Dior. And when I finally saw the photo, I went through a rainbow of emotions: confusion, concern, and then full-scale alarm. But my very first thought was that the sunglasses actually didn't suit me at all.

4

Rajeev G

BY THE TIME RAJEEV AND I had dinner at Per Se, September was in full swing. I had attended three other events as part of my year of yes but missed the one I wanted to go to the most: his runway show. Initially I had believed that he was showing in the tents at Lincoln Center. But he was actually one of several designers who had been selected as "fashion's future" by SeeUsNext, a collective that offered support and showroom space to people of color starting out in the industry.

Rajeev's show was taking place on a Sunday evening in SoHo, and I had spent the entire day deciding between several designer dresses that I hadn't worn yet, finally opting for a black Anna Sui dress with spidery, lacy sleeves. I had just tugged it over my head when Mallory let out a yelp from our kitchen: she had somehow ignited a small fire while heating Trader Joe's asparagus risotto on our rickety gas stove. We frantically doused the flames with baking soda, but black clouds of ash stained the walls and the smell of smoke was baked into our hair and skin. It would be impossible to get cleaned up and make the event on time. So after we disabled the fire alarm and called our super, I dashed off an email: Keiko, I can't make it tonight. Woefully delayed by traffic. Please give Rajeev my best. Hope to see you both soon.

I had never written the word "woefully" in my life, but that seemed right for Downtown Lata, the kind of woman who would be stuck in a black car on the West Side Highway because she couldn't possibly take the subway.

The following day at work, I looked up the SeeUsNext show online and saw that Rajeev's part of it had taken place second to last and received a lot of positive write-ups on fashion blogs. The show was also featured in *Page Six* and *WWD* because of Aqua, who had worn a glittery red eyepatch along with her ruby necklace as she walked the runway. Even as she seemed to be evolving her talents, Aqua couldn't quite leave her kitschiness behind. I hoped that Rajeev believed all attention was good attention.

One of the best parts of my job at TriviaIQ was that no one noticed or cared about my online browsing. Any and all of it could be related to digging up new trivia questions for the various mobile games contracted by my employer, and so I never worried about anyone looking over my shoulder. This aspect was what had made it so easy to stay at TriviaIQ for the past three years. As long as I came up with my weekly two hundred questions, I was left alone. I spent hours online shopping and occasionally working on a short story or essay to submit to contests and literary journals. Yet the number of emails in the "Shopping Roulette" folder outnumbered the ones in the "Writing Projects" folder by a wide margin.

At times the stagnancy of the trivia content specialist role drove me crazy, as there was zero creativity involved and no upward mobility toward a better title, a higher salary, or new responsibilities. And I felt this stagnancy acutely while reading all of Rajeev's glowing press clippings. Would anyone ever call me "a bright spark of potential and innovation"? I glanced over at my boss Dana, half-asleep behind her giant iMac screen, her coffee mug perilously close to her desk's edge. Not likely.

Just as I reached the depths of my self-pity, I received an email from Rajeev, sent to both me and Keiko. He wanted to schedule our thank-you dinner. Charmingly, he addressed only me.

Please let me know when I can take you out to dinner, Lata. The show went well, and I have you to thank (and not Aqua, and certainly not Keiko). You may bring anyone you wish, but if you must bring Keiko, please tell her not to bring the furball.

Neither Keiko nor Rajeev had my phone number yet, which I think added to my mystery. I waited a day before sharing a few dates and times I would be free.

Ten days later, I finally met Rajeev in person, wearing the same Anna Sui dress I had meant to wear to his show. We met in the restaurant's reception area, waiting for Keiko to join us. He wore navy-blue slacks and a white button-down shirt, with the top two buttons undone. A rakhi bracelet flashed on his wrist, which made sense, since Raksha Bandhan had been only a few weeks earlier. As an only child and a girl, I had never given or received one. I made a mental note to make sure to ask Rajeev about his family.

"Does it feel like we're on a blind date?" I said after we exchanged air kisses, which I regretted immediately. That was the kind of awkward joke I would make, not Downtown Lata.

"Sort of?" He laughed, showing off his excellent white teeth. The goatee was also mercifully gone, replaced by closely cropped stubble. It suited him so much better. "You look smashing, by the way." Rajeev's cheeks reddened. "Sorry, I'm not British, but that's the first thought that entered my head."

"I like that. It makes me feel like I'm in a Hugh Grant movie." I gave him a reassuring smile, even though exposing my teeth always made me self-conscious of my overbite. "And I think you're ... the bee's knees. And considering that bees don't have knees, well, I guess that was an old-timey way of saying you're one of a kind."

"I'll take it." Rajeev grinned. His phone buzzed first, then mine. "It's Keiko. She's going to be an hour late."

"That's too bad." Her email to me said the same thing. "She didn't say why."

"I think she's struggling a bit with Hanae. She's never had a pet before, and she works long hours. But she'll get the hang of it." My stomach chose that moment to rumble like a bowling ball scoring a strike. I had been to a handful of top-tier restaurants before, but never Per Se, the finest in fine dining in New York City, where the bill could go as high as four or even five figures. Which meant that for the previous eighteen hours I had limited myself to a scrawny plum and a fun-size bag of Cheetos in anticipation of consuming every single pricey crumb on my plate. Rajeev kindly responded to my whiny stomach with "Let's go ahead and eat. We should start, and hopefully Keiko can join us for dessert."

He gave me his arm, which had never happened to me before. But I accepted it airily, as Elizabeth Bennet would have upon first meeting Darcy, enjoying the sensation of having my arm linked with his. Without Keiko there, and with Rajeev ten times more attractive than his photo, it was hard not to feel like we were on a date. Actually, with our immediate rapport and our gorgeously expensive setting—we were seated near the floor-to-ceiling windows offering a dramatic view of Columbus Circle and the outer edge of Central Park—it actually felt like we were celebrating our one-year anniversary.

After we both opted for the tasting menu, I congratulated Rajeev on his show and asked about working with Aqua.

"Can I admit I have a slight case of PTSD and would rather talk about anything else? I mean, Aqua was fine for the ninety seconds she walked the runway. But she was a nightmare before and after, and honestly, after working six months straight on my collection, I'm starving for the chance to *not* talk about it."

"Sure. Of course." I would just have to wait for a one-on-one with Keiko, who would enjoy filling me in and, as a bonus, would have juicy details that Rajeev wouldn't know about. "Well . . . so. How long have you lived in the city?"

I already knew, of course. (He was a lifelong New Yorker:

born in Astoria, raised in Jackson Heights, currently residing in Chelsea.) In fact, I could write twenty trivia questions about Rajeev G based on what my online sleuthing had turned up so far.

He answered my question, offering the exact amount of detail I already knew. Hungry to know more beyond what the internet had told me, I gingerly returned to the topic he had begged off discussing.

"Forgive me, I just have to ask about…how you became you. Fashion design is such an interesting career choice. It seems like a difficult path to pursue, especially for desis."

"You're right about that." A trio of stress lines briefly deepened on his forehead, and I was about to regret the question, when a smile flourished on his face. "Do you know the designer Naeem Khan?" While the name was only semi-familiar to me, I nodded anyway because Downtown Lata would have known. "I've always loved clothing design—garment construction and draping in particular. I was the rare son who loved accompanying his mother to sari boutiques and asked to look at every single bolt of fabric."

He shared that while pursuing a graduate degree in civil engineering at Columbia four years ago, he read that an Indian designer had dressed Michelle Obama when she and President Obama had held a White House state dinner honoring the Indian prime minister and his wife. Rajeev described the custom-made gown in glowing detail, as well as his obsession with the fact that an Indian designer had been granted the opportunity to dress the First Lady for such an important occasion.

"I read up on everything I could about Khan and his career. When I learned how he had apprenticed with Halston before starting his own line, I understood it could be a real possibility for me. I quit Columbia to attend FIT." He grimaced as he said this. No doubt his leaving a renowned university for a two-year fashion-focused college was a sore spot with his family.

I recalled how Keiko had Rajeev saved as "Halston Junior" in her phone, and was just about to mention it to him when I noticed the pained, faraway look in his eyes and the reappearance of his stress lines. It was time to change topics. Remembering his rakhi, I pointed at it and asked about his siblings.

"I'm an only child, so I have an unending fascination with anyone who has brothers or sisters," I said, with a self-effacing shrug. "And I still don't understand why only boys get one."

"Well, my sisters never did either. So I created this"—he held up his wrist, and I noticed the braided red threads had a paisley-shaped silver clasp—"and gave them ones too."

"You made your own rakhi?" I asked if I could take a closer look, and he extended his arm on the table. The rakhis I had seen were careless red threads tied with a knot, barely surviving past a week. But this was expertly made, and I couldn't imagine it ever disintegrating off his wrist. "Wow, a Rajeev G original! Were your parents offended? Mine would never tolerate a break with custom."

"They don't know." Rajeev dropped his arm away, then shifted in his seat. "This is something that Shay and Mazzy and I did ourselves this year." Dying to know more about Shay and Mazzy, including why he had such affectionate nicknames for his sisters, I opened my mouth to ask, but Rajeev spoke first.

"Actually, I'd love to ask you something," he said, just as our waiter brought over our first course, oysters and pearls. Noticeably, Rajeev hadn't ordered anything to drink, so I hadn't either. From personal experience I knew how alcohol could be a touchy subject. And the fact that he didn't even glance at the wine list told me he wasn't a drinker.

"Sure." I picked up my oyster shell and dipped it to my lips.

"Keiko mentioned that you summered at New Moon Farm." *Shit.* I gulped down the oyster and had to swallow three times before it went all the way down my throat.

"Yes, yes I did." I stirred my remaining pearl tapioca in its tiny bowl, unable to meet his eyes.

"I've spent some time there too. It's one of my favorites. Whenever I go, I always make sure to visit Emily." I looked up from my plate and saw a quick twitch of his eyebrows, a cocky grin ready to burst on his lips. "But I avoid Aunt Elizabeth at all costs."

I doubled over with laughter. The last thing I ever expected was for Rajeev G to call me on my bullshit, and the only way he could was because he adored the *Emily of New Moon* series just as much as I did. If L. M. Montgomery's *Anne of Green Gables* was Kim Kardashian, then her *Emily* books were her sister Kourtney, well known but never destined for global popularity. Never in my life had I met a man who had read L. M. Montgomery's novels, let alone my beloved *Emily*.

"Busted," I said, coquettishly framing my face with the palms of my hands.

Rajeev chuckled. "You have no idea how much I wanted to laugh when Keiko dropped that factoid on me. You are hilarious. Don't worry, I kept your secret."

I blushed. Our second courses arrived, and as we busied ourselves with the caviar and sunchoke custard, we shared our childhood favorites: Nancy Drew and the Hardy Boys, the Encyclopedia Brown books, *Harriet the Spy*.

"We both were really into kid detectives, weren't we?" I took a dainty bite of my blini smothered with caviar. "Which reminds me, do you know Enid Blyton?"

Rajeev put down his spoon and solemnly looked me in the eye. "We are the Famous Five . . . "

The sound that came out of my mouth could be best described as a happy yelp. I finished the song with him: "Julian, Dick, Anne, George, and Timmy the dog!" We sang it so loud that we elicited confused looks from the other diners.

"I watched that show religiously. It's way better than *The Secret Seven*." I eagerly leaned forward. "So you spent summer vacations in India too?"

"That is the only way for a desi kid to be indoctrinated into the world of precocious British kids solving mysteries in the countryside." He briefly raised his eyebrows. "But are you an ABCD? I thought you were from Mumbai."

Shit, shit, shit. I had been enjoying our evening together as plain old me, not even as Downtown Lata. And now Uptown Lata had to butt in. How best to proceed?

"I'm not from Mumbai, any more than I vacationed at New Moon Farm." I settled back in my chair, twisting my napkin in my hands. "I was at this party a long time ago. Someone heard my last name and got it mixed up with Mumbai. How? Who knows." I shook my head. "But then like a bad game of telephone, this info was passed along until everyone at the party thought I was from Mumbai. It didn't seem worth correcting them." This half-truth happened at my Seton Hall freshman mixer, when some of the kids thought I had said my name was Lata Mummy.

"Definitely been there, so I get that." He ran his fingers through his thick hair, soft, undulating waves that I longed to run my fingers through too.

"And then, just for the hell of it, I decided to speak with an accent for the rest of the night." This was a total non-truth. I'm not even sure why I said it, and the second I did, it seemed a step too far. So I tried to course correct by adding, "I imagine there are all kinds of stories out there about me."

"So you like playing with reality." Rajeev sat back in his seat, slightly nodding, as if satisfied by something that had clicked into place for him.

"Maybe more like with people's assumptions? Which you know can be so easy to do, especially in the circles we're in."

"Agreed. It can be maddening sometimes, the cheerful ignorance of certain people. I usually react with avoidance, but I like that you have fun with it."

Our third courses arrived, a colorful salad with endive and cucumbers. There was a lull in the conversation, and as I crunched my greens, hoping they didn't get stuck in my teeth, I worried about the whole Mumbai aspect of my supposed backstory. At what point would this all become too convoluted? I couldn't have Rajeev think of me as the woman who spreads fake stories. I needed him to know at least something genuine about me.

"Just so you know, my family is from South India. I've never even been to Mumbai. We were too busy circulating among all our relatives in Bangalore to go anywhere else."

"My dad's side is from Chennai, and my mom's family lives in Hyderabad, and that's where we'd spend the most time. So I'm a Southie too."

We exchanged grins and simultaneously pushed our half-eaten salads aside. The blood orange vinaigrette was a smidge too tart for me, and seemingly for Rajeev too. We obviously had so much in common! Which emboldened me to ask my next question.

"So, as a fellow Southie, can I trust you with my real origin story? And if you hear about me being from Mumbai or, like, I dunno, descended from royalty or something, will you just go with it? It's how I get my kicks."

"Sure thing. As long as I get to know the real you." Rajeev smiled, his gaze so smoldering that both my arms dimpled with goose bumps. He raised his glass to me. "I'm so happy we met, Lata. I meant it when I said I needed a break from myself, my brain, my work. And this is the most fun I've had in a long time."

"Same." The word came out half choked, because I tried to say it in the distantly amused way I imagined Downtown Lata would have, but my own relief and pleasure vaulted through, so that it sounded like "sa-AIM!" If Rajeev noticed, he didn't comment on it.

Just as I raised my glass in return, Keiko entered the dining room. We both welcomed her vociferously, but deep down, I lamented her arrival. Before she joined us, my thank-you dinner with Rajeev was mere millimeters away from becoming a first date. And if it had, it would have ranked as the best first date of my entire life.

5

Tory Burch

I LOVE A MOVIE MONTAGE. You know, when the plot pro-
gression occurs via several zippy scenes featuring people
constantly on the move. They're shopping, they're dancing, they're walking up staircases while carrying boxes.
Throughout it all, they're smiling. And there's a bubbly song
soundtracking it all, communicating "everything is going
great!" After that dinner at Per Se, my life changed rapidly
in so many different ways, and I didn't fully realize it until I
was literally paging through a calendar, counting the months
backward and shocked by how much had changed in so little
time.

It was all so rapid-fire, the changes. I had permanently
entered a new realm, and doing so felt like learning Narnia
really existed. Some of it was my own doing. I finally made
moves when it came to my career. Namely, I quit my job.
This was two months after Per Se, when I had gone to enough

birthday parties and art shows and concerts and dinners that
Keiko and Rajeev's circle became mine.

Knowing that original Lata's backstory hinted that she
was some kind of Mumbai socialite figure of untold wealth,
I decided to lean into it by positioning myself as a princess
who had elected to move out of the castle. I confided to Keiko
that I was having some difficult family problems for reasons I
could not say. And that this had resulted in me trying to stand
on my own for the first time in my adopted home of New York
City, the good news being that they could no longer dictate
my choices, but the bad news being that I no longer had the
powerful Mumbai Murthys' financial backing. I had to keep
all of this as quiet as possible, so as not to cause further strain
with my family or bring them shame. Keiko nodded know-
ingly, as Asian families are well versed in the concept of con-
cealing all dirty laundry and pained secrets under a veneer of
respectability so as not to invoke gossip from our peers. And
while I had means, I had confided with my chin quivering, I
did not have unlimited means. If she ever heard of a job opening that fit my skill set—writing, communications, and event
planning (I pulled this one foolishly out of my head, thinking
that Lata the socialite might have some experience with it)—
then I would be forever grateful.

And just as I'd predicted and hoped, this story was quietly
disseminated to others in the circle. For those who had actually heard of Lata the haughty socialite, the one Charmaine
Von Bon seemed to know, this new element to my story made
me seem a little more earthbound and approachable. But honestly a lot of people didn't know anything of the original Lata,

and except for Keiko and to an extent Rajeev, there wasn't a lot of overlap between those snooty snootertons of the Upper East Side and the Hamptons, and the hipster party scene of downtown Manhattan and Brooklyn. Which meant I didn't have to worry about proving my Mumbai bona fides by speaking with an Indian accent, thank the lord.

Not long after I confided in Keiko, she informed me that her coworker's cousin had an opening at her boutique PR firm because one of the publicists was going on maternity leave. When I spoke to the coworker's cousin, she revealed that based on how much the mother-to-be was already bemoaning returning to work after her "precious bean had entered the world," the maternity leave might become a permanent one. And so even though the placement was supposed to be only temporary, I chanced it and was rewarded with the news in February that the position was mine permanently if I wanted to take over. When I accepted, I uttered a silent thank-you to the precious bean.

Even though I was now earning close to $75,000, much more than what I had earned as a content specialist, that still was not a comfortable enough salary to survive on in an expensive city. Especially when balancing my friends-fueled lifestyle upgrade with my spiraling credit card debt, the latter preventing me from getting my own place. More worrisome was that Eleanor (the one who stole my Vitaminwaters) had gotten engaged over the holidays and had moved out not long after, and Mallory was pressuring me to let her childhood best friend take Eleanor's place. A "getting to know you" lunch at my favorite Thai place, two blocks away from our apartment, quickly made that an impossible idea. Once the best friend announced that she refused to eat anything if she couldn't pronounce its name, then visibly gagged while sampling her pad thai, it put the kibosh on that idea. But only for me. Because as Mallory huffily pointed out, we were in desperate need of someone to take over Eleanor's lease in order to be able to afford staying there.

"Unless you can manifest someone with a 750 credit score and a stable job, we have no other choice." I couldn't help taking this as a personal attack. Mallory, who prided herself on budgeting and spreadsheets and balancing her checkbook (which, what does that even mean?), had noticed the regularity with which I received mail from Amex and Mastercard. I think she was always a little worried I wouldn't make rent each month. Still, I seethed at what I took as an attack on me, especially when in our apartment dramas, the two of us had always been aligned against Eleanor. It was easy to see that once the best friend moved in, I would become the new Eleanor.

And then, I kid you not, a week after that conversation, the New York real estate gods smiled upon me. On a dreary Saturday in March, a new friend from my new social circle named Anita Chatterjee-Menken invited me to lunch at a rooftop sushi restaurant in Midtown. Even though she had Indian heritage ("my mom is a former Bollywood star, my dad produces basically everything on Broadway"), we had never spent any one-on-one time together. Frankly, she intimidated the hell out of me. Born and raised on the Upper West Side, Anita oozed wealth and style and a disdain for those without either. I worried not only that she knew the real Lata Murthy, but also that she would have a radar for my anxious need to fit in among her casually rich friend group. And noticeably, Anita and Rajeev could often be found huddled together in corners at parties, Anita whispering into his ear and Rajeev reacting with amusement and occasionally roaring with laughter. Which was another reason I had kept my distance. But I couldn't resist a lunch invitation, especially when it came with the words "my treat."

As I sat across from her in a newly purchased Tory Burch shirtdress from Saks Fifth Avenue, my woefully unmanicured hands fidgeting in my lap, I waited for Anita to coolly announce to me that she had figured me out, she knew I was a fake, and she was going to tell everyone, starting with Rajeev. Before the meal arrived, we made small talk, but mercifully it was mostly about herself: what movies she had seen lately, how much she was looking forward to celebrating her thirty-third birthday with a getaway in Cabo in a few weeks. Usually it would be annoying if a new friend showed little interest in your life, but I couldn't be more thankful that Anita was too self-involved to care about me.

The only time we talked about anything related to me was when she complimented my Tory Burch dress.

"The color is great on you. What shade is that? It's such an earthy green."

Was that a compliment or a dig? Coming from Anita's lips, it sounded like both. "It's called dark rainforest."

"I love it!" Anita flicked her wrist and snapped her fingers upward. "That's Tory, right? She can do no wrong." Relief flowered inside me. Prior to our lunch, I had fretted Anita would immediately suss out my lack of generational wealth by witnessing me up close and without the company of other friends to shield me from scrutiny. Which was why I had splurged on a $600 shirtdress better suited to afternoon tea at the Plaza than a sushi lunch in Midtown. Yet even with my damp underarms and the side zipper digging into my waist, the dress had conjured its intended magic. During my freshman year in college, I'd had a pink Post-it tacked to my laptop with the Edith Head quote "You can have anything you want in life if you dress for it." After lunch with Anita, I'd order the quote as a customized framed photo from Etsy.

Once our sushi-and-sashimi platter had been delivered to us in a gigantic wooden ark, Anita sipped from her tiny glass of sake and eyed me for several moments.

"Okay, Lata, here's the deal. I'm wondering if you could do me a favor." It was sort of hard to see her past the vessel holding our sushi, but her long braid languored down her shoulder like a lazy snake, and her kohl-rimmed eyes sparkled with curiosity. "I feel like you're the only person who'll understand, which is why I'm trusting you with this."

Plot twist! Anita trusted me? I leaned forward. "Okay."

"My parents have this tradition of buying condos for me and my siblings on our thirtieth birthdays. For mine, they got me a two-bedroom near the High Line. It is a brand-new building, and my dad is friends with the real estate broker who had the exclusive. I personally think he suckered them, because it feels like living in a human zoo. I hate it." She explained that the sixth-floor unit faced a public walkway she described as "a runway for the dregs of humanity," her face puckering at the mere thought of it. "I can't take it. It's fanny packs and sneakers and selfie sticks all day long." Anita delicately plucked a spicy tuna roll off the ark. "I basically have the blinds closed at all times. It's a claustrophobic way to live."

As Anita paused to chew, I selected a shrimp sashimi and thought about the area near the High Line, an elevated park created out of an old rail line located on the West Side of Manhattan. To give some perspective, I was living in a walk-up in the 50s between 8th and 9th Avenues, literally steps away from Times Square. But the West Chelsea neighborhood was thirty blocks south and all the way in the boonies, near 10th and 11th. But Rajeev lived somewhere there too, which was a plus in its favor.

I wondered what he thought about living there. We hadn't spoken nearly as in depth as we had that night at Per Se, but that was mostly me holding back, not feeling secure enough with myself yet, especially when I saw the closeness between him and Anita. (One time I ventured to ask Keiko about them, and she shrugged. "She's a princess, but she's a nice one. At least nice to Rajeev. She has great style, though.")

"I'm moving in with my boyfriend in a few weeks. But I'm not telling my parents, because they would have a shit fit." I would come to learn that her boyfriend was Francesco, a fifty-something theater director with an astonishing silver mane. He also played tennis with Anita's father every month. "And Rajeev told me that you're in the process of remodeling your place and need somewhere long term to stay in the meantime."

I almost choked on my sashimi. Where had he gotten that

idea from? I swallowed hard and lunged for my glass of water. In that brief period of time, I recalled that Keiko and I had recently gotten drinks at a bar in my neighborhood. I had slipped up and said I lived nearby, though it was not nearly a glamorous enough location for Lata Murthy to live, even if she had lost access to her parents' unlimited pools of money. Though Keiko hadn't asked, I had covered my tracks and said that I was subletting while remodeling my place in Tribeca. Like an idiot, I had even said my unit was in the same building as Beyoncé and Jay-Z's. (Luckily we'd had so many martinis that night, this lie had escaped Keiko's notice.)

"That's right," I said, summoning the haughty confidence of my wealthy alter ego, even as I smarted at the idea that Keiko had shared this info with Rajeev, who had then shared it with Anita. "And honestly, with renovations dragging on, I've been on the lookout for somewhere more comfortable that takes me as far from Times Square as possible."

Anita clasped her hands together. "Then this works for both of us." She bent forward conspiratorially, and I emulated her. "I know about your situation," she said in a hushed whisper, as if my estrangement from my rich parents were as shameful as a teenage pregnancy, "and I know how renos can cost a fortune." She snapped back up in her chair so fast that the chopsticks on her plate rattled and fell to the table. "I just need to have a presence in the building, you know? It should feel like someone is there every day. My parents never drop by, you won't have to worry about that. But it's like they have eyes everywhere. And sometimes my dad's broker friend will come by and make conversation with the doorman. You know what I mean?" I nodded, despite not having any idea what she meant. "As long as someone who vaguely looks like me comes and goes each day, keeps things status quo..." Anita didn't finish the sentence, and I couldn't understand her logic. We looked *nothing* alike. No one would ever mistake me for Anita. If she was glamorous Padma Lakshmi, I was cute Mindy Kaling. But why should I tell Anita that if she thought otherwise?

And so it was decided. I would move into Anita's apartment near the High Line to continue to present the notion that someone lived there. All I would have to do was pay for its utilities, and the place would be mine as long as Anita and Francesco wanted to keep their relationship secret from her parents. ("I know there's a diamond in my future, but it won't be for another year or so. And I need to get into bridal shape before I could even think about it.") If Anita needed to come over and stay for any reason, she would give me a twelve-hour heads-up and I would have to relocate elsewhere until she gave me the all clear. I had visions of marble countertops and solo living dancing in my head, so I didn't stop to think what that would mean for me if that happened.

As we clinked our glasses, I triumphantly imagined sharing this news with Mallory. When Eleanor had announced she was moving out with little notice, Mallory and I had bitched about her privately for hours. But over sushi and sake with Anita, with a rooftop view of the city that glowed in the midday sun, I understood. Eleanor had declared she had to move out because she "couldn't wait for her new life to begin," I now knew exactly what she meant.

6

Armani

IF THE WINTER AND EARLY spring of 2014 were my upbeat movie montage, then Taylor Swift's "We Are Never Ever Getting Back Together" would be the soundtrack for it. The song, of course, is a triumphant kiss-off following a breakup, and in my head that breakup was occurring with my sad little life of writing trivia questions, dining on takeout, and shopping at discount stores. And having done so gave me a swell of victory on par with the way Taylor squeals "wee-EEE!" in the song's chorus.

By April, I had officially moved into Anita's gleaming two-bedroom apartment in West Chelsea, anxiously toting two suitcases and seven enormous shopping bags over the threshold within the span of a week. I needn't have been so cautious. With twenty-five floors and over two hundred units, nobody seemed to know or care that I was a secret subletter. Plus, every single doorman who saw me enter merely nodded at me as I went by. I made a habit of checking Anita's mailbox, hoping that this would help imprint the notion that I was her. (To preserve the charade that I was Anita, my actual mail arrived at a PO box, and I had all my packages sent to my work address.) But I soon understood that although Anita's name might be on the mailbox, she had made little impression on anyone in the building.

And then there was the fact that I rarely saw another South Asian person while living there: no residents, no staff, not even any guests. I was able to slip neatly into her place, which likely meant many of them simply mistook me for Anita. This despite how different we were in terms of height, weight, and complexion (you can guess who's the more genetically gifted of the two of us). I've experienced this before, though. While I was in my teens, my parents and I would vacation with family friends in New England hamlets, and the white people there would constantly get us mixed up, even though we were various ages and shades of brown.

It comes down to this: if somebody isn't looking to see a difference, they simply won't notice.

In any case, as long as I dressed in a manner that indicated that I could afford to live there, and checked Anita Chatterjee-Menken's mailbox daily, the staff and residents didn't question my identity.

———

Living in Anita's high-rise reminded me of growing up in New Canaan. To be among wealth but not to have it yourself, and to be reminded of this fact at all times. At Anita's, I could pretend I was one of them and get away with it. That could have never happened—and I would have never even bothered trying—in New Canaan.

To grow up there was to always have an awareness of the markers of being middle class. Like our white-shingled town house, cozy on the verge of cramped even with just three people, when my classmates grew up in estates easily valued over $2 million. Or my parents' Subarus, which were boxy and efficient enough but would never be the kinds of vehicles spotted in my high school parking lot overrun with Lexuses and sports cars. Or how my mom dragged me with her on monthly Costco runs in Norwalk to stock up on cereal and tube socks and laundry detergent. Whereas my peers were treated to shopping trips in the city and given Daddy's credit card to ring up charges at Abercrombie's and Nike's flagship stores on 5th Avenue.

It might be hard to believe, but I never really cared about fitting in. Books were my refuge, and I squirreled my way inside their stories, which were always guaranteed to be more interesting than growing up in a town that politely refused to acknowledge your existence. It's a town that is overwhelmingly white, after all. And a Main Street straight out of a Norman Rockwell painting, with cobblestones, charming boutiques, and American flags waving at you from every corner. I had my three friends (all belonging to New Canaan's 2 percent Asian demographic), and from grade school to high school graduation what bonded us was how much we disdained our hometown. When your skin color and hair and clothes and parents' accents marked you as other, why even bother trying? When we went to college, we all lost touch, as if we didn't even want to be reminded of what connected us.

My parents didn't seem to grasp how weird it was to live in New Canaan and not be white or super wealthy. As pharmacists at the sole independent pharmacy in town, they worked twelve-hour days, six days a week. And on the rare occasions they weren't working, they left New Canaan to spend time with friends in (relatively more) normal places like Wilton and Stamford. For Ashok and Diya, New Canaan was the five-mile area that encompassed our home, their pharmacy, and my school. All other activities, from grocery shopping to socializing, took place outside the city limits. If they experienced any kind of othering and outright racism, they never told me.

They actually never told me much of anything. Even once I turned eighteen and the law considered me an adult, Ashok and Diya did not. As I was their daughter—and an only child—they treated me as the vessel for all their hopes and dreams, and therefore I wasn't privy to any part of their shared world, be it workplace concerns, financial decisions, or even their opinions on their friends. It was as if they were co-CEOs and I was the perennial intern, only to be given instructions, without having any of my issues addressed, let alone allowed in the boardroom.

And I would have likely remained a reclusive bookworm if not for Blake Stinley. He was a senior with stringy blond hair and a goatee of acne, and after we spent two trimesters as chemistry lab partners, he asked me to be his prom date. We weren't romantic, and we were barely friends. But he wasn't out to his parents yet, and they had demanded he attend at least one high school dance before graduation. He offered to take care of all of it—the tickets, the dress, the corsage—if I would go to the dance with him, including photos. Given that I was a brown-skinned junior with braces and masses of untamed curly hair, there were plenty of more palatable options to impress WASPy parents. When I asked why he didn't ask all the Sydneys and Madisons at our school, he responded blankly, "They already have dates." So I accepted but told myself that I was going as an anthropological experiment, something I could witness with smug eyes to report back to my fellow outcasts.

And instead, I got infected.

From the moment Blake drove us to the prom in his dad's silver Porsche Stinger, surprising me with the luxuriousness of the leather seats and the pleasurable speed as we wound our way to the Four Seasons in Greenwich, it began seeping into me.

Want, desire, envy.

I experienced that whole night as if watching everything happen behind a wall of glass that I could not penetrate. Once we had arrived at prom, Blake ditched me to huddle with his ruddy-faced lacrosse teammates, and so I spent much of the evening sitting at a table by myself, sipping from a cup of warm ginger ale. To see my classmates in tuxes and short candy-colored dresses jumping and scream-singing along to the music was more surreal and isolating than I had ever expected.

Even though I had known most of them since grade school, I had regarded them like Koopas in *Super Mario Bros.*: nui-sances to be avoided as much as possible while on my journey toward, well, not saving Princess Peach from Bowser, but let's call it my journey toward a more diverse and egalitarian adulthood. It was a classic defensive mechanism—I didn't have to worry about being left out of their cliques if I kept my distance from them first, right? I'd seen the Sydneys and Madisons and Jacobs and Blakes countless times in school settings, rarely running into them in the outside world, because honestly, I couldn't afford the places they went. My version of New Canaan was as narrow as my parents' in that way.

But to see so many of them gathered together at prom, their camaraderie even more bone-deep on the dance floor than what I had seen in over a decade of sharing the same classrooms with them, all my defenses collapsed. They had won, and they hadn't even known they were at war with me. They also didn't even seem like my classmates anymore, but a multi-tentacled monster of tanned legs and hairspray and strappy heels radiating a euphoria I had never experienced one second in my life. The thought that circulated nonstop in my brain was *Everything is so easy for them.*

And then there was also my dress: black velvet Armani. My first designer label. Before that night, my wardrobe could best be described as shapeless. And my relationship to my body was defiantly perfunctory. I had valued my brain above all else back then; feeling smarter than everyone else was the one thing that gave me a sense of self beyond my constant invisibility.

The gown transformed my vision of myself—it *gave* me a vision of myself. Rather than trust me to pick my own gown, Blake had his mom buy a dress for me from an Armani retail store in Greenwich. Which was why I was attending prom in a dress that was better suited for a classical pianist performing at Lincoln Center. But the sleeveless dress was like a magic trick: not only was it my size, but it also made my outsize chest and hips seem like desirable qualities. In that dress, I was no longer a slump-shouldered brace-face, but instead Marilyn Monroe. The week after prom, I took on two part-time jobs I worked all through the summer just so I could repay Blake in full before he left for college. Because every penny of that $4,000 dress had to be fully mine.

But it was also the bite of the apple in the Garden of Eden. I now knew things I could never not know again.

Which only made me that much more dead set on going as far from New Canaan as I could. For once, Ashok and Diya had indulged me and let me go to Seton Hall, the only out-of-state school I had been accepted to that offered me financial aid. They also paid the remainder of my tuition in full, for which I'll always be grateful. But the original sin, the fact that we had to live in a place like New Canaan and I had to perennially feel on the outside, forever wanting. That I couldn't quite forgive.

Which meant I never invited Ashok and Diya to visit me at the High Line condo. By that time, they were barely functioning as a couple, but were instead two sweat suits sitting stone-faced on a faded sofa. They didn't belong in the new life I'd created for myself; they'd barely belonged to me during the time we lived under the same roof. I had a family, but I was alone. And for once, that didn't feel oppressive or sad. It felt like freedom.

7

*Rachel
Comey*

THE FIRST THING I DID after moving in was invite Mimi over to celebrate my new place, explaining that I was subletting from a family friend. Mimi already knew about my new job with Initiate PR and had taken me out for margaritas to celebrate. But it's one thing to hear about a fancy new job, and another thing for her to tour an apartment carved out of marble with floor-to-ceiling windows. Her eyes were huge and skeptical as she took everything in, and I mean, could I blame her? She was well acquainted with my unkempt Hell's Kitchen apartment. And now I was living in a pristine condo overlooking the High Line, complete with herringbone floors and two crystal chandeliers? (Although the High Line view was obscured by heavy cream curtains. Like Anita, I didn't enjoy the sensation of being observed in my apartment by the people walking past, as if I were in a human zoo.)

But it was the photos I had put up all over Anita's apartment that most caught her eye—and her disdain. Anita luckily had hated the apartment enough to decorate with stylish but inert furnishings while barely making her own stamp on it. A few hours before Mimi's visit, I had set about making the apartment seem more my own while also not upsetting the expensive decor. As a result, no doubt it looked like I had moved into a glamorous Airbnb in which a small tornado of my personal belongings had been haphazardly spun out in all directions.

The fridge was the most cacophonous in terms of photographs. I had accidentally selected all of them from my time with Keiko and Rajeev's friends (*My friends now*, I kept telling myself, as Mimi scanned the pics), without including anyone from the past.

"Did you join the cast of *Gossip Girl*, Lats?" she said as she looked at the smiling, laughing faces of my new friends.

"No, just a guest star," I joked. I handed her a glass of the Riesling she had brought over as a celebratory gift. (Her favorite white wine, not mine.)

"Seriously, though. Who are these people?" She hopped up on the marble countertop facing the fridge, driblets of wine sloshing out of her glass. I cringed to see her act so casually, as if I were still back at my Hell's Kitchen walk-up, where you could tread on the ragged hardwood in muddy boots and not leave it much worse for wear. When she gave me a pointed look, I saw that she meant that I should literally explain every face in every photo.

So I did. And with a measure of giddiness and pride I couldn't contain, I talked about Keiko and her fancy job at

Yves Saint Laurent first, glossed over Rajeev as "her work buddy" without more details, then addressed the others.

Micheline, a curator with glossy brown hair and aquamarine eyes, who had her arm around me at one of the art openings at her gallery, whom Mimi dubbed "Angelina Jolie's Mini-Me, like, super mini."

Zaila, a photographer and fashion blogger whose close-cropped hair and dramatic beauty led Mimi to call her "Halle Berry–ish." In the photo, the two of us were singing dramatically into a microphone at a karaoke spot on St. Mark's.

David Jay, a junior exec at an A-list movie star's production company, dressed as Jack Sparrow, pretending to walk me off a plank (I was miniskirted Cady from *Mean Girls*), prompting Mimi to opine that he was wearing too much eyeliner. I didn't bother to tell her that David Jay was blessed with long, curly lashes that permanently gave him that look.

Kingsley, the son of a famous author, and in his words, the "literal redheaded stepchild" of a Fortune 500 CEO, which meant his full-time career was partying and spending his stepfather's money. Our photo showed me towering over Kingsley in skis at the Burlington slopes on New Year's, leading Mimi to describe him as "Billie Joe Armstrong crossed with a leprechaun."

Anita, of course, who I neglected to mention was the person who owned the apartment we were standing in. In the photo, we were both dressed in lehengas and bindis while at a garba dance party in the West Village. ("Are her eyes violet?" Mimi said, taking the photo off the fridge to examine it more closely. "Are those contacts?" When I said yes, she snorted.)

Usually I enjoyed Mimi's biting observations, which she deployed while watching reality television or against our college frenemies. But I liked them much less when they were aimed at my new friends. In our ten-plus years of friendship, Mimi and I had run the gamut of emotions and moods but had never dealt with this strained distance. It made me itchy, like a too-tight sweater. As we sustained a conversation with the bumpy back-and-forth of two amateurs lobbing a tennis ball at one another, I thought back to Zaila's visit a few days earlier. Due to our shared interest in fashion, we had the kind of immediate ease Mimi and I had once shared. Even so, I hesitated when Zaila asked to see my closet.

"I do a photo essay series about them. It's always fascinating to get a peek inside, you know?" Oh yes, I was very aware. Since becoming friends with her, I had followed Zaila's site religiously and loved her *Up Close(t)* series. To have her take an interest in mine was a thrill. Zaila was not someone who featured just any person's closet. She certainly would have never featured my previous one, a space so narrow that I had to double all my clothes on the hangers—thick cardigans over my smattering of formal gowns, raincoats over maxi dresses—to make everything fit.

At last I had a place where my clothes could coexist without being smooshed or layered atop one another. It was the size of a Macy's dressing room, with built-in cabinets and shoe racks and plentiful drawer space, a perfumed lavender sachet tucked in each one. I could do a three-hundred-sixty-degree twirl inside the closet, with my arms extended out, without touching the walls. (And several times, I did.) It was the kind of space that honored clothes as if they were art pieces. To have Zaila assume that I'd have a closet worth photographing made me fizzy with gratitude.

But that was also the problem. Back in my Hell's Kitchen days, my closet had contained a mishmash of designer and discount. But I wasn't aware of how much the discount dominated the designer until I unpacked my wardrobe, showing me how my Isabel Marants and Reformations were outnumbered by Gaps and Uniqlos. It felt impossible to let Zaila photograph it in its current state, so I begged off, citing privacy concerns. But as a fashionista herself, she still wheedled for a peek, and so I gave in but came up with a reason why I had only about thirty pieces hanging in my closet.

"I have a lot of things still in storage and just haven't found the time to bring it here. I'm not sure what's worse: unpacking or having to operate with only a third of your wardrobe."

"Ugh, right?" Zaila said, glancing around, her hand lovingly curled around the sleeve of a gray puffed-sleeve Rachel Comey sweater. Thankfully, upon moving in, I'd had the good sense to give hangers only to the high-end pieces, while the mass-market stuff was squirreled away in the drawers. "So hard to say." And then, after a beat, we both said, "Unpacking."

We spent the rest of the afternoon laughing and sipping iced teas while Zaila toured my closet as if visiting a museum, asking thoughtful questions about the prized items I did have. Mimi didn't have the same regard for clothes; she shopped near exclusively at H&M and Buffalo Exchange. No one had ever made me feel smart before due to my taste in apparel.

And to have someone with the background and expertise of Zaila exude approval made me acutely aware of Mimi's sour-eyed judgment.

"If only this were true, right?" Zaila said, pointing at the pink-framed Edith Head quote I had placed between two succulents on the main cabinet. "Dressing for the life you want. I've seen a variation of this quote in about a dozen closets I've photographed."

"Oh really?" My cheeks colored to the same shade as the frame. When she lingered on it, then picked it up, I added, "I can find it irritating, though. Especially on Monday mornings when I'm sleep deprived and late for work and I'm tired of all my clothes."

"Exactly." Zaila returned it to the cabinet. "I didn't know Anita to be so twee."

"Ha. Yeah." After Zaila left, the Edith Head quote was relocated to the bottom drawer.

———

"Everyone you know is so beautiful and snobby. I mean, they seem rich." Once the photo tour concluded, Mimi and I had settled on opposite sides of my living room sofa. We hadn't been spending a ton of time together since she returned from Craterfest, but even so, I'd never imagined our paths would diverge in such a striking way. Mimi had always had an all-American quality, with her cherubic cheeks, her light brunette waves, and the sprinkle of freckles on her nose. But she now had the look of a rocker girlfriend who had skipped a shower or two. It wasn't just her ripped-at-the-knees jeans and black Nirvana tee, but also her brown hair being longer and stringier than it had been during our dormmate days. Contrary to my prediction, her and Evan's time on the road together had brought them closer, and they were now saving up to move in together. It was hard not to think that Mimi felt one-upped by me, because I was partying at pricey hot spots and she was going to her boyfriend's shows in dingy hotboxes in Brooklyn.

"I mean, they are rich but surprisingly not that snobby." This was true, at least when it came to Keiko and Rajeev, possibly Zaila. "It's been nice just experiencing a different part of the city, you know?"

"Sure, sure." Mimi took a big gulp of her wine. I set aside mine. I could sense she was about to tell me something big, but I wasn't sure if it was about her or directed toward me. "Look, I'm glad you're having such a good time. I know this is what you wanted, all this fun and glamour and *Gossip Girl* kind of lifestyle."

"Um, I never really watched *Gossip Girl*, that was you," I teased, even as I tersely pushed up the sleeves of my sweater. "I was *Sex and the City*, all the way."

"Whatever. But honestly, Lata, how can you afford all this? I can't imagine you make that much money at your new job. The last thing you want to do is make that hole deeper."

I flinched. Only Mimi was aware of my credit card debt and the fact that I described it as a hole that I was sinking into inescapably with every passing day. Last time she heard, I was $8,000 in debt. Since that time, I had gotten a new credit card with a whopping-high APR and inched ever closer to doubling the amount she thought I currently owed.

"I get your concern, Meems. And I appreciate it. But the PR job salary is sky high compared to the peanuts of the trivia job." A half-truth. I was making $20,000 more at Initiate than I had at TriviaIQ, and was told that after three to five years' time, I would have the opportunity to break into a six-digit income. "And I'm working on the hole, chipping away at it. I'm not perfect, but I'm working on it." A full truth. Besides dutifully paying the minimums, I was balancing my newly expensive lifestyle with selective Rent the Runway options and even more selective shoplifting.

"If you say so." I turned away from her to pick up my glass of wine, not waiting to witness her dismissive shrug, which would match the tone of her voice. We spent the rest of the afternoon making polite small talk about our lives and were both relieved when Mimi had to leave early in order to catch Misfit Slime's show in Bushwick.

And after she did, I finished the rest of the Riesling by myself, sipping straight from the bottle while I toured my roster of outfits—which was much easier to do in my new walk-in closet. I had my own plans for the night, and luckily I didn't even have to go very far. Definitely not somewhere that would necessitate Mimi's three subway transfers or even one.

Rajeev was hosting a party at his condo that night at a building only five blocks away from mine. And I was desperate to make sure I arrived before anyone else and finally had a chance to be alone with him again.

8

Sergio Rossi

I MIGHT HAVE BEEN ABLE to magically find myself a new
dream life, but the one thing that continued to elude me was
a deeper connection with Rajeev. As much as I had been welcomed into his friend group, he was often missing from our
nights out. The Fashion Week show, coupled with Aqua's
stunt, had caused a splash, and he was now highly sought
after for designing couture pieces for the famous and wealthy.
("B-list famous and hipster wealthy," according to Keiko,
which apparently was an important distinction.) And all the
while as he fulfilled these custom orders, he was working on
the concept for his next fashion line, hoping to secure a spot
in an actual Fashion Week tent that fall.

Every time I went out with his (now my) friends, a pitter-
patter of anxiety would erupt in my chest in anticipation
of Rajeev possibly being in attendance too. Four times out
of five, he would not be. And then when he did emerge out

of his work cocoon, he seemed standoffish and distracted. There were a few times we spoke, wryly bantering about New Moon Farm or the Famous Five or my faux-Mumbai back-story, but it was frustrating that we weren't able to discover anything new about each other, leaning on inside jokes that were starting to get stale. Most of the time, my insides would be aflame as Anita would gather Rajeev to her, her long, slim arms wrapped around his shoulders, chattering in his ear as if soothing a fussy child. Even Keiko didn't speak to Rajeev as much as Anita did, and I felt too awkward to ask Keiko what she thought of Rajeev and Anita, or the reason behind their closeness.

So discovering that Anita was enmeshed in a romance with an older man was arguably a bigger relief than Anita offering me the opportunity to live in her apartment. Which was why when I arrived at Rajeev's doorstep in a fuchsia Anthropologie sweater dress and leather boots, my armpits and forehead perspired as if I were wearing a parka on a hundred-degree day. Carrie Bradshaw famously once said that every woman in New York City is always on the search for three things: a boyfriend, a job, and an apartment. Miraculously, I had secured the latter two. And I was ready to finally land the most elusive one of them all.

I managed to blot my sweaty face right before Rajeev opened the door and beamed at me.

"Lata, hi!" God, why did he have to be so handsome? He was wearing a gray tee and black jeans, and his Jon Snow hair was downright lustrous, like it had just starred in a shampoo commercial. "Thank you for coming, so great to see you. You are absolutely glowing." This last part was said sheepishly, as if he had caught himself by surprise by saying it out loud.

"Great to see you too," I said, hoping to sound casual rather than elated by the sight of him, the brief warmth of his touch from his welcoming hug, the alluring scent of his cologne. "To be honest, even though you're the one throwing the party, I wondered if you would actually attend."

Rajeev chuckled. "Honestly? Same." He ruefully rubbed his knuckle under his chin. "But Keiko and Anita basically held a joint intervention for me and said since I had skipped celebrating my birthday last year, they demanded I throw myself a half-birthday party."

With a hand on my back (not quite lower, just underneath my shoulder blades), Rajeev guided me around his place, a one-bedroom loft space with brick walls and wooden beams, which was as stylish and low key as him. As he showed me around, Rajeev explained that his birthday had landed one week before his NYFW show with Aqua, and he was so busy he had forgotten about it until days later. Technically, his half birthday would have been in February, but that had been a busy time, with Fashion Week and its attendant parties, plus awards shows such as the Oscars and Grammys and all of their satellite events. Which was why Rajeev was finally getting around to celebrating himself in the relative calmness of mid-April.

My tour of Rajeev's home was the most time we had spent together since Per Se. We were alone for approximately eleven minutes, and I hoped our time by ourselves would last longer because I lived the closest out of everyone. But once people began to arrive—and they arrived in a flurry, like a fast-moving snowstorm that dropped ten inches before moving on—we didn't really speak again. On occasion, the two of us were in the same group, chatting about upcoming Easter weekend plans or various social occasions that were approaching on our shared calendar. Yet with the music blaring and the multitudinous flutter of conversations in the packed living room, there was no opportunity to pull Rajeev aside.

Instead, the one person I got to know a whole lot better was the one person I had until that point managed to successfully avoid. About an hour into the party, I had left the cacophony of the living room for a smaller den area. While sipping a gin and tonic and gazing out at the view of the West Side Highway and the Hudson River beyond it, I contemplated how much I enjoyed seeing New York gradually rouse itself from winter as the first touches of spring manifested in the white blossoms on the bare, severe trees.

"Well, look who it is," said a familiar voice, which was accompanied by the distinct scent of eucalyptus and cedarwood. The tall, lanky reflection of Charmaine Von Bon appeared in the glass.

"Oh, hello there." Startled, I wobbled in my Sergio Rossi boots. But I recovered quickly and leaned in to give him an air kiss. This time our exchange was much less awkward than when we had first met at his East Hampton home. One of the most surprising things I'd learned about myself since I began leading my life as Downtown Lata was how spry and adaptable I could be in social situations. Many years ago, when I first moved to the city, I threw myself into what

I thought of as various New Yorkish activities, trying to find my thing. That included taking improv classes at the Upright Citizens Brigade. But I had been a mediocre student because I was too self-conscious about saying the wrong thing and was unaccustomed to having eyes on me while fumbling to find a way to be both off the cuff and funny. But the "yes, and" improv training had finally kicked in with each encounter with new people and unfamiliar environments. To be Downtown Lata was just one long improvisational exercise and was crucial to my success in ensconcing myself in my new social circle.

Charmaine would be my biggest challenge, but strangely I wasn't nervous, despite the fact that he actually knew—or seemed to know—the other Lata. I was no longer some mere interloper, but was actual friends with these people. To me, the bigger question was what Charmaine was even doing here.

"Can the last time we saw each other really have been at the Summer Sayonara?" He raised his thin, streamlined eyebrows, a glass of Scotch balancing on his palm.

"So, a million years ago, then," I said with an easy laugh. "How is everything with you?"

"Fair to middling," he responded with a straight face. I couldn't tell if he meant that or not. "How is life treating you? I hear you're now a West Chelsean too. Why anyone would live this close to the West Side Highway is beyond me. Although, I do now see some of its charms."

"I'm settling in." I nodded toward a love seat in the corner, and we moved to sit down. "Anita has been so gracious to let me stay with her right now. Honestly, a lifesaver." Anita her-self had not been able to attend Rajeev's party, even though it had been partly her idea. Instagram showed her at a bridal shower in Westchester.

"That dramatic, huh?"

"More like saving me from drama." *Good answer*, I thought, giving him a cocksure grin. I was fairly positive that my vague family issues had been taken up by the winds of gossip and floated over to the people who knew the actual Lata. Char-maine indicated my assumption was correct when he cocked his head to the side in an appraising sort of way, then gave me an agreeable nod. After clinking our glasses as we remarked how nice it was to see each other again, we took long sips of our drinks. The pause in our conversation coincided with the dramatic thud and crash of something heavy, followed by a chorus of "oohs!"

"I didn't know I was attending a frat party." Charmaine winced, then briefly whipped off his glasses to press his fin-gertips over his eyes with the weary irritation of a substitute teacher facing an unruly classroom.

"I didn't realize you knew Rajeev." I crossed my legs and enjoyed the buttery smoothness of leather sliding against leather. These boots were a purchase of true indulgence, the first time I'd owned knee-high boots that weren't made from pleather.

"You probably know him for the same reason I do."

I nodded. "We could definitely play a game of Six Degrees of Keiko Sasaki. No doubt everyone in this city is connected through her somehow."

And guess what? That's what we did. We each began naming people we knew and tracing them back to Keiko and, in doing so, learned that we were acquainted with some of the same people. And with relief I noticed that the hipster chef and the handbag designer and the mixologist were closer in degrees to me than to Charmaine. He was only a visitor to my social stratum, while I had established residency and spoke the language. The distance between Downtown and Uptown Lata seemed even wider.

And then we added celebrities to the game, the kind of bold-faced names that popped up in *Page Six*. It devolved into silliness as we came up with increasingly outlandish ways of how stars like Al Pacino and Cher would be connected to Keiko. By the time she walked through the doorway, the two of us were laughing like old friends.

"What did I miss?" Keiko strolled toward us, a walking ray of sunshine in her pale yellow jumpsuit. Charmaine and I doubled over in laughter each time we tried to explain, but we were a few drinks in by that point, so what seemed uproarious to us wasn't the same for her. Even so, Keiko smiled and nodded gamely. I think she liked seeing two of her friends getting along. Neither of them would realize this, but Charmaine and I were the most random people to connect via Six Degrees of Keiko.

"How's the birthday boy?" I asked. "I really haven't seen him since I arrived."

"He's kind of in hiding," Keiko said, a hint of concern flickering over her face. "Once Anita realized she couldn't make Rajeev's party, she invited a ton of people because she wanted this to be an over-the-top blowout. So of course he's in his bedroom, wearing headphones, bent over a sketch pad."

"Always a good sign when the birthday boy escapes his own party," Charmaine said dryly. "I have a dinner party to get to. Can you lead me through the frat boys so I can wish him well and get on my way?"

"Ditto, actually," I parroted without thinking, even though I had nowhere else to be except with my hopes and dreams of finally stealing some time with Rajeev.

The three of us wove through the crowd and entered Rajeev's bedroom, which was stark and spare, as if in the process of being packed up for a move. The conversation was stilted and brief, as Rajeev seemed to be in a daze, finding it difficult to break his concentration while in the midst of sketching something that seemed, at least to my eyes, to feature an outfit that included boots very similar to mine. When we hugged goodbye and he thanked me for coming, his arms lingered just a second longer than necessary. Although it was very necessary to me.

Charmaine left immediately afterward, while I stayed a few minutes to chat with Keiko in the hallway outside Rajeev's apartment. As she told me she would stay on to watch over Rajeev and put the kibosh on the party, my mind was whirring from what I had experienced a few minutes before. The boots. The hug. It had to mean something. He liked me. He just didn't have *time* for me. I couldn't rely on Rajeev to make the next move, not when he barely had the time to celebrate his birthday on the actual day.

Yet for all my liberal attitudes about sex and dating, I remained weirdly conservative in one particular way. I had never in my life asked a guy out. Not because I had the values of a stodgy Miss Manners, but simply because I had always been too shy to do so. And even though I had transformed myself into Downtown Lata, I hadn't done so overnight. My "year of yes" pledge had brought me this far, but it had also taken time and resources, money and luck.

And so I made myself a second pledge. If Rajeev didn't ask me out by Memorial Day, then I would ask him out instead. By that time I surely would have the courage and confidence to tell him how I felt, and also would have mentally prepared myself for his response, whatever it would turn out to be. And by waiting until Memorial Day, I could also plan for exactly where and when: Kingsley was hosting us for the holiday weekend at his parents' estate on Long Island, and I had over-heard Rajeev ask Kingsley a question about its square footage. Why would he ask if he wasn't planning to go too?

As I bid Keiko goodbye and walked toward the elevator, I was already dreaming up ideas about what to wear on the fateful weekend away—and how I would pay for it.

9

Moda Operandi

DURING THIS CINDERELLA PHASE OF my life, there were still other Lata emails landing in my inbox, but not with the same frequency as last summer. And any that weren't actually for me were deleted without a second thought. That was one of my satisfying achievements of that time too, the fact that so many of these glamorous and exclusive invitations were truly meant for me.

The most notable one to date was the invite to stay as a guest at Dove's Landing, a fourteen-bedroom estate in Great Neck that sat on five acres of perfectly manicured lawns and had its own tennis court, indoor *and* outdoor pools, a greenhouse, and an English garden modeled after the one in *Howards End*. Kingsley had invited only the inner circle of our sprawling, interconnected friend group. Zaila cracked me up when she likened us to planets: Earth, Mars, Venus, and the gang were allowed to stay the weekend, while stars and moons that orbited around us like hangers-on could come only for the blowout party taking place Saturday.

The difference between Friday and Saturday could be described only as bacchanalian. Late Friday afternoon, when we arrived, was an amalgam of chill: steaks on the grill, Lorde on the speakers, our feet happily lazing in the pool as we watched the sunset. Rajeev wasn't among us, but he was supposed to arrive the following morning with David Jay. And I was actually relieved, because it gave me a little time to relax and take in my spectacular surroundings with Anita and Keiko. Zaila and Micheline had both brought their partners, and so while that foursome plus Kingsley played poker inside, the three of us passed a bottle of champagne back and forth while hanging in the hot tub. Anita gushed and complained about her boyfriend in equal measure, while Keiko confided that she had been texting with a childhood friend from Kyoto and that their texts were getting increasingly intimate, even risqué—a confusing but also beguiling development she hadn't seen coming. Hoping to head off any discussion about my romantic situation (or lack thereof), I steered the conversation toward Anita and me advising Keiko on how to navigate her evolving situationship, even if her person was halfway across the world. Looking back, that might have been the one perfect night I experienced as Downtown Lata.

It also marked the demarcation point of Before and After, when it all tumbled down like a tower of Jenga. The fact that it took only one small movement to destabilize my carefully crafted life showed how unstable it all was. Not to mention the inevitability of the crash.

—

By three p.m. on Saturday, there must have been over two hundred people at Dove's Landing. ("Way more stars and moons in our galaxy than I thought," Zaila said upon surveying the overrun grounds.) Kingsley had expected a sizable crowd, but he hadn't thought about what that would mean in terms of parking, and so he was spending the entire day outside on the phone, trying to manage the situation before things got so out of hand someone would complain to the police. There was nothing the rest of us could do to help him, although we offered. Zaila, Micheline, Anita, Keiko, and I instead hid out in the English garden, which thankfully was hard to find unless you already knew it existed. It wasn't that we were trying to be unsocial. But we hadn't expected so many people to show up, and the steamy weather made it difficult to circulate among acquaintances and strangers. We sat together in a semicircle under a willow tree, which provided us some respite from the merciless heat.

"Nika and JJ had the right idea," I said to Zaila and Micheline about their respective significant others. "I'd much rather be golfing, and I've never held a golf club in my entire life."

"Is it me, or does it feel like we're Marie Antoinette and everyone out there are the French peasants storming Versailles?" Anita could tend to talk in this snotty way without realizing she was snotty.

"Kingsley has way too many friends." Keiko sighed, kicking

off her dainty gold flats. "He's had parties before, but never like this. He must have invited everyone he attended prep school with, all of his frat brothers, and everyone he's shaken hands with in the past six months." She shook her head. "Thank god I didn't bring Hanae."

"What's up with him?" Micheline said. A lifelong New Yorker, she had a slight French accent from attending boarding school in Marseilles, which was where her family went back generations. "He seems a bit manic lately. Like he's always on."

"Or do you mean on something?" Anita asked, tapping the right side of her nose.

"Who amongst us," Micheline retorted. Anita and Micheline were friends, but not in the sense they spent any time alone together. As for what Micheline said, only Anita and I could say we hadn't ever partaken of nose candy. We'd become much closer since I moved into her place, and we'd bonded over how our square upbringings (she had been largely raised by a strict, traditional grandmother) had precluded us from ever trying or wanting to.

The two glared at each other, and to break the tension, I thought of asking, "Anyone hear from David Jay yet?" But I didn't know if I wanted an answer. Whether Rajeev wasn't here yet or he already was, it wouldn't prevent the frenetic stutter-stop of my heartbeat and nerves. The sweat dripping rivulets down my back wasn't just due to the ninety-degree temps. Yet it was also really hot, getting unbearably so. We were all cranky and tired, with only one water bottle to split among the five of us. I decided to take one for the team.

I scrambled up, hoping that my white denim shorts hadn't been besmirched with green from sitting on the grass for so long. "I'm going to get us something to eat or drink. And survey what's going on out there." Of course, a part of me hoped that Rajeev had arrived and needed to be rescued from the partying throng. If that was the case, I didn't want anyone else to join me.

My friends thanked me while also peppering me with requests for Evian and Corona and those "yummy lobster cakes," none of which I would bring back. The last thing I heard before exiting the garden was from Anita. "Don't let the peasants find you and drag you away," she warned. "None of us are heroic enough to come save you."

I had my purse with me, a Moda Operandi tote bag made of rainbow-striped raffia. It was the most expensive item in my whole weekend ensemble, as my shorts, blue off-the-shoulder cotton top, and cream espadrilles had cost $250 combined, thanks to an afternoon of diligent shopping at Woodbury Common. But the purse had cost double that, which wasn't a lot for purses usually but nevertheless felt like an extravagant purchase when I knew I'd use it only a handful of times.

But as I threaded through the sea of people in the expansive lawn area, sidestepping giggling girls in tube tops and overly tanned dudes in shorts and baseball caps, I was so happy to have the tote. It would be roomy enough to bring back a bottle of wine, several cans of LaCroix, and whatever snacks I could scrounge up from the kitchen. If I could just survive getting through this crowd first. In the months to come, I would mentally try to recall every step, every moment I felt a shoulder bump against mine, every foot that smooshed my poor toes, every careless elbow that brushed past me. It took me nearly twenty minutes to move from the outdoor grounds, climb the tall stone steps, go around the outdoor pool, past the indoor pool and greenhouse, and finally into the kitchen, where an overwhelmed catering company did its best to keep the snacks flowing. (A barbecue was supposed to also be happening somewhere outside, but I hadn't seen any sight of it.) I deftly maneuvered over to the pantry area that had all the foodstuffs and drinks. I was mopping my forehead with my sweaty arm, ready to go to work, when my phone buzzed. It was our group text, and the message was from David Jay.

> Sorry guys, not going to make it. We had a rental car snafu, and we're hearing there's an ugly traffic jam on Rt 878.
> Rajeev and I are calling it—this just doesn't feel meant to be.
> See you back in the city!

Ughhhh. This weekend was not turning out how I'd hoped. I returned my phone to my pocket, blearily gazing at the stacks of Pringles and Cheez-Its. All the energy drained out of me, and the idea of going back out into the madness with chips and sodas held zero appeal. I slowly slid to the floor, grabbing a LimonCello LaCroix on the way down. I dropped my purse as I did so, and my belongings skittered out all over the tile. With a sigh, I crawled on my hands and knees to reclaim my sunglasses case, makeup bag, and sunscreen. As I returned them to my purse, I noticed a piece of pink paper lodged at the bottom. It was folded in half, and scrawled on top in all caps was LATA.

How odd, I remember thinking before I opened it. And then a lightning crash of emotions: a mixture of shock, confusion, and terror that could be described as OMGWTF.

The note said:

You stole my life.

Next to those words was a phone number with an unfamiliar area code. The phone number was underlined several times with an angry hand, the pen pressed so deeply against the page that it had left a tiny, jagged rip at the center.

10

Callae

FORTY-EIGHT HOURS LATER, SAFELY BACK home and alone in my apartment, the curtains drawn against the never-ending parade of High Line tourists and the blazing midday sun of Memorial Day proper, I placed the call. There hadn't been instructions on when to call, but I imagined she would be waiting to hear from me whenever I got up the nerve to reach out.

It was a Baltimore area code. I had Googled it prior to dialing, thinking that this info might be helpful, although she might be using a burner phone. What I remember most from those final moments before I spoke to the other Lata for the first time was that sitting beside my terror was a gaping loneliness: whatever I was about to face, I would have to do so alone. There was no one I could confide in about this, no friend to whom I could relay the facts of what was about to happen, no one to ask for advice or go to for support. An utterly miserable feeling, reflected in my jagged fingernails, all bitten down to the quick, and a newly born stress pimple blooming at the tip of my nose.

Three rings later, she picked up.

"Lata," she said. Her voice was smoky, quiet, a tad hoarse.

"Yes. I mean, this is she. Me."

"Us," she responded in a smirking sort of way. "Enjoying it so far? Taking a walk in my shoes?"

"I really don't know what you're talking about." I figured denial was my best move here. What did she actually know about me?

"So you thought you could just parade yourself around this city, taking my invitations, and pass yourself off as me? Oh, sweetie," she purred. "Did it ever occur to you there was a reason I was not out there myself?"

On her side, a horn honked far away, and for a moment I thought I heard the tinkle of an ice-cream truck. I did my very best to channel my inner Nancy Drew and try to ascertain where she was placing her call from. Turns out she had a much better idea of my whereabouts.

"You're living the good life right now, aren't you? An apartment on the High Line, a PR job in Midtown East, making new friends at all those fancy parties you attend. All because of me."

I slumped down on my bed, my bare legs hugging my pillow and my stomach roiling. But it was what she said next that had me gasping out loud, as if I'd opened my bedroom door and Jason from *Friday the 13th* had been revealed on the other side.

"You dress very well, Lata. I like your style. We have similar tastes. Except you don't always like to pay for things, do you? That Callae bracelet, for instance. Very clever how you were able to slide it inside your sleeve. Although, you were smart to target Callae." She laughed, throaty and dry, like scraping tree bark. "Their security measures are basically a 'No Shoplifting' sign. Which obviously worked on you." Another throaty laugh.

This woman had been *watching* me. My visit to Callae, a new jewelry boutique in SoHo, had happened two weeks earlier. Zaila and I had met up for brunch, followed by shopping in the trendy boutiques that lined Prince Street. I had immediately noticed the exact same thing about the lack of security measures in the busy store, with twenty people trying to maneuver inside a space the size of a walk-in closet. Without even giving it serious thought, I had picked up the double-threaded 14-karat gold bracelet and stuck it on the inside of my cardigan sleeve, holding it in place by affixing it to the thick silver cuff I had already been wearing. That was how easy taking things came to me now. If it was ripe for the picking, I just plucked it and moved on with my day. To have this woman observe me doing so made me sick. Sickened for myself, the illicit ease of my actions. But also to be caught like a fish thrashing in a net, with no chance of escape. And sickened too that whoever this woman was, she had been so nearby. The store had been so suffocatingly small that no doubt I could have smelled her perfume, even felt her breath on my neck as she watched me take the bracelet. Goose bumps chased along my arms as I watched myself through her eyes: all dressed up in designer clothes and brazenly stealing to maintain a chic facade, committing a crime that landed certain people behind bars while others got away with a slap on the wrist. Before speaking to Other Lata, I'd had a hundred justifications for myself about why shoplifting was necessary. After this conversation, I never did it again.

"You are a smart girl, Lata. I enjoyed watching you in action. And you might be surprised, but I want you to continue being me. The Mumbai socialite who so obviously has never been to Mumbai but was raised on McDonald's and MTV and Barbies," she scoffed. This irritated her, I could tell, the fact that no one questioned my story too closely. For the first time, I sensed that we were not the same age. Part of her derision for me came from the fact that she looked down on me, like an older sister scolding her younger sister for trying to raid her closet or wear her makeup. There must be a clue in there somewhere.

"Listen, I—"

"No, you're going to listen. And do exactly as I say. And if you don't follow my instructions to the very letter, I'm going to turn you in. Expose you to your friends, get you fired from your job. You'll go back to being a nobody. Worse than that, even."

She was viciously angry, and no longer trying to hide it. Her distant affect, like the ones you would see in films noirs, femmes fatales holding cigarettes and leisurely blowing smoke, was how I had initially pictured her. But this Lata was now all fire. Not just fire, but lava pulsating out of a volcano. My palms were so sweaty I nearly dropped my phone even as I pressed it against my ear.

"Write this down. And when you're done, recite it back to me."

With my heartbeat stuttering like a tap dancer, I wrote down exactly what she said. This included "@fauxperdante," which was a Twitter account. Not long after we hung up, I would do a Google search and find out it meant "fake loser" in French.

"Good chat," she said, her voice slinking back to acrid amusement. "Look forward to seeing how you do." Then silence. She had hung up.

This would be the first and only time Other Lata and I would speak on the phone. We would talk again, but not for some time. Instead, she had other ways to communicate with me that would indeed make me feel like a fake loser.

Otterhand
& Co.

11

MY ONLY TWITTER ACCOUNT AT the time had been created for my job. I had used it to dutifully retweet Initiate PR's tweets, largely press releases that not many people paid attention to. My account was simply @LataInitiatePR, which goes to show how work-dictated my usage of Twitter was at the time. I followed about a hundred accounts, had thirty followers in return, and when I got off the phone that day, I had a thirty-first: @fauxperdante.

I followed back, but since it was a private account, access was not immediately granted to follow. Nearly a week passed before @fauxperdante finally accepted my follow request. Waiting for me was a tweet that had a time stamp of Wednesday, June 4, 2014, 2:28 a.m. The new phase of my life as Lata Murthy had begun.

Zaila's girlfriend Nika was the only person I knew who had her own boat. Not a canoe or rowboat or dinghy, the kind of vessel that could easily be stored in a large shed. But an honest to goodness luxury yacht. The kind I had seen only in music videos and *Sports Illustrated* shoots. Nika, the grand-daughter of an Albanian hotel magnate rivaling the Hiltons, shared the yacht with her twin brother, Dan, who usually claimed it to sail along the East Coast every summer, jour-neying to the Florida Keys and beyond. But he'd broken his ankle while riding his skateboard, and Zaila said that as soon as Nika received news of her brother's injury, she had imme-diately started planning a party on the *Dannika* (a name that combined those of both siblings).

Because it was hastily thrown together, only about ten of us were actually free to make it to the yacht party on the first Sat-urday of June. And I considered it a true mercy that the party was so small, considering what was being asked of me. It also marked the first time I prayed up to my eyeballs that Rajeev G would not attend an event I was going to. After David Jay's apologetic text for missing the Memorial Day party, Rajeev had also written that he was sorry to miss out and hoped to see us soon. When I had replied **we missed you guys!** along with a smiley face, Rajeev had replied **next time** along with his own smiley face. It was amazing how a simple :-) could feed me for days.

My yearning to see Rajeev at the yacht party lasted only a day before Other Lata's first tweet scuttled all my hopes, replacing them with a slimy dread. I tried to think of a way out of it, but I didn't have enough information about her to try to evade her plans for me. And this time there would be no selecting my outfit from my overstuffed closet or from a big department store like Macy's or Bloomingdale's. I spent the rest of the week in a mad dash, visiting every thrift and consignment store in a forty-block radius. As I completed my expedition on a late Friday evening at an Upper East Side Goodwill, I wished that I hadn't become so adept at shopping.

———

It was an unseasonably warm ninety-four degrees the day of the party, and so to save myself from embarrassment—not to mention heat stroke while waiting for the subway—I took a cab all the way to the Brooklyn Marina in DUMBO, where the *Dannika* was docked. The cab driver had eyed me warily as I clambered into the cab with my rainbow tote, not yet wearing my full ensemble. As a way to give myself some kind of dignity, I had arranged my hair into a topknot, but that couldn't possibly assuage my nerves as the cab inched along the West Side Highway to DUMBO.

On the way there I tried giving myself a pep talk, but I was too out of sorts to do anything but dab at my sweat-stained forehead and dig my toes into the cheap plastic of my pink flip-flops. By the time the cab dropped me off, I felt close to a panic attack. The only thing that prevented me from fleeing altogether was the new tweet Other Lata had fired off that morning.

I'LL BE WATCHING.

Nika spotted me first. I took short, uneasy steps across the cement dock toward the *Dannika*, which resembled an edgy three-layer wedding cake. She peered at me as if she didn't recognize who was approaching her, then waved while laughing.

"Sweetheart, did someone tell you this is a costume party?" Nika came down to the dock to welcome me. Unlike me, she was dressed appropriately, in a lace-trimmed poplin mini dress that I immediately coveted.

"Hey, Nika," I said. We exchanged air kisses. "I just felt like doing something different."

She raised an eyebrow. "Well, you definitely did that."

And so for the first time in my life, I arrived on an actual yacht. This would usually be the kind of triumphant moment that would make me think about my past selves, how New Canaan Lata and Seton Hall Lata would have dreamed about a moment like this, though scarcely believing it would be possible for them.

And they wouldn't have believed it, nor the fact that I was attending a summer yacht party while wearing a brown fur coat that stopped at my calves, pink flip-flops, several gaudy gold chains, and a pink bikini the same color as Pepto-Bismol. My sunglasses were also pink, but heart shaped with white polka dots.

Zaila approached, and her jaw dropped as she took me in from head to toe.

"Why are you dressed as J. Lo?"

There were six other friends of mine who witnessed that first Other Lata–induced task/humiliation. Besides Zaila and

Nika, Anita and Francesco, Keiko, David Jay, Kingsley, and, yes, Rajeev, all got to see me dressed as "J. Lo" or "Park Avenue Minnie Mouse crashing spring break." (The latter comment came from Kingsley.) Zaila and Nika also invited two of their couple friends, so their first impression of me was that I was a weirdo. I kept up the ruse that I was "in the mood to change it up" and liked "experimenting with my style." Once the *Dannika* set sail, heading toward Manhattan before sailing up the Hudson River, two things happened.

One, I was happy to have the fur jacket. It was actually a faux-fur jacket, discounted at 80 percent from a sustainable clothing line called Otterhand & Co. The yacht moved so quickly through the waters that the jacket kept me warm as we stood on the top deck, the winds whipping at everyone else, in shorts and sundresses and bare feet. I hugged it close to my bare skin, feeling snug inside.

Two, after everyone had a few glasses of champagne, the novelty of my outfit wore off. At least, no one was making comments to my face anymore. There were conversations about upcoming parties and summer trips and stories in the news. No one was really talking to me, though. I think they found it too awkward to make conversation with someone who looked so silly but was also possibly on the verge of a mental breakdown. Rajeev shot me a few concerned glances, but I looked past him, jutting out my slightly quivering chin.

After about an hour, as the group started to pose for photos, I left for the empty lower deck swamped in shade. As I took in the view, I tried to look like someone entranced by the beauty of the sky and the sunlight bouncing off the water. Not someone avoiding the other guests and hiding my shame and watery eyes behind my stupid sunglasses. Dior they were decidedly not.

I felt a tentative tap on my shoulder. It was Zaila, holding two cans of LaCroix. I accepted one from her, and she stood next to me.

"Sooo," she said, her eyes quickly skipping from my pink sunglasses to the fur coat. "Do you feel out of place here sometimes? Is that what this is about?"

I longed to tell her the truth. That "what this was about" had to do with a tweet from the @fauxperdante Twitter account that said:

For the yacht party: wear a dark brown fur coat, pink bikini, sunglasses and flip flops & five gold chains. Take a photo of yourself in the yacht's bathroom mirror and text it to me.

Upon seeing the tweet earlier that week, I had responded, as instructed, by favoriting it, as if I approved of the absurdity of what Other Lata was asking. Good thing I had written down her directions on a Post-it, because a few minutes later, the tweet had been deleted. I had already taken care of the photo upon boarding the yacht, because it gave me a few precious minutes to check my emotions and avoid the stares of my bemused friends. I had texted the photo to Other Lata but never received a reply.

To answer Zaila's question, I gave a noncommittal shoulder shrug, then looked out on the lapping waves.

"Sometimes all of this can feel like being the best friend in someone else's movie," Zaila said. "You know *Clueless*, right? Dionne and Cher? I'm the Dionne, everyone else here is Cher."

For the first time since arriving at the *Dannika*, I took off my sunglasses to regard my friend. In terms of style, Zaila was undoubtedly Dionne, always effortlessly chic, usually in bright colors and eye-catching patterns, whereas her girl-friend preferred a minimalist wardrobe of beige and black. As a teenager Zaila had modeled in Paris and Milan, and her walk still had that kind of purposeful strut that caught every-one's attention as she went by. But Zaila seemed much hap-pier behind the camera, snapping photos for her popular blog capturing the street style of herself and others. Of our friend group, there were several of us who weren't white, but Zaila was the only one who was Black. And to my shame, both at that moment and in thinking about it now, I never really thought about what that was like for her.

"Before modeling, I went to an all-girls boarding school in Millbrook, but on a scholarship. I'm used to not fitting in for many reasons. I wasn't born into all this," she said, tapping on the yacht's railing. "My mother married my stepfather when I was in college, so now I'm more used to it." Zaila's mother was married to a media mogul who owned several cable networks that Google claimed had a combined net worth of $12 billion. "But it's not comfortable. You remind me of that sometimes. That this doesn't always feel easy for you."

"Thank you for saying that. And I'm sorry that it never occurred to me to ask about you." She gave me a matter-of-fact nod, acknowledging but not excusing. "I guess we're opposites. I started with all of this luxury and then had to scale way back. It's sort of like being a princess exiled from her castle. Sorry, that sounds so gross." I laughed apologetically. "So at times, I feel like a poser." To be able to say the word, to be able to nod in any way toward the truth of Other Lata and the awful Twitter account, was a momentary balm to my soul. I ached to be able to share more, to tell her everything.

"What was it like, to be that wealthy and then suddenly on your own?" She raised her rainbow-print sunglasses, exposing two worry lines between her perfectly arched eyebrows.

I compared it to a free-fall ride, the kind that hurtles you five hundred feet upward and suspends you briefly in the air before the stomach-churning drop back to Earth. But my words sounded hollow to my ears. Not just because of my fake Mumbai origins, but because of my true story. I might have never been uber-wealthy, but we never lived hand-to-mouth either. My parents had worked hard to provide me a comfortable upbringing. And although I never asked them for financial assistance after they paid my college tuition, if I truly needed to borrow a month's rent, they would be able to help me without being burdened by it.

"Why do you ask?" All around us were blue skies and shimmering ocean, plentiful sunlight drenching us as a Katy Perry song bounced out of the speakers, her plastic-sweet voice awed that she was living a teenage dream. Even so, Zaila's melancholy matched my own.

"Because I'm always telling myself not to get too comfortable with all of this. Like, I'm here, but none of it actually belongs to me. This is my girlfriend's yacht, and my parents own my condo." Zaila snapped her fingers. "It can go away just like that."

To shake off my sadness, I tried embodying Downtown Lata. I put my sunglasses back on, lifted my chin, and elongated my neck, a haughty princess in thrift store clothing. "I know this all too well." But my eyes had welled up while I was thinking about my parents, and a tear glimmered on my eyelash. I dipped a finger underneath my pink shades to blot it out.

Zaila eyed me carefully. "So … is this you acting out? Like, do you need to talk with someone? Maybe a thera—"

"Oh no, but thank you." I hugged the fur coat closer to my body. "This is just me trying to figure myself out. Who I am now, without my family? But also trying to have a little fun at my own expense, if that makes sense."

"Yes and no." Our eyes met, and after a beat we both laughed, a shared gale of merriment that also felt like a release. "But know you always have a friend in me. If you need to talk, I'm here."

"Thank you. And ditto too, okay?" I told her. Zaila nodded.

When I had come to the yacht, I had expected laughter and stares and jokes made at my expense. I had never once thought someone would approach me with compassion. I took her hand and squeezed it, the tears in my eyes finally breaking through. She squeezed mine back.

12

LuxTress

AFTER THE YACHT DAY, KEIKO and Rajeev reached out to me separately too. Both messages were sweet and tentative, check-in texts that came with offers to meet for coffee. I responded warmly to Keiko, and with a bit of distance to Rajeev. Because even without the chaos of Other Lata interjecting herself into my life, I was tiring of Rajeev running hot and cold. No doubt he was preoccupied; Keiko noted that Rajeev was tunneling back into his "work cave" as he worked on orders from clients and prepped a new line. Rajeev was a focused and intense guy, and I respected his work ethic.

But did he think of Per Se as often as I did? I replayed our conversation in my head constantly, sometimes chuckling to myself when recalling a joke one of us made. It's frustrating to meet someone you really think could be that person for you, and still see him on occasion, but never actually go further than that one blissful and perfect interaction. And I didn't want our first meeting after so long to be a discussion about why I had been so weird on the yacht.

Especially when I was only going to get weirder as the summer went along. The first few weeks of June were busy with typical summer things: parties and events, openings and more parties. And Other Lata seemed preternaturally aware of my social calendar, making me paranoid. I kept all the curtains and blinds in the apartment permanently closed, never letting in even the smallest slat of sunlight; I fretfully peered behind me while out and about, doing this so often that I nearly walked into bicyclists and lampposts on several occasions; I stopped posting on Facebook and tweeted only when it was work related.

Prior to Other Lata, I had been indifferent to Twitter, preferring Facebook. Now I hated Twitter. I hated and feared receiving a notification marked by that stupid blue bird appearing on my home screen, informing me, "New tweet from @fauxperdante." She could have sent her missives via DM, but for whatever reason she just tweeted them out from her private account. I was her only follower, although a quick glance through the accounts she followed revealed random commercial brands like Pepsi and Target. Other Lata was very good at masking any revealing facts about herself.

There also seemed to be no rhyme or reason for her demands, except to invent new ways to humiliate me. And she was very good at that. At a Sunday barbecue at a beach house in Montauk, she had me juggling hot dogs for the entire length of the party. I don't think it mattered to Other Lata that I had no idea how to juggle, because whether I was adept at it or not, I was still the butt of the joke. Kingsley and David Jay filmed me on their iPhones as I stood in a shaded corner of the brick-floored patio, sweaty and red-faced as I attempted to juggle the franks. When not doubled over with laughter, David Jay commented on the action as if he were a sideline reporter at a sporting event. (Kingsley later uploaded a brief clip of me to Instagram with the hashtag #lataplayswithweiners.)

"Why, Lata? Do you have dreams to be a clown?" Kingsley asked with a hint of exasperation once they got tired of making fun of me.

"I just always wanted to try," I sputtered grimly, collecting the dirt-speckled hot dogs from the ground. "And can you not do that?" I added, throwing a hot dog in the direction of their phones before stalking away. I was hot, tired, and thirsty, and Other Lata couldn't begrudge me a five-minute break from humiliating myself.

So of course I received a double dose of humiliation while hiding out in a guest bedroom. The room was nautical themed to an absurd degree, including a corner bookshelf designed to resemble a ship's prow. Needing a moment to myself, and with all the bathrooms occupied, I crouched behind it while glugging from an Evian bottle. As I tried to psych myself up to go back outside and resume my foolish task, two familiar voices arrived in the guest room.

"Ahoy, matey," Anita said, with a treble of laughter. "This room is ridic. Like that bookshelf. It's as if half the *Titanic* is bursting out of the wall."

I held my breath, the water bottle nearly dropping from

my grasp. With at least ten rooms in this house, why did they have to choose to come in here?

"Whose house is this again?" Zaila replied.

"Who knows? David Jay's friend of blah-blah-blah." Some rustling and unzipping sounds. "It's hot as balls out there. Do you have any sunscreen?"

Zaila said something, but I couldn't make it out. Whatever she said, it caused Anita to laugh.

"Remind me to never come back to Montauk. By the way, what is up with Lata? Is she drunk or something? I don't get the hot dogs at all."

"It's weird, but I think that's just her. She likes trying new things." Zaila didn't sound convinced of her own reasoning.

"I think she's on something. Or she likes being the center of attention." Something plastic dropped to the floor and rolled in my direction. "Shit. Stupid lipstick."

"Sounds like someone I know," Zaila teased as the click-click of Anita's heels stopped inches from where I was cowering.

"Um, hello? I don't need to pull any stupid stunts. I can command attention just by...I don't know, putting on lipstick." To my relief, the click-clicks pivoted in the opposite direction. "Nika thinks it's a cry for help. She said she's seen people lose all their money and act out just like this."

"She's not hurting anyone, is she?"

"Chill, Z. Those are your girlfriend's words, not mine."

"I know. It's just that when you're born with money, it's so much different. You and Nika have no idea what it's like not to have that safety net. If Lata needs to act out, then let her."

I uttered a silent prayer of thanks to Zaila, while also agonizing over earning empathy I did not deserve.

"I'm letting her stay at my place while she renovates hers, what more do you want from me?" Anita huffed out of the room, her click-clacking across the hardwood reminding me of an angry woodpecker.

"To not be blinded by your privilege," Zaila said softly. A few moments later, she left the room too.

Overhearing Anita and Zaila's conversation put me in a fighting spirit. After reapplying my lipstick and rearranging my sweat-streaked hair into a tight bun, I returned to the patio with a new packet of hot dogs nabbed from the kitchen. With the *Rocky* theme song in my head, I resumed juggling with the intensity of someone auditioning for the Barnum & Bailey Circus.

And after about thirty minutes, can you believe I actually started getting the hang of it? As the minutes passed, more and more people stopped to watch me, until I had a full-on crowd cheering me on, Anita and Zaila included. And eventually, miraculously, not only did I successfully juggle those hot dogs, I did it for one minute straight. Still recording me on his phone, David Jay led a cheer of "Lata! Lata!" as I bowed with a flourish. When I rose up, I caught Zaila's eye and we exchanged smiles.

Rajeev and Keiko had missed my antics, as they were huddled elsewhere, discussing something related to Rajeev's work. But they came up to me afterward and congratulated me.

"You're full of surprises!" Keiko beamed. Rajeev nodded,

but he was as usual his distant, preoccupied self. I thanked them and then got myself an overflowing glass of white wine. Two thoughts occurred to me at the same time: *Oh shit, I did that* and *Screw you, Other Lata*. For once, I hoped she was snooping around somewhere, so she could witness my triumph.

———

The next few weeks passed this way. I'd receive an invitation from a friend, or a friend of a friend, then a few days later, there would be a @fauxperdante tweet with a new command, and a few days after that I would do it. And if Other Lata's intention was to continue humiliating me, it was actually starting to have the opposite effect.

My friends were now expecting me to act oddly. I think by the end they were even starting to look forward to it.

I did the Macarena nonstop at a Tribeca rooftop party— while chatting and smiling for photos and waiting in line for the bathroom—until eventually half the crowd joined me, prompting the bemused deejay to play the Los del Río song for us. I wore a sash and tiara over a tank top and jeans to the swanky after-party of a movie produced by David Jay's company, and in the middle of a chat with Micheline, Anita, and some others I didn't know too well, I interrupted the conversation to give a pageant speech about why I should be crowned Miss America (my platform was "world peace and unlimited pizza for all"). For Micheline's birthday party at Gramercy Tavern, during which JJ surprised her with a proposal, I wore my hair in an enormous beehive (created with the help of pricey LuxTress hair extensions and a You-Tube tutorial) while speaking about myself in the third person, which meant that after the applause and handing out of champagne, I approached them and gushed, "Lata is so happy for you! You guys are so sweet together, Lata knew it was only a matter of time. Total couple goals. Congratulations! Lata aspires to have what you have one day."

All of my shenanigans could have driven my friends crazy. And based on what I'd heard Anita say back in Montauk, I knew there was still a chance they would ice me out. But not only did they warm up to my antics, I actually began enjoying them too. Thinking back, I realized that as much as I'd been enjoying my new life as Downtown Lata prior to Other Lata's arrival, all of it had been tinged with the anxiety that Zaila had sensed from me. Even as my friendships deepened and my invites got more exclusive, I couldn't quite shake the feeling that I was a mere interloper, a pretender. I mean, I was all of that, but the knowledge that my new career and friendships were built on a shaky lie that no one seemed to interrogate kept me jumpy. But to now be embraced for my wackiness, to have my friends just come to accept it and even encourage it, helped me settle into myself. I liked myself more and felt a blossoming confidence that I had never known.

Rajeev was a different story.

After I walked away from Micheline and JJ, Rajeev approached me, holding two glasses of champagne. He never drank alcohol, but I guess he made an exception for the occasion.

"That's impressive." He gazed upward to the top of my hairdo, and there were noticeable worry lines cropping up near his eyes.

"Um, thanks." My cheeks reddened. With a trembling hand, I accepted the glass from him. We never talked anymore, just the two of us. Lately, that was my preference.

"What inspired this? It's so... specific."

"I like experimenting," I mumbled. A glimpse of my reflection in a nearby window showed me that the beehive had started lolling to the side.

"You remind me of Saira Banu. She wore her hair like this."

"You mean the actress?"

Rajeev nodded. I knew of Saira Banu because she starred in a lot of my mother's favorite films. The following day I would be making the trek to New Canaan to see my parents, a visit that had gradually become biweekly, then monthly. A stab of guilt pierced me as I thought of how little I'd seen of them lately.

"Yes, but Saira wore winged eyeliner." He was taking me in, not in an appreciative "I find you so attractive" way, but as if he were appraising a statue or painting. And at that moment, I lost patience.

"Well, I'm not her," I snapped, pushing my sliding hair upward. I saw him flinch and instantly regretted my tone (the fact that I forgot to speak in third person, less so). Before I could apologize, Keiko and Anita encircled us and started asking me questions about my beehive extensions. As Anita noted that Lady Gaga favored the same brand, Rajeev slipped away.

By the time July arrived, I was exhausted with thinking about Rajeev and wondering how he felt about me. At the same time, I had kept my distance too, and so my own once-fervent feelings were now on a low simmer. Mostly he was on the outskirts of every stunt I pulled, but I often felt his eyes on me, even if he was standing far away. Whenever our eyes would meet, there would be a connection that set off sparks underneath my skin. But after our quick conversation at the birthday-turned-engagement party, I convinced myself that I had to move on and let our magical night at Per Se be a lovely memory, its only purpose to bring me closer to everyone else in our circle.

Maybe it's just not meant to be, I thought right as my phone buzzed with Other Lata's latest tweet, this time about the upcoming Fourth of July weekend.

13

Kate Spade

THE FOURTH OF JULY WAS never a holiday that held fond memories for me. In New Canaan, every July 4 was marked by a painfully long and boring parade that my parents and I watched go by while waving tiny American flags. I would have preferred to spend the holiday at the pool or accepting a neighbor's invitation to a barbecue, but my parents believed it was important to show our faces each July, so no one could ever doubt our patriotism. No matter how much I reasoned, begged, or pleaded, Mom and Dad were adamant that we show up each year. (We did the same at the Indian Independence Day parade in Stamford, but that was more of a social event than proving our loyalty to our homeland.)

Once I moved to New York City, I found the Fourth of July to mostly be a pain in the ass. The iconic fireworks switched from east to west every year, and whether they were set off over the East River or the Hudson River, I'd inevitably be on the wrong side of the city. To actually see the fireworks with an unobstructed view was a near impossibility, at least for me. The closest I got to achieving it was my second year in the city, when my then boyfriend Dinesh and I raced up to his six-story walk-up in the East Village and emerged onto the roof just in time to see the Macy's fireworks give one last triumphant hail of red, white, blue, and gold. It was a triumphant moment for me too, as someone still new to the city. But then we couldn't get the rooftop door to open and ended up stuck up there until three in the morning, sniping at each other as a never-ending cold drizzle soaked us to the bone. We broke up two weeks after.

So yes, I'd never had any great excitement in celebrating America's independence. And certainly not this year.

Weirdly, this was the one occasion that Other Lata took a break from tormenting me. Her tweet was brief, dryly stating, **Taking this week off. Enjoy your independence, for now.** It didn't exactly feel threatening, though, more like a tired aunty brushing me off after we had arranged to meet. But why was Other Lata giving me a reprieve? Was she that looped in to my schedule that she knew I had no real solid plans for the long weekend, and so it wasn't worth crafting my humiliation when there would be no audience to see it?

All my friends had taken off for different locales, luxury beaches and cabins and resorts. Anita and Zaila and Keiko and David Jay had all kindly extended invitations, and I had reluctantly said no to all of them. My overextended credit cards needed the break. I was dangerously close to being maxed out, even though I had long since given up clothes shopping, with all my income instead devoted to socializing and, more recently, Other Lata's blackmail. If Other Lata was giving me a break, then I was truly going to treat the next few days as a mental spa day. My plans for the four-day weekend included soaking in the bathtub and curling up on the sofa with *Sex and the City* reruns and cold pizza.

About six episodes into my *SATC* binge, my phone lit up with a text message.

Hey Lata. Are you in the city this weekend?

It was Rajeev.

I scrambled up in my seat. I texted back, **Yes, are you?**

From there, we had a text exchange in which we lamented that we were the only two people left behind in the city as it was flooded with tourists, and decided we needed to band together to survive, acting as if the bridge-and-tunnel crowd were a zombie horde. The Rajeev in these text messages was warm and funny, the man I first met nearly a year ago, and just like that, my day did a magnificent turnabout. Rajeev invited me over to his apartment that night to watch the fireworks, which happened to be taking place on the West Side that year. His upstairs neighbor had a penthouse, and Rajeev had volunteered to stop by over the holiday weekend to tend to their gigantic aquarium of saltwater fish. In exchange, Rajeev was granted access to their private rooftop, which had clear and shimmering views of the Hudson.

With nine hours before the fireworks started, I used seven and a half of them to prep every inch of my body and every fiber of my being. Having *Sex and the City* on in the background was a comfort, as if Carrie, Samantha, Charlotte, and Miranda were gabbing away to keep me company while I got ready. My ensemble came together immediately: a red J.Crew sundress, Kate Spade slides with three white roses embroidered on each strap, and blue-beaded dangle earrings, a favorite pair of jewelry that I used to wear a lot in my pre–Downtown Lata days. While I didn't want to look like the American flag, I at least wanted to give an approximation of patriotic fun. When examining myself in the mirror, I was pleased that for once my reflection accurately reflected how I felt within. Not abuzz with butterflies that made me jittery and nauseous, as I had felt so many other times going out hoping to see Rajeev. This time I was merely hopeful for a good night with a good friend, and happy not to be spending the holiday alone.

The sky was glorious and clear, even if the weather was a bit humid. Fourth of July parties were happening on private terraces to our left and right, which we could hear but not see over the white fences that partitioned each space. Rajeev and I were seated side by side on the edge of a plastic red picnic table, the sole piece of furniture on his neighbor's terrace, which was otherwise surprisingly sparse except for several wilting plants and a stroller in the corner. Even if the terrace felt more like a storage unit than a rooftop Eden, neither of us cared. We also agreed that having parties beside us but not having to be among a crowd was the most ideal situation.

"I'm the lucky one, though. When I left my studio this morning to get coffee and realized what day it was, I considered just going back inside and keep working. If you weren't here, that's where I would be now." Rajeev, clad in light blue jeans and a black button-down shirt, gave a rueful laugh. "Pathetic, right?"

"Not at all," I said before tipping an oyster to my lips. Doing this reminded me of our dinner at Per Se and the first course of oysters and pearls. A part of me wanted to take this as a good omen for our night, and the other part of me retorted, *It's just an oyster, chill out*.

"Work has consumed me lately, more so than usual. I've been a workaholic since I was ten, but that was more about doing math homework and playing my Nintendo. My work ethic hasn't really changed, but my focus has." Rajeev took a swig of ginger beer. "I know I've been..."

"MIA?" I teased.

"Yes, that." He set down the ginger beer and scanned the sky, wisps of clouds moving above the horizon at a tortoise's pace. "I don't think I've had such a beautiful view of the Hudson like this before." He seemed lost in thought, and even if Rajeev and I hadn't spent a ton of time together, it was easy to recognize when the gears were turning in his head as he pondered a new idea. I swung my feet carelessly back and forth, waiting for him to return. Honestly, I didn't even mind. It was enough just to be there with him and only him, and the beautiful view.

As I got lost in our sky and surroundings, Rajeev abruptly turned toward me. We were sitting close together, and so when I swiveled toward him, our eyes met and he held my gaze. It was the most intense eye contact I had ever experienced in my life.

"I wanted to apologize for not being around a lot. That night at Per Se, I still think back on it a lot as my last pure moment of fun. Before the deluge, when my life turned into a treadmill of sketches and fabric and sewing. I'm happy for the work and the interest I'm receiving. But I got so caught up in it, I let other things slide. And that's one of the reasons I wanted to see you tonight. To apologize and let you know that our dinner wasn't just a dinner to me." At this last part, he tilted his face downward, his eyebrows raised slightly.

I drew in a deep breath. My feet swung at a faster clip. None of my daydreams about this moment could have been scripted nearly as perfectly. Before I could respond, my Kate Spade slide rocketed off of my left foot, ricocheting off the terrace wall before landing in a giant planter that held a ficus tree.

"Whoops." The word "whoops" did not begin to capture the one hundred and fifty-two levels of embarrassment rippling through me. I retracted my bare foot and hid it behind my other leg.

"Wait right there. I got you." Rajeev hopped off the table and rescued my sandal. Rather than handing it to me, he gestured for me to hold out my foot. He slid it on, and the warmth of his fingers on my ankle lingered as a warm charge exploding around my heart.

"Um, thank you," I said as he sat down next to me, still dizzy from his brief touch. "And I totally get how busy you are. This must be such an exciting time right now. It could change your whole life!" Not able to meet his gaze (seriously, so intense), I addressed the ficus tree. "But that wasn't just a dinner for me too. It's really nice to hear you say that."

On either side of us, each party cranked its music higher as we neared the start of the fireworks display. The parties seemed to be opposite in every possible way, as if Rajeev and I had crash-landed a time machine between two distinct eras. To our left was jazz, swing, and rockabilly, as classy as a vintage gramophone. And to our right, it was full-on eighties party music. Beastie Boys, Madonna, Bon Jovi, and anything else that hinted at white powder and rolled-up dollar bills on a glass coffee table.

Rajeev started to respond, but I pointed to my ear and asked him to speak louder. Instead, he moved closer. His breath against my ear and the scent of his cologne were so potent that I viscerally understood the meaning of the word "swoon."

"Even if I've been in my work cave or stressed out or lost in thought, I always looked forward to having the chance to see you. Honestly, to be in the same room with you was enough for me."

I blinked back tears. Then I pinched the inside of my wrist, which was a cheesy thing to do, but how else could I be sure I wasn't dreaming?

"After Fashion Week and the drama with Aqua, there was so much pressure to equal all the nice things people were saying about me. And so with every passing week, I felt further away from myself. I wasn't designing for me, but for what I want people to think about me. It's a constant stomachache, thinking that way.

"These past few weeks, when you started acting differently, at first I was concerned about you. I talked to Keiko, and she had talked to Zaila, and they both said you were fine. Acting weird, to be sure, but fine. But after the party in Montauk, you had a different energy about you. And it's infectious. None of us can get enough of it." He said that when Keiko told Charmaine that I wasn't accompanying her to Sea Cove for the weekend, Charmaine was disappointed because he was dying to know what I would do next.

"Oh god." I shook my head. "I'm a running joke. I'm like the Naked Cowboy that everyone gawks at."

"No! I didn't mean it that way. We all like being a part of . . . your thing. If joy was a fireplace, we all like to be gathered around you." He paused, then added, "I can't imagine what it was like before we met you. You make everything . . . better."

And now I was blushing so hard I imagined my face looked as if I had swept my entire compact of Maybelline Sweet Berry from hairline to chin.

"You've inspired me, Lata. That's what I wanted to tell you. Seeing you let loose and be your weird, wonderful self reminds me not to take myself too seriously. And especially not to let my anxiety about my career overtake the joy my work gives me."

Rajeev exhaled as if he had been holding these thoughts in for a long time. And of everything he said that night, it's the exhale that stays with me. Because he had been carrying that feeling for so long, and each time I had seen him at a party, when our eyes would meet before I slinked away in embarrassment, this was on his mind.

It was my turn to speak into his ear. "That I could be that for you... I'm... Wow. I'm speechless."

On either side of us, the battle between neon eighties and sepia jazz came to a halt, as both parties switched to the radio station providing the musical soundtrack for the Macy's fireworks display. So Rajeev and I were treated to a double-booming chorus of patriotic songs like "You're a Grand Old Flag" synced to the dazzling sparkle and crash of lights spanning miles of sky. For the next twenty-five minutes, we watched them together, our faces pointed upward as the fireworks did their ballet routine for us, lights exploding, then fading, then blooming anew. A few minutes in, Rajeev reached for my hand, and to have my palm enclosed in his was the kind of tenderness I had never felt in any relationship, parental or romantic. I tried my best not to give in to my emotions, but by the finale, a one-two punch of "America the Beautiful" and "The Star-Spangled Banner," my tears were in freefall. Too awed by the fireworks to wipe them away, I let the tears travel southward, off my chin and down my neck, past my clavicle.

"Lata, you're crying!" Rajeev exclaimed, handing me a napkin.

"Happy tears, I promise," I said with a weak smile.

"Are you sure?" he asked as I patted down my face and neck, the napkin soon tainted with the browns of my foundation and powder.

"Yes." I smiled again, but this time with exuberance, because I imagined my surly teen self, bookended by her parents, while she listlessly waved a flag on the sidewalks of New Canaan, hoping against hope that exciting days were ahead of her.

The pair of outdoor parties roared back to life with their own music, but the eighties party seemed to bring reinforcements via additional speakers. Whatever the classy party was playing, it was quickly drowned out by Belinda Carlisle's "Mad About You." Even though the main fireworks show had ended, from our vantage point there were still mini fireworks displays that could be viewed from every angle, small pockets of color exploding all around us, spanning the East Side to across the Hudson. Despite my tearstained face, my whole self was beaming, as if perforated by a thousand sun rays. And I had a thought.

I didn't make my move on Memorial Day, but here's a new holiday, and a new start.

Life doesn't always offer moments that could be lifted straight out of a romance movie. But when they do arrive, you have to take your shot. That was what I did when I heard Belinda Carlisle and watched the tiny fireworks bursting in every corner of the sky.

I leaned toward Rajeev, ran my fingers through his wonderful silky hair, and kissed him.

And I was rewarded with the kind of kiss Shakespeare had penned sonnets about. And if he hadn't, he really should have.

14

Elephantine

HOW COULD I BE SO lucky and unlucky at the same time? This was the question that prodded at me for the rest of the four-day weekend, as I reveled in Rajeev's affections while also dreading Other Lata's next missive once real life resumed when Monday arrived. And I couldn't get over the fact that Other Lata's blackmail demands were the spark that finally brought me and Rajeev to admit our feelings to one another.

That irony became uncomfortably clear over those next few days. We spent the entire weekend together, starting the night of the Fourth. The West Chelsea streets were tricky once the fireworks ended, because the hundreds of people who went to watch the display along the West Side Highway took forever to leave, a slow-moving mass that was a nightmare to navigate. So Rajeev suggested that I stay at his apartment ("I mean not like that...just as a sleepover," he added shyly) and return home a few blocks northward the following morning.

We curled up side by side on his bed, his strong, calloused hand on my elbow and the covers tucked snugly around us, and spoke into the early morning hours. Rajeev asked me about the specific inspiration for my getups, particularly the fur coat and the beehive. Though he couldn't see me—I was the little spoon to his big spoon—I squeezed my eyes shut as I called them "random ideas, kinda reflecting how I felt at the moment." While Other Lata's blackmail had brought us closer, it also had built a wall between us, because everything Rajeev admired me for was built on her instigations, forcing me to lie to him.

But Rajeev bought my flimsy excuse and explained that over the past few weeks, his stalled creativity had been reawakened by my "random ideas." To the point that he had mostly scrapped what he had been working on so far, and was designing several new pieces inspired by my mischievous energy.

"You're kidding," I said, turning over to face him. I had never been so close to him before. I could see a faded scar at the corner of his left lip, a red irritation blooming underneath his nose. It was all intoxicating, this sudden intimacy with someone I had yearned for at a distance for nearly a year.

"This new line has to be a mission statement, especially if my goal is to get into the tents." He went quiet for a moment and then shook his head with two terse movements, as if reeling himself back from getting lost in thought over his work. "I watched you be so liberated and free, not taking yourself seriously. I'd like my clothes to exude a similar feeling." Again, the blank stare. Just by mentioning his clothing line, Rajeev traveled far away. This time, I reeled him back by taking his hand and running my thumb over his thumbnail. He came back to me, returning this time with a chagrined grin.

"You haven't known me very long, but I promise you I'm not always such a robot," he said with a laugh. "I feel like all you've seen of me is 'Work. Fashion. Boop be boop boop.'" At this last part, he moved his arms like a robot. I giggled in his face, then nearly clapped a hand over my mouth, hoping my breath hadn't been affected by all the ginger beers and oysters. But my breath was fine, because Rajeev leaned in and kissed me.

"I love your laugh, Lata." He smiled dreamily, and my insides got all fizzy.

"I'm glad to be an inspiration in any way. It's an honor," I replied. "I hope it means that I'm going to see beehives and flip-flops on your runway."

"You know it." Rajeev winked.

"But you shouldn't feel bad about being a robot. You're working toward a dream, and of course that will take all your focus. How could it not?" Our hands were still married together, and he tightened his grip on mine.

"That's nice of you to excuse my rudeness, but it's all about balance. My sisters have told me that there is Work Rajeev and Regular Rajeev. Whenever the three of us make plans, they insist the invitation is for 'Regular R' only. Which means I've only seen them about three times this year." The worry lines around his eyes deepened. "I have to work on it."

I nodded, wondering if I would have the chance to meet Shay and Mazzy. He spoke so little of his sisters that I still didn't know their real names. But the way he spoke of them sounded very big-brother-esque, which endeared Rajeev to me even more. The only reason I didn't want to ask him about his sisters was I feared the reciprocal question about my own family. Rajeev remained the only person in the Downtown Lata friend group who knew that my Mumbai backstory was false. No doubt Keiko had informed him of the estrangement between me and my wealthy parents. At some point, though, Rajeev was going to ask about me, the real me. And I needed to stave off that reality for as long as I could.

"But what about you?" Ah crap. "How do you like working in PR? When we first met, I don't know if we talked about it at all. Work Rajeev is obviously to blame," he added ruefully.

How to answer, how to answer. "It's good. I have a knack for it, but it was never exactly my dream." I needed to walk a tightrope of talking about myself in a genuine way without ever tilting toward the truth. I took a few moments to think about how I could do this, before saying the words I rarely allowed myself to say out loud.

"I've always liked writing, almost as much as reading. Reading is my number one with a bullet, and if there was a career to be a Professional Reader Curled Up on the Sofa on a Rainy Day, please let me know, because I'll apply immediately." Rajeev gave an appreciative chuckle. "I think I could like writing more, but I've never really tried, you know? I mean, we're not exactly raised to pursue a career in the arts. There's no clear and defined career path in a creative profession that our parents—"

Shit. The last thing I wanted to do was bring up Diya and Ashok Murthy. Nothing to do but keep going, though.

"—that our parents can understand. Which is why I find what you do so admirable, by the way!" How I longed to ask him how he navigated such an unusual career choice with his parents. But I couldn't puncture this bubble we were in. Not with Rajeev gazing at me with his vivid brown eyes, the oaky scent of his cologne and the silky warmth of his sheets creating the haze of a cocoon. Instead, I allowed myself to speak honestly about my ambitions, something I rarely did, even with myself.

"Public relations is a really good way to make a living. But I want to be a writer with a capital *W*." My feet kicked under the sheets, as if they knew what I was about to say and wanted to flee in embarrassment. After a deep breath, I dove in anyway. "The problem is, all I have is the want. Some days I want to be Arundhati Roy. Other days Agatha Christie. And then sometimes Amy Tan or Isabel Allende or Anita Desai or Joan Didion. I can't decide on what kind of writer I want to be. All I know is that I want to say something." I broke eye contact with him and stole my hand back, twisting my rings back and forth, first on the left hand, then on the right.

"Where does that want come from, you think?" No one had ever asked me this, because I had never admitted this out loud before. I found it hard to answer. I glanced up at the ceiling, as blank as my writing career to date.

"I love words and sentences. When I read something beautiful, I want to write something equally beautiful. And I've tried to," I said, thinking of the tiny scrawls in notebook margins during college courses and, later, the Post-its at my old job at TrivialQ. "And what seems so profound in my head looks dull on the page."

"You're really hard on yourself," Rajeev said before dead-panning, "I can't relate to that at all."

"Ha," I replied. "And even if I could decide what writer I want to be, or what I want to say, reading a thousand books doesn't mean I'd make a good writer."

"That's the foundation, though. You can only be a good writer if you have done that," came Rajeev's immediate—and surprisingly impassioned—reply. The conviction in his voice briefly dissolved my shame. I had never thought of it that way before. Especially since I had made time to read only one book in the last six months, and it was just a comfort reread of *Harriet the Spy*. When I told him this, he shook his head.

"You've got it in you. I think you just have to give yourself permission to really try. And know that it's going to be hard, and you will fail. But if writing is something you love, you're going to keep going anyway." He reclaimed my hand and ran his finger along the dark brown curve of my lifeline. "At least, that's what Work Rajeev would tell you."

"How about good ol' Regular Rajeev?" I wiggled my fingers. "What does he see in my future?"

"Hmm, well, let me see." We both sat up cross-legged on the bed, and he guided my hand to the top of his knee. "I see a bright young woman who is ready to take her future in her own hands. No pun intended."

As I watched him examine my palm with the urgency of a surgeon about to make an incision, I wanted to freeze the moment and stay inside of it forever. Just me and Rajeev talking about our hopes and dreams, exchanging stupid jokes and blushing smiles. There was nothing waiting for me outside this room that could match the enveloping euphoria that all spelled out the same thought: *You're safe here. You're understood.*

"Lata Murthy is going to come across a moment of inspiration and seize it. And once she does, her life will never be the same." Rajeev uttered this with so much sincerity that his words had the gravity of an oracle. He was about to say something else when his phone rang on his bedside table. To my delight and his sheepish expression, the ringtone was the theme song to *The Famous Five*.

"Wow, you really did like that show, didn't you?" I laughed as he checked his phone. "That's adorable."

"I'm adorably embarrassed," he said, grinning as he looked up from the screen. "It's Keiko. She must be up this early because she's walking Hanae." With the curtains drawn in Rajeev's bedroom, I could have sworn it was only four a.m., but a quick check of his alarm clock indicated it was six thirty a.m. "She wants to know how my Fourth was. I guess you didn't tell her you were coming over?"

I reached over and checked my phone and found a similar message waiting for me. "I didn't want to put pressure on this, in case it turned out to be anything else but two friends hanging out."

After some discussion, weighing the pros and cons of what to say and how much, we decided to keep our blossoming relationship under wraps for now. Yet there was no harm in indicating we had hung out platonically. After an hour passed, Rajeev replied, **L and I watched the fireworks, it was fun.**

How about you? Having fun in the Hamptons? Two minutes later, my phone buzzed with a text from Keiko. **You and Rajeev hung out last night! How was it?????**

The number of question marks gave me pause, same with Rajeev. ("Oh boy. Her radar's already pinged.") Since I was known for being the opposite of an early riser, I waited until nine a.m. to respond:

Fun! The view from his building was incredible

When are you coming back? Free for dinner this week?

Between those two texts I sent her a photo of me and Rajeev standing on the rooftop, the scarlet-and-gold sky sprawled behind us. The photo had been snapped before we admitted our feelings, when we were still in awkward platonic mode. I thought it was safe to send.

Yet while Rajeev and I snacked on potato chips and pretzels while waiting for our breakfast delivery from the corner diner, I learned otherwise.

"Crap." With a jittery hand, I passed him my phone.

YOU GUYS ARE THE CUTEST!!!! It was only a matter of time

We've all been taking bets on when.

Rajeev laughed. "If I knew there was a pool, I would have timed this to happen so anyone but Kingsley would win."

"You're not nervous? That they all already know? We haven't even had our first date yet." Double crap. Was I being too presumptive even talking about first dates?

He groaned, but his eyes glinted with humor. "We were the last to know this was fated, I guess." When he noticed my anxious face and the phone lodged tight in my fist, his voice softened. "This still belongs to us, Lata. They don't need to know anything if we don't want them to. We'll have our first date; if it's okay with you, I already have an idea of where I want to take you." He held up his hand as if making a Boy Scout pledge. "No one is going to stick their noses in our business. I won't let them. We'll have our first date, and we'll take it from there."

But as I nuzzled against his shoulder while he put his arms around me, the uneasy feeling didn't fade, but flowered.

———

After the long weekend ended, I commenced playing defense with Other Lata. There was too much at stake now to continue blindly taking her commands without knowing why, especially when she had the power to reveal my true self to the people I cared about the most. Actually, I had already mounted small insurrections against her control. Starting with the second tweet, the one ordering me to juggle hot dogs, I'd taken a screenshot of every tweet she'd sent as soon as I read it, since Other Lata deleted her tweets after I favorited them. There was a hidden photo album in my phone titled "OL" where I saved the screenshots. After a busy two days at work, all the while parrying Keiko's probing text messages asking for an in-person catch-up, I used the entirety of my Wednesday evening to examine the tweets and see if I could start brainstorming ideas on how to extricate myself from Other Lata's control.

Unfortunately, a new tweet from @fauxperdante popped up while I microwaved a frozen pizza for dinner. Several tweets, actually.

Hope you enjoyed the week off. You'll be making up for it now.

This is bigger than wearing a bikini and flip flops, but I have faith in you

You've turned lying into an art form

The microwave beeped four times, each one sounding like a fire alarm. I didn't want to keep reading. But there was no choice.

1. You're going to get the Mars Marble from Aqua's collection. I'd like it very much

The Mars Marble, the Elephantine party, and Aqua seemed so long ago it was as if it had happened in another lifetime. Yet without all three, I'd still be at a dead-end job while sharing an apartment with Mallory and her BFF. I definitely wouldn't have Rajeev sending me cute texts about how excited he was for our first date the following Monday. Aqua was the impetus for my Downtown Lata existence, and now the obstacle to having it continue.

I had no idea where the Elephantine necklace was after Aqua wore it in Rajeev's runway show. But it couldn't be as simple as asking for it.

A cold chill laced around my heart. Did Other Lata want me to steal it?

If this was her first demand, I shuddered at what else she might want from me. With mounting dread, I read the rest of the tweets.

2. You need to be reminded of your Mumbai roots. And remind everyone else too.

You're going to publicly pledge $1 million while attending the annual MoonRose Benefit. You'll be receiving an invitation shortly

(It was meant for me, but I'm generous enough to share.)

I took the screenshots, put my phone in the microwave next to my cooling pizza, and slammed it shut. I then made a beeline for the bathroom, turned on the shower, and stepped inside the glass cube fully clothed. The scream I let out, long and delirious and painful, was muted by the water jets that filled my nose, mouth, and ears from all sides.

15

Fabindia

ACCORDING TO *VANITY FAIR*, THE MoonRose Benefit was one of the most highly anticipated events of the summer season for snooty blue bloods and their spoiled offspring. (I'm summarizing, obviously.) The cost of buying a table was $10,000, and then attendees were encouraged to donate further by participating in the silent auction and simply writing a check. I didn't see anything about people taking the stage to announce a donation, but Other Lata was never keen on following the rules. This year's benefit would take place in ten days.

I learned all of this after I soaked myself to the bone in the shower, sobbing and howling in a mad catharsis. Yet my brain was steadfastly working away at the problem anyway, as if attempting to undo one hundred knots in a silken thread, because taking a shower always helped relax my mind. When I had fled to the bathroom following Lata's latest tweets, I'd been seeking only solace and release. But the hot water deluge worked its magic anyway, and that was where I had my first concrete idea on what I could do to fight back.

After hanging up my sopping clothes over the shower door so they could dry, I retrieved my phone from the microwave and crawled into bed wearing only my Fabindia orange kaftan and a red towel wrapped around my head. My mom had purchased the kaftan for me during her last visit to Bangalore but misjudged the sizing, and so even though it had a tie that cinched at the waist, the ankle-length fabric was still looser and more voluminous than it was supposed to be. When I wore the kaftan, it usually meant I was in full retreat mode: phone turned off, snacking on Pringles on the couch, romcom movies all afternoon. But now I donned it because the kaftan's roominess helped me feel like my mind could further relax yet remain focused—sort of like working on a *New York Times* Sunday crossword puzzle during a spa day.

I opened up Twitter and favorited each of the new tweets. For the first time, I noticed the resentment exuding through each word. Usually, Other Lata's instructions were just a list of things I must do. But this time she let her emotions seep through. For the life of me, I couldn't understand her anger and what had upset her.

The thought that occurred to me in the shower was a simple one: Whom else does @fauxperdante follow on Twitter? I was her only follower, yet Other Lata followed 522 other accounts. After researching the MoonRose Benefit, I returned to @fauxperdante. I examined each of them. At least half the accounts were those of random brands like Zappos and Häagen-Dazs and Clinique. But they were a little too studiously random, as if she had followed those brands to mask whom else she followed. So I homed in on the non-brands, meticulously Googling each username. An hour into my search, I spotted an account that triggered a tingle of familiarity. The account was called @thefoxandlion. Now why was that so familiar? The Twitter account's photo was simply the letter *M* in cursive font. My brain did the mental scroll, the one I had cultivated over years of writing hundreds of trivia questions. When it hit on something, my body jerked with so much force that the towel flew off my head.

"Charmaine," I said out loud.

———

After Rajeev's party, I had determined that Charmaine was innocuous, and he either didn't actually know or no longer cared about the original Lata Murthy. A few days afterward, we ran into each other at a photography exhibit held at Micheline's gallery. The exhibit showcased photographs of people with unusual body modifications, including head-to-toe tattoos, and while waiting in line at the open bar, we got to discussing our own. I told Charmaine I had only one tattoo but, because of the intimate nature of its location, would never show it to anyone.

"Never?" Charmaine laughed, raising an eyebrow. "If I wasn't gay, I would almost take that as a challenge."

"Ha." I twirled my empty martini glass as I awaited a new one. "It's kind of my life philosophy." That wasn't quite true, but true enough.

"Oh really? I have a tattoo like that." He pushed up the

sleeve of his polo shirt, and I peered at the image on his biceps. It was the outlines of a fox and a lion standing side by side. A simple tattoo, in my opinion, and not a very interesting one.

"What's the significance?"

Charmaine shook his finger at me as if I were being a naughty child. "You don't get that from me so easily. I'll trade my life philosophy for yours."

"Hmm." I reached for my refilled martini glass and swirled the stick of olives. "No deal."

"Then I guess we'll just never know that about each other," Charmaine replied. "Too bad. Mine would have blown your mind."

"Yeah, sure." We exchanged a laugh and then parted ways as the party took us in opposite directions.

———

Charmaine's life philosophy did not blow my mind. It was honestly pedantic. I hadn't cared to try to figure it out after our chat, but as I searched "fox lion philosophy" now, the first thing that came up was "The Fox and Lion in Machiavelli's *The Prince*." I went back to @thefoxandlion to read the tweets, but just like @fauxperdante, it was a protected account. But it didn't matter, because I knew all I needed to know.

Charmaine Von Bon was Other Lata's mole. I should have never trusted him after all.

It explained so much: how Other Lata was always able to keep tabs on me and my whereabouts, even though I'd stopped sharing on social media months ago to keep my whole Downtown Lata existence hidden from my family and other friends. Yet Other Lata had known to find me at Kingsley's Memorial Day party and slipped the note in my tote bag (or at least had someone do it for her). And she always seemed aware of my social calendar and tailored her blackmail accordingly. It should have occurred to me earlier that she seemed to hit upon the perfect kind of humiliation for each setting: fur coats and flip-flops on a luxury yacht; a tiara, a sash, and blue jeans for a star-studded movie after-party.

No one knew more about me than Keiko did. And Charmaine and I had bonded over our Six Degrees of Keiko game, marveling at how connected she was to everyone. For a brief moment, I worried that it was Keiko that was leaking my life to Other Lata, since she too was aware of the Lata Murthy mystique I had co-opted for myself. But that seemed impossible; she was too sweet and good-natured to be that deceptive. Sure, Keiko liked to talk and share freely. She was my very own Gossip Girl, always filling me in on everyone else's stories and secrets. If Charmaine wanted to know anything about me to pass along to Other Lata, Keiko would be an unwitting fountain of information.

—⁓—

The breeze coming off the water ruffled my skin, but my prickly anticipation interpreted its gentle touch as a foreboding one. It was a bright Saturday morning at South Street Seaport. Too early. Too early to even enjoy Pier 17's view of the Brooklyn Bridge, the best in all of Manhattan. Instead, I closed my eyes behind dark sunglasses to mute the sun, a cappuccino shaking in my hands.

"Hey, Lata." Charmaine sat down next to me, holding a cup of coffee of his own. My eyes flew open, and my cappuccino dropped to the ground with a splat, then rolled underneath the bench. "Didn't meant to startle you, sorry."

Rather than reply to Charmaine or try to retrieve the dropped cup, I quickly swiveled around, my eyes frenetically gazing around the rest of the pier. But the plentiful benches were populated by only a handful of people.

"She's not here," Charmaine said, sounding rattled. "And she doesn't know I'm here. I swear on my grandmother's life."

My shoulders and jaw muscles relaxed several millimeters when I heard this, but I kept up my icy affect. Charmaine had not done anything to earn my trust yet. "Tell. Me. Everything."

It had surprised me that when I texted **I know**, along with a link to the @thefoxandlion Twitter account, Charmaine not only had responded immediately, but also had known exactly why I had sent it to him. He was the one that had proposed meeting in person, as if he had a guilty conscience and had long been ready to confess. And when I asked him to tell me everything, that was exactly what he did.

16

Forever 21

"I MET LATA TWO SUMMERS ago. I can't recall what she looked like. She wasn't short or tall, slim or fat, gorgeous or ugly. She was just, I dunno, average; there wasn't particularly anything that made her stand out. But I can remember other things: the spicy scent of her perfume, her lilting accent when she spoke, how when she laughed, you didn't know if she truly liked you or was secretly mocking you. The last part made her a lot like other socialites I know. Which is why I never questioned her story about her family's stature in Mumbai, because she exuded the kind of hauteur that only the truly wealthy could project. As if the world existed to please her, to bend to her every thought and whim. My mother is like that, come to think of it. Maybe that's why I felt an immediate connection with her too. I just got who Lata was immediately."

Lata Murthy was said to be the only daughter of a wealthy Mumbai industrialist whose family's exorbitant wealth was derived from manufacturing fabrics and textiles. That was the only concrete thing known about her, with Charmaine using air quotes when stating the word "known." Charmaine stressed that wealthy people from other countries always made the social circuit at that time of year, so Lata was just one of many.

"She first appeared at Valentina Sheppington's tealight soiree, which is one of the most exclusive invitations of the summer season. I had been there because I was lucky enough to be the plus-one of an ex who was in a last-minute need of a date. There were about a hundred of us under the white tent, and somehow Lata became the white-hot center of attention even though she didn't seem to know anyone there. Eventually I was able to make my way through the crowd and spotted her in fervent conversation with Valentina herself. I saw Lata hand Valentina a glittering envelope. I can't recall her face, but I remember that envelope: it was sequined, gold and purple and green, and it wasn't a thin envelope either. There was definitely a wad of cash inside."

Over the next two hours, Charmaine told me that this would become a signature Lata move throughout the summer. She would receive an invitation coveted by all but shared with only a few, and at each event Lata would conclude the evening by making a donation to the host or hostess's pet charity or foundation, slipping one of her signature glittery envelopes into their hand before she made her exit.

"No one ever publicly spoke of the amount, which only added to the mystique. But I imagine it at least had to be five figures."

I moved my sunglasses to my forehead as the sunlight

shifted off us and cast us in temporary shade. "Honestly, that doesn't seem to be that much? If her family is supposed to be like the Vanderbilts or even the Hiltons."

"I've thought about this too." Charmaine scratched his chin. "And the only thing I can come up with is that once Lata was in full swing, the story of being handpicked for a Lata Murthy donation became more valuable than what she was actually giving."

As more and more people wanted the cachet of having Lata attend their events, Lata was seen less and less in the Upper East Side or the Hamptons. Charmaine saw her three more times that summer, and the first of the three occasions was the only time they had an actual conversation.

"My good friend Exeter was hosting a dinner party at his grandfather's home. And when I say 'home,' I mean it is a manor designated as a national landmark that only allows a few guided visits a day. And to preserve the architectural integrity, they rarely host private events there. But Exeter wanted to amplify the profile of his event to raise money for, I don't know, let's say endangered llamas. But every person who has an address in the Hamptons hosts a gala or a clambake or a shindig, and so with his parents' permission, he held his llama benefit at the Cosgrove. By that point, it was known that the only way to reach Lata was via email. And her email address got shared like a game of telephone: sometimes you got the right one, sometimes it was wrong and the email bounced back to you. Exeter got the right one. When he received her RSVP, you would have thought he had just scored tickets to a private concert with Madonna."

The dinner party was attended by twenty-five people, nearly all of whom had been profiled in a glossy magazine with a name like *Hamptons Style* or *Luxury Life*. Except for Lata, although there were rumors that *Vanity Fair* was running a profile of her in its September issue. ("Rumors ran with wild abandon. She was engaged to a Mughal prince. She was BFFs with Stella McCartney. All dumb stuff, but most gossip is.") Exeter didn't want Lata to be seated near any potential sycophants who would not-so-subtly bombard her with requests for their pet causes. ("Exy was reserving that for himself.") He had told no one she was coming, except for Charmaine. Exeter knew that Charmaine didn't have any charitable enterprises that would need Lata's backing, and that he would just treat her as a dinner guest.

"It's funny to think about now, but I had received that invite like it was a Willy Wonka Golden Ticket. Even though I had been experiencing some weird and mildly alarming vision issues: lots of blurriness, seeing spots. Normally I would have returned to the city to get it checked out. But I put it off, because...well, I wish I could say I was more immune to this whole mythology building around Lata, but I was just as curious as anyone else." Charmaine winced as he said this. "I almost invented a charity just so I could get a glimpse of one of those glittery envelopes.

"We were seated side by side near the head of the table, with Exeter at the head and me beside her. The two of us bookending her as if she was precious cargo." Charmaine laughed. "After I introduced myself, I was pleased that Lata knew exactly who I was and about my family. She asked me some questions about something related to them, I don't remember what. After a few moments, we had a lull in the conversation, and so it was my turn to surprise her."

Charmaine paused, as if he was waiting for me to fill in the blanks. The look in his eyes matched the way he had first regarded me the day I met him at Sea Cove.

When he spoke Hindi to me.

Charmaine nodded as he saw this realization dawn on me and continued.

"My family lived in the UK when I was very young. Between the ages of four and ten I had a nanny named Gigi—likely not her real name, but that is what I called her. She came to us from Delhi, I think. And Gigi loved to watch Bollywood movies, day and night, including with me. She would always translate for me, until eventually I started picking up Hindi on my own. I was fairly fluent by the time we moved back to the States, and think I'm decent at it now, though my accent is no doubt abominable.

"So I started speaking Hindi with Lata. And though my vision was giving me trouble, I could tell she was delighted. We spoke about everyone at the table, gossiping and insulting each of them. She asked me a few questions about some of the guests too, but I wasn't always adept at understanding every-thing she said. Still, the way we hit it off, I could feel every-one staring daggers at me. I have to admit I enjoyed our cabal of two, and that Lata was so witty in how she immediately understood each person's weaknesses. She was a very good observer of people, that's what I took away from that night."

There was a second thing Charmaine took away too,

which seemed like an interesting quirk at first and took on new meaning only later. After the guests had departed, Exeter asked Charmaine to linger behind and pressed him for details of his chummy conversation with Lata.

"Exy couldn't stop lamenting that she had not presented a glittery envelope to him or anyone else." Before she left, Lata had briefly opened her purse, an oval clutch made up of red-and-gold sequins that seemed to be of Indian design. Exeter said he had held his breath, certain that she was finally going to offer a donation.

"But when she opened it, he didn't see any glittery envelopes. But he swore he saw that purse's brand tag had said Forever 21." Charmaine blinked several times, as if he were seeing it himself. "And that always seemed odd to me. It's like hearing the wrong note played in a concerto. But what did I know about women and fashion and all that?"

Charmaine hosted a birthday party for his then boyfriend at his Upper East Side home a few weeks later and, on a whim, sent an invitation to Lata, hoping to get to know her better. By then, he had discovered that his vision issues were due to a detached retina, and had surgery to correct it. When he saw me react with horror, he chuckled.

"It does sound a bit gruesome, doesn't it?"

Charmaine added that it was easily corrected with surgery, but his eyesight could still get blurry while healing from the procedure. Which made hosting a party in their "spacious . . . okay, enormous" place on 70th between Lex and Park a challenge, since he had invited over two hundred people. "So there were many guests who were in and out throughout the evening. I think I at least had the opportunity to say hello to everyone, but a few fell through the gaps." That included Lata, standing on the staircase landing in a light yellow sari.

"I waved hello and she smiled and waved back. I had wanted to go over to her, because here was my chance to speak to her without being bothered by eye problems. My friends were showing me photos of the new bichon frise they had just adopted, and by the time I looked up again, Lata was gone. I never saw her again the rest of the night. And as a host, I felt bad that I had neglected to take time to speak with one of my guests. Plus, my then boyfriend was mad because he had heard all about Lata Murthy and was dying to meet her. I swear she was there—I can still picture her standing on the landing, and she waved like this." Charmaine held up his palm and moved his fingers slowly up and down. "But when I asked my other friends if they had seen her, they said they hadn't."

Charmaine set down his coffee cup between his feet, then sighed. "There's no way to say this out loud without feeling like a fool. I'm still embarrassed about my own stupidity. My great-grandfather owned a Rolex Prince. And it has been passed down to every male Von Bon in my family since then. Usually, I kept it in my safe. But that night I was in a rush and took it out to wear it, but then something must have distracted me and I left it on the dresser. The day after the party, I noticed it was gone."

"Whoa," I responded, my heartbeat tick-tocking wildly. With those words, I could already see where Charmaine's story was going, but it was even worse than I imagined. For those in Charmaine's upscale social circle, the summer had been marked by a series of robberies. Nothing too exorbitant, just small but pricey items that often were not noticed to be missing until weeks or even months later. A Rolex watch or a diamond-and-sapphire ring or a vintage letter opener with a 24-karat gold handle. The kinds of things that were easily slipped into pockets or purses. But Charmaine hadn't been aware that there had been a string of thefts when he saw Lata one last time toward the end of summer, at a Medici Artists benefit at the Southampton Inn.

"I was supposed to be in St. Barts at the time, but my boyfriend and I had split and I let him have the resort stay to keep things civil." Charmaine shook his head. "Not that he appreciated it, the little shithead. Anyway, that's why I was at the party when most everyone had assumed I'd be out of town. And right when I walked in, I saw Lata. I made a beeline toward her, wanting to apologize for missing her the last time. She didn't see me coming, not initially. Lata raised her left wrist, and I spotted her watch. It looked *exactly* like my Rolex."

Charmaine did his best to hustle over to her as quickly as possible, but by the time he approached the people encircling her, Lata was gone. "They had been so charmed by her, and just oozed with praise. One of them had just received a magical glittery envelope right before I got to the party. The last one, it turned out." Because of that interaction with the other guests, and the fact that one of them had just been chosen for her selective largesse, Charmaine decided that he had mistaken Lata's watch for his. Through the grapevine, Charmaine learned that Lata's family had summoned her back to

Mumbai, and although she was sad to leave, she was planning to come back the following year. But no one heard from her or saw her again, until...

"Oh shit. Me," I said with a groan.

"Yes, you." Charmaine gently elbowed me. "My defective retina meant I only had a fuzzy idea of what Lata looked like. So that's why—"

"That's why you spoke Hindi to me when you saw me." Charmaine nodded, then shared that when he first addressed me, he had asked about his missing watch.

"It was the only thing I could think that could help me identify her. Because even before you came to Sea Cove, and months had passed without anyone having seen the other Lata, I really began to believe that she had stolen it. A friend of mine is friends with Aqua's publicist, so when I heard that a Lata Murthy had accepted an invite to Aqua's jewelry party, I was absolutely gobsmacked. I had tried emailing Lata twice last year, but there had been no reply. So I asked my friend for the email address that had been used to invite you to Aqua's event and basically threw together the Summer Sayonara in a few days just so I could send you an invitation and see if you'd come. How you and Keiko became friends, I have no idea. But when Keiko told me she had met you too, it gave me hope that you would actually attend my event. But of course, it was the wrong 'you.'"

I nodded numbly, replaying our first meeting in my head. "But you still seemed unsure I was her. Do I look like her at all? Are there any photos of her, so I could see for myself?"

Charmaine shrugged. "Early on, Lata had made it clear she

would only attend gatherings in which she would not have her photo taken. She had hinted—to others, not me—that there were important reasons why her privacy had to remain guarded at all times, and they were related to protecting her family empire. And though it had seemed like the Summer of Lata, with everyone claiming to have met her or received a lavish donation from her, she only actually attended I'd say about ten or fifteen parties the entire summer. Not only that, they all made sure to respect her whole no-photos rule. Most of them seemed to be small and exclusive, not the major galas that attract hundreds. She was really good at making sure there was no record of her." He ruefully added, "Although she did show up to my ex's birthday party, but maybe she didn't know so many people would be there."

Charmaine then looked at me and asked me to stand up. We both stood. After a few seconds passed, he indicated we could return to sitting.

"Yes, you're both around the same height. Although now that I think of it, she might be a little older than you. Late-thirties-ish." So it wasn't my imagination about why Lata gave off annoyed older sister vibes. "The height thing was why I think I was initially confused by whether you were the Lata I knew or not. And your skin color."

"My skin color?"

"Yeah. Um, can I say this? I've met a lot of Indian people, and most of them are light skinned, like that Bollywood actress who attends Cannes? What's her name? Ashwarree something?"

"You mean Aishwarya Rai." I tsked.

"Yes, sorry. But your skin is darker, just like that Lata's was.

More brown, I mean, like coffee without cream. Okay, I'm going to stop now." His thin face turned crimson. "But anyway, that's why I thought you could actually be her, because those two things are what I remembered about her. But then you threw me off by not understanding my Hindi." He rubbed his hands together. "You can sense the depth of my confusion."

"Um, yeah." I gave him a half-hearted pat on the back as I tried to process all he had shared with me. At last I had confirmation that Other Lata and I vaguely resembled each other. Did that make it easier for me to take on her persona? Maybe. But it might have been a breeze no matter what, considering the surprising number of times I had been mistaken for statuesque, fair-skinned Anita.

Charmaine took out his phone, and I could tell that whatever he was about to show me, he felt really bad about it. The hairs on my neck prickled, then stood at full attention when I saw his phone screen. It was a photograph of me at Sea Cove, wearing the Dior sunglasses.

"You sent this to her?" I exclaimed, kicking the sidewalk and stubbing my bare toe. "Oh my god. That's why . . . That's why . . ."

"Yeah." Charmaine had emailed the photo to thelatamurthy@gmail.com, along with the message, This woman has the same name as you. Do you know her? "I didn't really expect a reply. But eventually, I got one."

A month after Charmaine sent the email, Other Lata responded by claiming that I was impersonating her. Still in Mumbai dealing with "family matters," she asked Charmaine to keep tabs on me and report back everything I did so she could build her case against me.

"It was the Hindi thing," Charmaine said with a sigh. "The other Lata and I had such a lively conversation that summer, but when I spoke to you, you were a deer in the headlights. Plus, my watch—it's a family heirloom, and my parents still don't know that it's gone. I just wanted it back so badly. And if there was even the slightest chance . . ." Our eyes met, and he seemed to be as anguished as me. He was either a very convincing actor out to win my trust, or just someone who had been hoodwinked and manipulated like I had been. "You can see why I believed her story, right?"

"I do." Then I put my head in my hands. Charmaine waited as I took several deep breaths. Once I felt ready to speak again, I asked him if he was getting a lot of his info about me from Keiko, and the guilt in his expression magnified.

"But she's not a part of all this. You know Keiko, Miss Six Degrees. Very sweet and very chatty. She adores you. And she loves talking about you." He fiddled with an engraved signet ring on his pinky, the cursive gold C winking in the sun. "And by the way, even before you texted earlier this week to ask about the other Lata, I had already made up my mind to stop talking to her. There was never any quid pro quo. Any time I asked if her investigation into you had turned up any leads on the stolen items, she had nothing to offer." Charmaine briefly cinched his forefinger and thumb around his wrist. "I've finally made my peace with the idea I'm not getting that watch back."

We both fell silent again. By this time, plenty more people

had entered Pier 17, gathering at the railing or at nearby benches to take in the Brooklyn Bridge majestically crossing the East River. And with every passing moment, the sunny day only magnified in beauty, as if to steep us further in our misery.

"So you've also been communicating over Twitter?" I asked him.

"Yeah. It's so dumb, but that's how she wanted it. I think she gets off on the cloak-and-dagger thing." Charmaine, who had been hunched over, staring at his sneakers, bolted straight up. "Wait. What do you mean by 'also'?"

With a pit of dread excavating my insides, I told Charmaine everything that had gone on these past few months (save for my shoplifting), culminating in Other Lata taking her blackmail from odd antics to theft and fraud. He gave me the most pitying look I'd ever received, and I began to shudder. Charmaine threw an arm around my shoulder, and I leaned into his sympathetic embrace. Despite the fact that Charmaine was partly the reason I was in my predicament, it was a relief to finally talk about all things Other Lata with another person.

"So you have actually been impersonating her. She got that right, I see." *Does it matter?* I was about to say, when he added, "Not that it matters. Since that Lata was all smoke and mirrors too."

I put my sunglasses back on as the sun's rays burst over us like a giant spotlight, but my face was growing hot for a different reason. "I never wanted to deceive people," I replied, unable to keep the defensiveness out of my voice. "I tried my best to keep my Lata existence separate from hers. I didn't attend soirees or fancy galas or silent auctions. I just wanted to go to a few fun parties. And it all just kind of spiraled out of control."

"Listen, we've all done things that skated just past ethical lines. I'm actually impressed by how far you've taken it." Charmaine sighed. "But how long are you planning to do this? I mean, you can't play the Mumbai socialite excommunicated from her family forever."

An excellent question, and one I could not answer. So instead, I deflected. "If I had known Lata was handing out glittery envelopes stuffed with cash, I wouldn't have done it at all."

Charmaine shrugged. My sullen mood intensified, and all at once I became desperate for something to drink, anything to wash the raw, burnt taste of the cappuccino from my mouth. Just as I got up to get a bottle of water, Charmaine grabbed my arm. "She wants you to steal, you said?"

I nodded.

"If that's the case, then Lata has to be responsible for all the robberies from two years ago."

"Right," I mumbled, sinking back down. "Oh shit."

"No matter what that woman says, she's the real fraud," Charmaine said sadly. "And whatever she has planned next, you're at the center of it."

17

Casamigos

MY FIRST DATE WITH RAJEEV was two days later, and as you can imagine, I was an outright mess. It didn't help that the day was chock full of fumbles, each mistake amplifying my distress. Knowing that I would be heading to the restaurant straight from my job, it took me forever to choose something equally work and date appropriate. I finally opted for a pale blue Vivienne Westwood dress that was too snug at my hips, only because I was 100 percent certain Rajeev hadn't seen me wear it before. I arrived to work nearly twenty minutes late, which my boss noted with a raised eyebrow. And then with Charmaine's revelations weighing on me, I whiffed on an important call with a client, causing my boss to scold me in a polite, clipped manner in front of the entire office.

By the time I arrived at Minetta Tavern, my nerves were so frazzled that I could not keep still. Particularly my hands: when not running them through my hair or checking my phone, I was constantly dabbing a tissue to my nose due to a summer cold. The only thing I had done right was arrive ten minutes early for the seven p.m. reservation. And so with a sigh, I plopped down at the bar to wait for Rajeev, barely touching the white wine I had ordered.

"Here," said the bartender, wearing a crisp white shirt, a black tie, and a boyish grin, sliding me a shot glass. "I can tell you're in need of something to take the edge off." I eyed the shot dubiously, then shook my head. Tequila reminded me of dorm room drinking games and blotto nights at dive bars that had me puking in grimy toilets by the end of the night.

"It's top-shelf tequila, very smooth. It's Casamigos. You know, the George Clooney brand?"

The name of a movie star shouldn't have been so convincing. But wanting to numb the chaos of the past several days before embarking on the most consequential first date of my life cinched the deal. I'll always be grateful for that bartender, because the tequila did help: by the time Rajeev arrived, I was calmer and in a steadier frame of mind. And the butterflies still bloomed as I saw him enter and speak with the hostess. By the time he reached me, I knew we shared matching grins, our faces overrun by our pure happiness at seeing each other.

"I hope I didn't keep you waiting long," he said after he kissed me on the cheek.

"Not at all."

"A first for me." He studied me for a moment and then swept his hand over my hair, delicately removing a piece of tissue the size of a gum wrapper. I stared in horror at the fluff, which no doubt contained remnants of my snot. Couldn't the bartender have told me? But Rajeev was so matter-of-fact about it that my mortification didn't last long. He simply dropped the tissue in a wastebasket, then took my hand, and we followed the hostess to our waiting table.

Is it weird that the snotty tissue in my hair was the highlight of our first date? I mean, of course it is. But it was a pure moment reflecting Rajeev's sweetness and grace. Plus, everything that transpired afterward would return me to a state of apprehension, which no amount of George Clooney tequila could assuage.

We were seated in a booth, thankfully, giving us an island of space and privacy in a bustling restaurant. Everything about Minetta Tavern was crowded and chatty, from the patrons to the walls, every inch covered with black-and-white sketches and old photographs reflecting the fact that the place had existed since the 1930s.

"I have officially found funding for my show," Rajeev blurted out once we ordered steak frites. He obviously had been holding the news in since arriving, and his unbridled joy buoyed my spirits too.

"That's wonderful! Congratulations." I slid out of the booth to give him a big hug, and we stayed locked together for a long time despite the waiters huffing past us with heavy trays. It was hard to let go; he was wearing a new aftershave that smelled so damn good, an intoxicating mix of pine and musk that had me wishing we were back in his bedroom holding each other, this time without any clothes.

"Thank you," Rajeev said once we returned to the booth. "Sorry, I really don't plan to go on and on about this all night. But this has been a big stressor for me, and we only got official word a few hours ago." Rajeev shared that one of his clients had been so impressed with the bespoke gown he had created for her charity fundraiser that she asked her husband's perfume company to underwrite Rajeev's Fashion Week show. He would be officially showing in the tents at Lincoln Center.

"Please, feel free to talk about it all night! That is such a big deal." A couple next to us had champagne cooling in an ice bucket beside them, and I nodded toward it. "Should we celebrate?"

"Uh, no." Rajeev went sort of stiff, then seemed to will his body to relax. "I'm not a big fan of alcohol. It's fine for other people. Ginger beers are as wild as I get." He must have seen me wilt in response (*How could you forget, you stupid idiot?* was the gist of my inner monologue), and he reached across the table to take my hand. "I have a history with it. Not me personally, but with my family. I like to abstain, but that doesn't mean you have to."

"No, that's fine. I'm good." I licked my lips, wondering if he had noticed the tequila on my breath. After we discussed his collection some more, Rajeev cleared his throat, then gave a stilted chuckle.

"No more about me. I refuse to let my work dominate this conversation. Let's talk about the most beautiful person in this room." Rajeev gave me a flirtatious smile, even as his fingers drummed incessantly against the table, joggling the silverware. "That was cheesy, wasn't it? I'm sorry."

"I like cheesy." I leaned forward and returned his smile, my elbow resting on the table. "So, why did you choose Minetta Tavern for our first date? You said you had this place in mind when we first talked about it, but you didn't say why."

"It's legendary, for starters. And Minetta has a great literary history. Hemingway used to come here, and Ezra Pound and E. E. Cummings—Mazzy loves his poems. All the great writers congregated here back in the day. I thought it would be fitting for you." He must have seen my face fall, because he hastened to add, "Plus I've never been here before, and you seemed like a perfect person to try it with."

"Yup, this is my first time too." I gave my dress, which was riding up midthigh for the umpteenth time that day, a sharp tug. I should have never worn the damn thing. "But you don't have to talk to me about writing, Rajeev," I added, trying to keep my voice light. "I love how encouraging you are. I'm just not...there yet."

Rajeev nodded and said he understood, his cheeks slightly pink. After he excused himself to use the restroom, our waitress brought over the white wine I had deserted at the bar. I stared at it and, after giving it a moment's thought, downed it in four gulps.

And these two exchanges sort of summed up our first date. We would have moments of levity and banter, and then one of us would say something that the other would take an awkward way. For me, it was any references to family or childhoods. In response, I would steer the conversation toward the most random of topics, because I had no way to discuss my parents without opening that Pandora's box.

The bombshell finally came during dessert. Over crème

brûlée, I asked Rajeev about the client who was responsible for securing funding for him.

"Marlena Santigold. Have you heard of MoonRose House? They offer shelter and resources for victims of domestic violence. There are MoonRose Houses all over the state."

The crème brûlée soured on my tongue.

Rajeev happily went on, sharing how much he admired Marlena and how proud he was that she would not only choose him to design her dress for the annual MoonRose Benefit, but go so far as to help his fledgling career.

"In fact, she's hosting a dinner for me on Friday. She said she wants to introduce me to some of her friends. Isn't that amazing? I tried to say no, considering she has the benefit coming up. But Marlena insisted."

"So amazing." I limply set my fork down on the plate.

"Oh! One more thing. I can't believe I forgot to tell you this. Do you remember the Mars Marble?"

My eyes became saucers. "Uh, of course."

"Remember when we thought Aqua would never part with it? How did you say she put it? 'I carved it from the depths of my soul,' something like that. But Marlena bought it from her. Apparently, Marlena's even more stubborn than Aqua and finally wore her down. I'm not sure anyone knows how to say no to her."

"That's impressive. Maybe she's a hypnotist?" I joked weakly.

"Ha, yeah, maybe. It is a beautiful piece of jewelry—I mean, it captivated me. But Marlena is even more enamored with it. For example, that dinner she's having for me? There's going to be Fort Knox–level security. She's not taking any chances."

"Why?"

He took a sip of his coffee. "I guess you haven't heard. There's been a string of robberies these past few weeks. Mostly jewelry, but some other things as well. I think Kingsley's dad's gold coin collection is missing, and he is pissed at Kingsley. He'll never be throwing any parties at any of his parents' places again. And at Leela Anoushka's—she threw the rooftop party where you did the Macarena." He went on to list several other events in the Hamptons and all over the city. "Oh, even Micheline's party, where you wore the beehive? Someone's wallet got lifted, and he had something like $10,000 in cash in it. His girlfriend lost a diamond bracelet, but she insists it was stolen. I'm not sure why you need to carry that much on you or wear diamonds to a birthday party. But yeah, so people aren't taking chances." Rajeev set down his cup, and the way it rattled against the saucer mirrored my own unease. "These kinds of things happen more often than we think."

I slid down a few inches on the banquette's soft leather.

Rajeev briefly startled, then pulled his phone out of his pocket and glanced at it. "Forgive me, I have to take this. They know to only call me tonight for an emergency, so I better see what this is."

"Of course," I said, the only two words I seemed to be capable of speaking. As he excused himself to the bar, I took out my own phone and glanced through my screenshots of Other Lata's tweets. The dread pooled out and spread its fingers over every inch of my body and brain, as if I were Fay Wray in King Kong's iron grasp. At last, the reasons behind Other Lata's blackmail became clear.

That bitch is setting me up.

Among the locations and parties Rajeev had named were eight I had attended while following Other Lata's orders. What had once seemed inexplicable now became all too clear. Because Other Lata had made me act in an identifiable way, with the Macarena and the beehive and the hot dog juggling, everyone would remember I had been at the scene of the crime each time. When it came to all the robberies in the city, I was the unifying factor for any that took place south of 14th Street.

Even as I felt new waves of revulsion and fear I didn't know it was possible to experience, I also felt a tiny bit of awe at how Other Lata had so expertly pulled my strings and positioned me to be her fall guy. Linking me to this summer's robberies, and those of two summers before, was almost impressive in its tidiness. And it also explained why she was now advancing her blackmail to crime... *specifically via Rajeev.*

But how could she possibly know about Rajeev and Marlena's connection before I even did? Let alone the Mars Marble.

I debated whether the inside info about Marlena and the ruby necklace had been funneled to Other Lata through Charmaine. But unless he was a psychic or a secret fashion blogger, it seemed highly unlikely Charmaine would know of Marlena and Rajeev's professional relationship either.

Rereading the tweets reminded me of their snippy, petulant tone. Other Lata was no longer just using me or toying with me, she was actively upset with me. Because of Rajeev?

Perhaps she was jealous that in using her persona, I had lucked into a romance.

"Everything okay?" Rajeev had returned so noiselessly I had squawked and dropped my phone into the remaining bits of my crème brûlée.

"Oh crap. Whoops." I rescued my phone and wiped off the cream, then put it away. "Work stuff. It never ends."

"I can't relate at all," he said with a wink, and we both laughed. Despite my current anguish, Rajeev's presence instantly made me feel better. "I wanted to ask you something, but I don't want you to feel you have to say yes. Honestly, you might actually have plans. I'm such a dolt."

"No you're not. What is it?"

"Would you want to be my plus-one to the dinner on Friday? Marlena is a truly kind person. But she's giving me entry into her social circle, and I find that really intimidating. I'm not used to being around these kinds of people. I'm just a kid from Queens. And I fear being around them will only make me feel that's all I am: a little boy in a suit, trying to impress the grown-ups."

"I get that." Marlena's dinner party would likely be peopled by a special kind of blue-blood snootiness that I'd been aiming to avoid since my visit to Sea Cove. My nerves twitched at the idea of being seated at a table with them. "But wouldn't it make more sense to go with Anita or Keiko?"

"Is it weird to say that seeing how comfortable Anita and Keiko are in those circles makes me feel less comfortable? Their naturalness exacerbates my lack of belonging. Even worse, that I'm an imposter." It shouldn't have been shocking to hear Rajeev say this, yet I still had to stifle a gasp, the word "imposter" an arrow shrieking through my heart. I took his hand in mine, our fingers quickly intertwining, hoping this gesture would soothe us both. "Honestly, it's even worse with the guys. Whenever I hang out with Kingsley and David Jay, I still feel that I'm auditioning to be one of them." He lowered his voice. "Sometimes I think they keep me around because I work with models. Or for the cachet of having a fashion designer in their clique. But I'm no saint either, because I know it's good for my career to be associated with them. Or so I tell myself."

Rajeev gave me a hopeful grin. "It's different with you. Your presence makes me feel better. Even during those times when we would be at the same party, but we didn't really talk, just knowing you were there put me at ease." He jolted again, seemingly from another vibrating phone call, but this time he ignored it. That was how important my answer was to him. "It would be a huge favor to me, and I'll repay you in a hundred and one ways. Starting with a new crème brûlée."

I nodded and nodded and nodded, not knowing what to say. Of course, in normal circumstances I would go without a second thought. But with my Other Lata life intruding on my Downtown Lata life, it just seemed too tricky to navigate.

"Is that a yes?" Rajeev asked. He turned to the drawing closest to him, a pugnacious-faced man named Romeo. "Do you think that meant yes?"

And in a flash, it occurred to me that Rajeev had just handed me a way to cut Other Lata's puppet strings and start making my own moves.

"Of course I'll go. I'd love to support you." Rajeev thanked me, radiating relief.

For the remainder of our night at Minetta Tavern, I tried my best to stay focused but my mind was elsewhere. And so I wasn't displeased when a work emergency bade him to cut short our post-dinner plans so that he could return to the studio. When I watched Rajeev hail a cab, a surge of protectiveness came over me. I couldn't let Other Lata hurt him. Besides, this was between the two of us. And it was time to change the rules of her game.

18

Channel

MY FIRST MOVE WAS INSPIRED by @fauxperdante. Specifically, if I was able to identify Charmaine through his Twitter account handle and avatar, couldn't it be possible to figure out who Other Lata was too?

Her Twitter page had a black background, but the account had an unusual yet strikingly familiar image: three thick white swooping lines that seemed to be attached, although the image cut off without showing whether they were actually joined together. As I studied it, then enlarged it, I couldn't shake the tickling in my brain that not only did I know this image, but it would seem so obvious to me once I discovered the answer. I had come straight home from my date to pore over the @fauxperdante image but three hours later hadn't come any closer to deciphering its identity. If only I could Google it, I thought to myself dejectedly, as the first stirrings of sleepiness overtook me. And as I was about to finally give in and give up for the night, a new idea had me leap out of bed and retrieve my laptop.

Maybe Google could help me after all, via its image search. I plugged in the three swooping lines and received about ten thousand search results. It was two a.m. by that point, and I didn't know if I had the ability to click through each result to find my answer. Only by chance did my eye catch on the word "art" in one of the search results, and thankfully it triggered why the image was so familiar: the swooping lines weren't lines at all. They were swans' necks.

I had studied Alissa Carroll's paintings in my 1960s Modernist Art class during my penultimate semester in college, an elective chosen by chance that ended up shaping much of what I admire about art. Carroll was a painter who specialized in depicting images from nature with a modernist flair, such as in the case of *Three*. Three swans sailed side by side in a lake of sunset-colored waters, their necks unnaturally elongated so that they resembled the braids of a friendship bracelet before splitting off in different directions. It was the swan necks splitting off that the @fauxperdante image captured. I did a fist bump in the air. At last I was getting somewhere.

And to my astonishment, identifying the painting quickly brought me to its location, and that of Other Lata. According to ArtNews.info, Carroll's goddaughter had gifted *Three* to the Tellworth, a private club in Tribeca, five years ago. So dedicated to preserving the exclusivity and privacy of its members that it famously sported a secret entrance so no one could espy anyone's comings and goings, the club was a favorite of the celebrity set as well as the supernova wealthy.

According to the news item, *Three* had a place of honor in the library, among paintings by artists such as Keith Haring and Andy Warhol. But Carroll always struck me as a salt-of-the-earth type, and so she likely would have been unhappy that her gift to her goddaughter could now be viewed only by those whose net worths exceeded eight figures.

I returned to the @fauxperdante image again and enlarged it as much as I could. I needed to know if this was an image sourced online or snapped in person. And to my relief, I could see the blurry outline of a silhouette reflected in the glass overlaying the painting.

"Okay," I said out loud to myself, since I had no Bess and George to bounce ideas off of à la Nancy Drew, "so she snapped the photo of the painting while at the Tellworth. Which means she's likely a member herself. So, she's super wealthy too? And does she use the name Lata Murthy or something else?"

I combed my fingers through my hair, completely stumped. It wasn't like I could hang out outside the club at all hours, hoping to catch a glimpse of her. So I once again appointed Google to be the Watson to my Sherlock Holmes, spending a few hours each day trying to dig myself closer to Other Lata's whereabouts. Three days before the Santigolds' party for Rajeev, I hit pay dirt in the most unexpected way.

For once, I knew something about Other Lata that she wouldn't see coming. And with some assistance, I knew just how to use it to my advantage.

The Santigold home was a five-story limestone-and-brick mansion taking up half a city block on 5th Avenue and facing Central Park. It was the kind of building that made you think you'd been thrust straight into an Edith Wharton novel. Despite being the guest of honor, Rajeev had to submit to an inspection from two stern-looking men in sharp suits and earpieces before being allowed to set foot inside the house, just like the other guests and I did. I imagined that if I ever somehow wrangled an invitation to the White House, its security measures would not be far off from the experience of having dinner with Marlena and Colin Santigold.

For such an important occasion, I wore a beaded midnight-blue Versace dress that made me feel like royalty, even though its still-affixed price tag was tucked inside my Spanx. I also wore a Rajeev G accessory, a braided bracelet of gold wires and black beads that he had gifted me during our first date. It had been meant to be worn by one of the models during his runway show last fall, but she had forgotten to wear it. Rajeev had designed the bracelet himself, but since it didn't fit into his vision for his new collection, he decided to give it to me.

"I'd like to see someone wear it, considering it took me a painful number of hours to construct it," he said when he passed me the box. "But no pressure!" he added quickly. "It might not be to your taste, and if so, I get it."

"I love it," I had told him at the time. And mostly, I did. The bracelet was a little poky and scratched lightly against the inside of my wrist; it was easy to understand why the model had "forgotten" to wear it. But the design was uniquely gorgeous, and a few hours' discomfort was not much to endure when it made Rajeev so happy to see the piece finally worn.

Marlena obviously adored Rajeev just as much as I did. The best way I could describe her was as a posh Morticia Addams with the personality of Mrs. Claus. She greeted her guests with the wide-eyed joy of a kid with a mountain of Christmas presents to unwrap, with Rajeev being the biggest one under the tree.

"Darling, hello! Colin, look who's here. It's our Rajeev." Air kisses abounded as they all said hello before they turned to me.

"It's wonderful to meet you, Lata," Marlena said, taking both of my hands within hers and giving them a squeeze. "We didn't meet by chance a few summers ago at the Mayhews' party in Sagaponack?"

"No, I don't believe so." I nearly yanked my hands away, not expecting my nemesis to come up in conversation. But I should have expected that Other Lata might have crossed paths with Marlena. I took a breath, then said, "But it is so nice to meet you now, and on this occasion. To celebrate someone so deserving." I gave Rajeev, who stood by me while engaged in animated conversation with Colin, an affectionate glance.

"I agree." She released my hands with a dazzling smile, then invited us inside.

If only that night's guests had been as pleasant as the hostess. Thirteen of us were seated at a dining table as enormous and stately as a redwood, and every single item in the room, from the rugs to the silverware to even the napkins, could have been exhibited at the European Sculpture and Decorative Arts collection at the Met. To be amid such incredible affluence, wearing a Versace dress marked down to 40 percent off at Bergdorf's along with my Channel clutch (which, in my defense, is the best Chanel knockoff on the planet), gave me the severest case of imposter syndrome I had ever experienced. In the face of such immense wealth, my ensemble no doubt betrayed me as a wannabe. But my shame mutated into anger the longer the meal went on, as I learned how the super rich liked to talk when ensconced in their privileged bubble.

"It has to be the help," said Barney Bigmouth. Even though I was introduced to everyone at the party, I quickly forgot most of their names. (In my defense, they definitely forgot mine too. At least one of them called me Lottie.) So it's easier to refer to them based on my first impressions. And my first impression of Barney was that he liked hearing his own voice, but not as much as he liked smacking his lips after every bite of our four-course meal.

"That's my thinking." Ernest Snobbucket picked up his glass and held it in the air, and it was swiftly refilled. "I mean, the whole concept of 'the butler did it' exists for a reason."

"But that refers to murder mysteries, not our little string of thefts." Lydia Van HuffyLips twirled her silver fork on the tablecloth in uneven arcs. "And these robberies took place all over the city, plus the Hamptons. We have a serial robber on our hands, not a serial killer." This last part was said with so much self-satisfaction that I let out a quiet tsk. Luckily, no one noticed, because no one had glanced in my direction once we had sat down. Rajeev was at the far end of the table, sandwiched between Colin and Marlena, while I was exiled to a dim corner near the doorway where the staff entered and exited with our meals and drinks. Each time one of them brought in a course or topped off a wineglass, I examined their faces to see if they were as affronted by the unfolding conversation as me. But they were too used to it, or too well practiced to show any emotion.

The whole table was abuzz over the burglaries, as they compared notes and traded suspects with the relish of those who fancied themselves amateur detectives because they had played a few games of Clue. The dinner had started with the conversation focused on Rajeev and his "wonderful fashions," and how excited Marlena was to wear one of his looks to her signature benefit. But the mention of the event prompted Barney to launch into praise for the Santigolds' security measures at their home and to ask how they planned to keep out the "wanton thieves" from the MoonRose Benefit. And the conversation never got back on track after that. Both Marlena and Colin tried at times to steer it back to Rajeev, and then other topics of general interest, but their guests had an interest only in rehashing the details of the thefts. I caught Rajeev's eye a few times, and we both had bemused expressions on our faces. It escaped neither of us that we were the only people of color in the room, and that included the Santigolds' waitstaff.

The one benefit of the dinner guests' flapping mouths was that they gave me a better sense of the robberies themselves. Seventeen thefts had been reported, with fourteen of the victims knowing each other socially, leading everyone in their interconnected orbit to believe their subset was being targeted. Which meant Other Lata and I had truly been operating as Uptown and Downtown Lata. When not blackmailing me to act like a fool in front of my friends, she had been spending time in neighborhoods with either "Upper" or "Hampton" in their names, absconding with pricey, pocket-sized items that sometimes weren't missed until days afterward.

"Nannies!" Ernest thundered.

"Excuse me?" Marlena had been caught so off guard that she had spilled a few drops of wine on her dinner plate.

"Lydia said that it can't be the help, because the robberies were in so many locations. But if they're not a gang of coordinated thieves, why couldn't it be a nanny? They travel everywhere with kids and with those big handbags. What if they weren't filled with diapers and apple juice? They could easily transport something as large as your candlesticks, Marlena." He spooned a big portion of potatoes au gratin into his mouth, then added as he chomped, "Just a theory, of course."

I made a disgruntled noise, an "ugh" mixed with an "argh." I didn't realize how loud I had been until the woman to my left spoke to me for the first time.

"I'm sorry, dear, did you say something?" Evangeline Drunkface was staring at me as if she wasn't sure whether I was a trick of her imagination or actually existed. Eleven other heads swiveled in my direction.

I actually did have something to say. I had planned on doing so during a private moment with Marlena, not in front of these idiots. But as Evangeline squinted at me, it occurred to me that doing it now, and in such a public way, would serve me even better.

Twisting my napkin in my hands, I stood up. Rajeev's face fluttered with surprise, and I experienced a half second of hesitation and fear. Then I dove in.

"I have an announcement, actually. Tonight is about Rajeev, of course," I said pointedly, looking each guest in the eye, "and celebrating his work and partnership with Marlena and MoonRose. I was going to wait until the actual benefit to do this, but I am just too excited."

For the first time since donning the Dior sunglasses at Sea Cove last year, I channeled my inner Uptown Lata.

"Marlena, Colin, I'd like to pledge a half million dollars to your foundation. Actually, it would be my honor to do so."

Gasps and cheers and applause followed, and the conversation finally latched on to a new topic. I ignored the whispers of "Who is she again?" as Marlena and Colin rose to thank me, a confused Rajeev following close behind.

"But I hope you don't mind, the donation comes with a request."

"Anything, anything!" Marlena clapped with delight. The four of us moved into a smaller antechamber to continue the conversation.

"Ever since I saw it on the runway at Rajeev's last show, I've wanted to wear the Mars Marble. And if you wouldn't mind," I said as casually as if I were merely asking to borrow a cup of sugar, "I would love to wear it just for one night. Charmaine Von Bon is hosting a black-tie event next month—"

"Done! Done and done," Marlena said, embracing me. "I would love to see you wear it, my dear. You would be a stunner."

"If you don't mind being trailed by two security men all night, that is," Colin added. "With all the robberies going on…"

"Of course! I wouldn't dream otherwise." More nice words, more hugs. Rajeev stood watching the Santigolds and me coordinate details as if he were suddenly thrust into an alternate reality in which he didn't know the language. Only once we left an hour later did Rajeev finally have a chance to ask me about it.

"What are you doing? I didn't understand any of that. You weren't even at my show! Are you… are you pretending to be from a rich Mumbai family?" He shook his head. "I know you like to prank people, but it's not appropriate with them." Even in the darkness of our Uber, I could see his face darken with anger.

When I had come up with my grand plan, I'd known that Rajeev would likely—and rightfully—have this reaction. I had an answer prepared for him but didn't know how much it would do to quell his concerns.

"I promise I will explain it, and all of this and all of me, after Charmaine's party." My fingers traced the bracelet gently piercing my wrist. "Do you remember the night at Per Se, when you said you wanted to know me, the real me? I want you to too, more than anything. And until then, I hope you can trust me. Because I have the utmost respect for you and your work, and would never do anything to jeopardize it."

Rajeev stared off into the distance, then assented with a curt nod. "Tell me one thing: Are you really going to make that donation? Can you?"

"Again, please, just trust me."

The car ride home was very quiet after that.

19

Converse

SO HERE'S WHAT I HAD discovered that set all of this in motion. It was a Facebook page. After scrolling through, I kid you not, eighty-seven pages of search results for the Tellworth, I had my breakthrough when I came across a Facebook page from a rich teen who had filmed inside the social club (which was a big no-no, to guard the privacy and security of its members). The Facebook post was dated six months ago and was titled "OMG!!!! Spotted at the Tellworth." It was secret camera footage of an A-list heartthrob sitting near a window, smoking a cigar. And in trying to film him, she caught something else that would be of interest only to me.

Thirty seconds into the clip, an Indian woman stopped by the heartthrob, blocking the teen's view. "Move, dummy!" the girl whispered loudly. The woman looked up and seemed to purposely stand there a few moments longer than necessary.

"Ugh!" The camera revolved to the ceiling. And that was where the clip ended.

The woman in question was not a member chatting with a fellow high-worth individual. She was one of the wait-staff, delivering a glass of amber liquid to the heartthrob. I had paused the video, taking in her height, her skin color, her unremarkable features. If glancing at her quickly, I easily could have mistaken her for myself. But it wasn't me, of course. It was her.

Other Lata wasn't a member of the Tellworth. She *worked* there.

As someone who had waitressed at a diner in high school and swiped cafeteria cards in college, I knew how much you could overhear about other people's lives because no one considered you a person. There was a time I used to write down the juiciest tidbits that people carelessly dropped like bread-crumbs, thinking I could fashion them into a short story some-day. Some of the conversations I overheard were truly wild, and that was just at a diner. Imagine what Other Lata overheard as a service worker at the Tellworth. Such as the fact that Marlena Santigold had acquired the Mars Marble. Or that she was plan-ning to wear a Rajeev G dress to the MoonRose Benefit.

Other Lata had majored in upper-crust rich people for at least two years, then applied that knowledge to turn herself into one. Again, as much as this woman was the bane of my existence, I couldn't help but admire what she had done too. It wasn't so dissimilar to me and my Downtown Lata exis-tence, although larceny had never been on my agenda. Well, it hadn't been until Other Lata wanted me to take a page from her playbook and go down for her actions.

———

After arriving home from the Santigolds, I sent a DM to the @fauxperdante account. I told her that I had publicly pledged a six-figure amount to their charity, not seven, and had announced this to the couple at their home instead of at the benefit. After informing Other Lata that I had disobeyed her orders, I revealed that I would be wearing the Mars Marble to Charmaine's end-of-summer party. **If you want it, you'll have to come and get it yourself.**

Eighteen minutes later, Other Lata saw the message. Forty-eight hours later, she liked the message. When she did that, victory surged through me. My hunch had proven correct. Other Lata had overheard someone at the Tellworth talking about me and the donation and the necklace, and she wanted it so badly she let me change the terms of the agreement. But then she did one more thing that I had not predicted.

Ten minutes after liking the DM, Other Lata deleted the @fauxperdante account.

———

Charmaine's end-of-summer bash was markedly different than the previous year's Summer Sayonara. Rather than a barbecue with beach balls in the pool and guests dressed in linen shorts and sandals, this summer he was switching it up to a white tent festooned with chandeliers, a live brass band,

and a very exacting dress code: "Black tie and evening wear only. Dress to impress, kids."

My ability to dress to impress was limited. Credit card limits had officially been hit, and even Rent the Runway was proving too expensive for my budget. I had no choice but to wear something I owned. Thankfully, the Mars Marble was such a statement piece, I didn't need to be extra in terms of my fashion choices. And so I turned to the sole designer dress in my wardrobe no one had yet seen me wear: my velvet Armani from prom.

It didn't quite fit as perfectly as it had in high school. The sleeveless gown was roomy at the bust, which meant that I would be constantly hiking it up to keep from having a nip slip. But of everything I owned, no dress would impress more, especially when paired with the Mars Marble.

Keiko and I got ready together at her summer rental, and she was thrilled when the Mars Marble arrived on her doorstep accompanied by two men in *Men in Black*–type suits and sunglasses.

"You look gorgeous," she gushed as I did a slow turn in front of her three-way mirror. It was so strange to be wearing the necklace that had launched me into a new life that included my friendship with Keiko. "How full circle, right?" she added, echoing my own thoughts. "Rajeev's whole fashion ascendency started when you figured out how to get this necklace for him. And now you're wearing it. And you and Rajeev!" She sighed dreamily. "It's like a fairy tale."

Ah yes, Rajeev. Whom I had barely spoken to in the past three weeks, largely owing to how busy his collection was making him, as the runway show was quickly approaching. His dress for Marlena, a cream column of silk with gold detailing, had been a big hit, appearing in several fashion blogs as well as the papers that covered high-society events. So anticipation for Rajeev's show was reaching astronomical proportions, and during the few times we had texted, it was obvious that his stress levels were high. His texts were also direct and short, no winky faces or hearts, and it was obvious my own actions were causing him additional anxiety right before the biggest moment of his career. If there had been any other way to rescue myself from Other Lata without adding to his stress, I would have done it. But this was the only plan I had.

"So, the donation," Keiko said, hair-spraying her sculpted updo as Hanae nipped at her bare toes. "Does that mean you and your parents are back on good terms?"

"Uhhh, we're getting there." My life as Downtown Lata was nearing its end. By launching this scheme, I was also dismantling my current existence, one Jenga piece at a time. I could only hope that the tower didn't crash down until I saw my plan through.

"I'm so glad." Keiko squeezed my arm. "Oh, did you hear about Anita and her parents? They found out about her and Francesco yesterday, and they went ballistic. They walked in on the two getting it on at the clubhouse where Francesco and her dad play tennis. Anita called it World War Fifty."

"Oh no. Poor Anita." Another Jenga piece that was holding up my life had just loosened.

"Yeah. To keep her trust fund, they told her she has to break it off. And as much as Anita loves Francesco . . . "

"For sure." Anita had already sent me two text messages earlier that morning, asking if we could talk, and now I knew why. The Jenga piece officially fell. Cinderella was about to be asked to move out of her palatial home.

———

We arrived at Sea Cove sandwiched in a phalanx of SUVs, a slowly snaking sea of black vehicles that briefly paused at the gated entrance decorated with glittering fairy lights. Charmaine had truly gone all out for this evening, and even in my state of prickly trepidation, I couldn't help but be awed by the show of old-school, careless wealth on display. It would likely be the last time I ever attended a party like this, and I tried to soak it all in as much as I could. Apparently the Mars Marble could feel my anxiety, because it cast shimmers of red light in the vehicle's interior as if sending out "Danger, danger!" alarms. The car behind us had the Santigolds' security detail, and when Keiko and I exited our SUV, they followed us immediately, keeping six feet behind me. It was kind of funny, actually, because although it was a gorgeous piece of jewelry, the Mars Marble was not on the same level as what Oscar nominees wore on the red carpet, items that actually necessitated a security detail. But the wave of thefts had everyone jumpy, and no one wanted to be the next victim. And so I entered the end-of-summer party with one friend and two beefy escorts, my famous ruby necklace earning appreciative stares that I could only hope would not turn into daggers by the end of the night.

After forty minutes, I spotted Other Lata. In fact, she made sure that I saw her. Standing at the perimeter of the dance floor, I was scanning the party for Rajeev, who hadn't arrived yet. Waves of people approached me on and off to engage in conversation and take in the Mars Marble up close. It had become a fascination piece because of Aqua's runway stunt and the fact that so far this year, she had eloped in Vegas with a country singer, annulled the marriage in about thirty-six hours, gone to rehab, and started dating a smoking hot actor who was in the same facility as her, and now both were off the grid, reportedly "finding themselves" somewhere deep in the Amazon rainforest. For all we knew, the Mars Marble might be her defining work. When it came to Aqua's jewelry oeuvre, the Mars Marble was the oil painting in a portfolio of pencil sketches and crayon drawings.

Yet even through the crowds, I finally caught sight of Other Lata. There were a handful of people of color at Charmaine's party—in a crowd of one hundred we were about fifteen. But there was only one Indian woman working as part of the staff. In looking back, it was sort of like a scene out of *Halloween*, seeing Michael Myers standing in broad daylight, except Other Lata was much shorter and wore a simple uniform of a white button-down, a dark vest, and matching pants. Our eyes locked as she stood outside the tent, and even though I tried to photocopy her image in my mind, she wasn't there long enough for me to recall anything about her except the intensity of her stare and that her dark hair was worn in a tight chignon. One moment she was there, and then I blinked and she was gone. I breathed a sigh of relief knowing that Other Lata had actually come, because the entirety of my plan hinged on that. And based on our past interactions, she would find a way to tell me when and where she wanted to meet.

Not that I wasn't nervous—oh god, my synapses were firing every which way, and my nerve endings were frayed. The band struck up a lively version of Daft Punk's "Get Lucky," and I moved aside as a good number of guests flocked to the dance floor. I stepped backward, my sweaty fingers brushing against my hairline, and stumbled right into Rajeev.

"Whoops. Oh, hi!" He of course looked handsome in his tuxedo and with a smooth, clean-shaven face, my first time seeing him without a hint of facial hair.

"Good to see you, Lata." Rajeev kissed me warmly on the cheek, but his trepidation was obvious. "You look...I'll need a dictionary to find the right word to do you justice."

"Rajeev, you are too sweet. And you're the most handsome person here. By far." We were a little awkward with each other, as if we hadn't had a brilliant Fourth of July night together, as well as a nice first date. But the specter of our strange second one hung over us, with so many unanswered questions creating distance between us. Distance that existed because of me.

"Thanks." He took a step back and scanned me, then broke into a genuine grin. "You make that necklace sing. Forget Aqua, you should wear the Mars Marble from now on. Every day."

"Even at the grocery store? Or the laundromat?"

"Especially." He cocked an eyebrow at me. "By the way, you inspired my own look tonight."

"You're kidding me! How?"

"It's silly, but..." Rajeev pulled on both sides of his bow tie, and it began to twirl like a high-energy fan. "I don't know why, it just appealed to me. I keep needing to remind myself about levity. Having a little fun. This reminds me of that idea, especially being around people like this. I'm not sure if I'll ever get used to it."

"Does anyone?" I said offhandedly, tickled by Rajeev's tie and the ongoing slightly offbeat clapping from the ladies in gowns and men in tuxes on the dance floor.

"Do you?" Rajeev shook his head. "I can never tell with you how much of this is normal. I really have no idea about where you're from, how you grew up. Will I ever?" He gave me a pleading glance, as if he needed to be right about me but could sense I was on the verge of letting him down.

"Soon," I said to his twirling bow tie, because it was too painful to look him in the eyes. "I promise."

For once, Other Lata's timing couldn't have been better. A waiter glided past us with two champagne flutes, and there was a folded piece of pink paper tucked underneath one of them. I quickly took the flute and note, not even caring if Rajeev spotted the latter. His plaintive questions for me made me even more determined to end this dance with Other Lata.

The note said: *Valet parking near the grove of trees. 8:30 pm. Don't be late, and come alone of course.*

"What time is it?" I looked at my wrist as if I had ever worn a watch before.

"It's ten past eight. What's going on? What is that?"

"Rajeev, I have to go. I just...just know that no matter what happens, you are such a special person to me. And so talented. I admire you a lot. And I hope we can talk more when I come back."

Underneath my Armani gown, I wore red Converse sneakers, not just to be a fashion renegade living up to my "kooky Lata" reputation, but also because it made it easier to speed away from the tent and up the rolling green hills to Sea Cove. I didn't have to turn around to know that the security detail was following close behind, nor did I have the heart to look back at a confused Rajeev watching me go, his bow tie still spinning.

20

DeLuxe Outfitters

OTHER LATA HAD SELECTED A very secluded spot, nearly a quarter mile away from Sea Cove. After stopping briefly inside the house to collect myself and prepare to meet her, along the way shaking the security men who'd been shadowing me, I stood underneath a giant oak, trying my best not to shiver. It wasn't that it was cold, with the August air having the perfect amount of warmth with none of the oppressive humidity I associated with this time last year, when this whole thing started. But I had never in my life experienced a showdown like this, the kind that you'd see in Westerns or high school comedies, when the good guy and the bad guy settled things once and for all.

"Lata." And as if a manifestation of my dreams, or worst nightmares, she was across from me. We both took a moment to peer at each other, and I could see why it had been fairly easy to call myself Lata Murthy and have no one question it.

Since we were both in flats, we were nearly the same height. Our features differed a great deal, but only if you cared to notice. She had a narrower face, with more rounded eyes and elfish ears, and whereas my lips were thin and forgettable, hers had character: a sensuous pout without a single stitch of lipstick or other cosmetic augmentation. Crucially, though, we were similar in coloring. To borrow Charmaine's graceless analogy comparing coffee and skin color, we were both mocha with a splash of milk.

"Lata Murthy," I responded. "Nice to finally meet in person."

"Is it nice?" She leaned against a black Mercedes-Benz, her loafers briefly catching the glow from the fairy lights dotting the surrounding trees. "I wouldn't say so." She paused and I waited. One of the things I had decided once I knew we would meet was that I would let her take the lead in the conversation. "So, no apology, then?"

"Apology for letting you blackmail me? Asking me to commit robbery and fraud?"

"Oh, Lata, don't be a victim. You are impersonating *me*." She let out a raspy cackle. "You can't stand there in your sad little black dress and sneakers and take the moral high ground." I felt her gaze move toward the Mars Marble. "Why anyone buys you as a Mumbai socialite princess, I will never understand. You so obviously shopped at Target and Walmart all your life." Another mirthless cackle.

"But I'm the one standing here in Armani, and you're the one parking cars." I shouldn't have let myself be baited by her, but the arch of her eyebrow and the dismissive gleam of her eyes were a finger constantly poking me in the ribs.

"True. That's true." She checked a thin wristwatch, and her eyes darted to the left, in the direction of Sea Cove. "Yet at the end of the day, only one of us is going to prison. And it's not going to be me."

I dug the toe of my left Converse into the ground, hoping to steady myself. This was where I needed the conversation to go, but I didn't want to push it there myself. I uttered a silent prayer that Lata's smugness would make her do what I needed her to.

"Hand over the necklace, Lata. I'm not wasting my time with you."

My mind briefly spun: I had seen so many good-versus-evil confrontations in the movies that I thought the two of us would have an extended conversation in which Lata would spell out everything. Very quickly, I decided that I had to push.

"I don't think so. Whoever you are, whatever you did, no one thinks we're the same person. Tonight has proven that." Nothing was further from the truth, but I hoped the statement would provoke Other Lata.

"My god, you're so naive. Where are your brains, little Lata? Did you scoop them out and leave them on the sidewalk when you decided to impersonate me?"

"Everyone loves Lata Murthy." I shrugged, which caused my gown to lower slightly. I hoisted it up so that the sides of my dress were tucked firmly under my armpits. "Your version had to throw around money. Mine just had to show up and make a few friends and be a friend."

"Oh. Oh, I see. These people are your *friends*." She tapped her temple with a rat-a-tat intensity. "Use your head. No one here is your friend. And by the time you figure that out, you'll be in handcuffs, and they'll all be jeering as they watch you leave."

"But *I* haven't done anything. Beyond the Macarena or juggling hot dogs, thanks to you." Playing dumb seemed the best move, especially since Other Lata found it so annoying.

She sighed at me as if she were an older sister who had lost interest in having her little sibling following her around, aping her every move. "Do I have to spell it out for you? Why do you think Lata Murthy, daughter of Mumbai royalty, even disappeared in the first place?"

I waited, my armpits ringed with sweat. *Tell me, tell me, tell me.*

Other Lata gave another quick glance to her watch, then narrowed her eyes at me. "I was out, free and clear. It's fun playing rich lady with these idiots, you know. They'll accept any story hook, line, and sinker if you look exotic and sound exotic." These last two words she spoke with a cartoonish Indian accent.

"I don't know how you fit in so easily with them," I said, sounding bruised. "Maybe I should have tried the accent."

"It wasn't just the accent. Money talks, first and always. I could come to a million parties in the Hamptons dressed as a clown, and as long as I made sure to have a donation to share, they all accepted me."

Now was the time to exude vulnerability. "At some point, though, you must have run out of money. I mean...even I'm flailing. My credit cards are maxed. It's been tough keeping up."

Other Lata rolled her eyes. "I never used my own money. God, that's stupid. I had my ways to secure big fat wads of cash."

"The Tellworth." Other Lata's mouth dropped slightly. For the first time, Other Lata's above-it-all demeanor faltered. Was it the right time to deploy that information? I wasn't sure. But I needed her to say the full story out loud. "I recognized the painting from the Twitter account."

Other Lata did a slow clap. "Bully for you, little Lata. Yes, the Tellworth. Those people cast aside large bills like Kleenex. They're in sofa cushions and jacket pockets and on bathroom countertops. Same with jewelry, watches, purses, et cetera. The amount of carelessness is staggering. Really, I was doing them a service: I was simply 'donating' their money back to them." Other Lata had returned to her default state: smugness. She seemed to like sharing her story. Who else would she tell about her exploits, anyway? I leaned into this.

"Ohhhh!" I semi-dramatically clapped my palm to my cheek. "I've been wondering about that. It sounds like you gave tens of thousands away."

"That was the point," she said in the tone of *Are you really that dense?* Other Lata let a smile escape her lips as she explained that the first two or three donations were genuine, give or take a thousand. But once she had established herself as a benefactress, the giant wads in the glittery envelopes had been bookended by big bills, with smaller bills, sometimes even ones and fives, filling out the middle. "You know, I didn't just hand them out randomly. I knew exactly who they were and how involved they were with their pet causes. How many of those old coots do you think counted them out to see if my professed amount matched the actual cash? I would see them literally hand the envelopes off to their assistants, to be handed off to who knows where."

"And I imagine whoever ended up with the donation didn't want to have to tell their bosses the real amounts either." This was me genuinely starting to put the pieces together about how her con worked. "They most likely would react in a 'shoot the messenger' kind of way."

Other Lata smirked as she leaned back a little farther against the car's hood, putting one foot on the bumper. "It suited everyone to believe what I said. To be the recipient of a Lata Murthy donation was the point. The actual amount?" She tsked. "Who cared."

I could see her point. Marlena was deeply involved with MoonRose, but so many people, including the ones gathered at Sea Cove, operated vanity charities without actually handling the day-to-day operations of their organizations. It was just another branding exercise for them.

"Everyone is so in awe of Lata—your version, not mine." I made sure to sound awestruck rather than fawning. "You built a real mystique about her."

"Thanks to you, there's now only one version of her. Which suits me just fine."

I contorted my features to reflect my supposed bafflement.

"You still don't get it?"

In between several glances at her watch, Other Lata told me that she had gone underground two summers ago for two reasons. First, she had nearly been caught stealing a diamond ring, but she was able to talk herself out of that predicament easily enough. What really sent her off the grid was a woman who headed up a newly established foundation benefiting "little kids with Lyme disease or something." Wanting the Lata mystique, the woman kept haranguing Other Lata to donate to her organization.

"She was the fourth wife of some sort of important fat cow, and desperate to prove she had a brain cell and a work ethic. For whatever reason, she got it in her head that she needed a donation from me to legitimize her sad little charity." Other Lata laughed derisively. "I could tell she was the kind of woman who wouldn't let it go. The summer season was ending anyway, so it was time for me to cut out and send Lata back to Mumbai. I really didn't expect the invitations to keep coming once September arrived. I went back to my life... and then one year later you came along." A smile worthy of Cruella de Vil crossed her lips. "And if you wanted to play the Lata Murthy game, then you might as well take all her baggage too. I'm happy to dump it off on you and be free and clear of it forever."

"But why even do it at all?" I didn't know I was going to ask the question until I heard it come out of my mouth. "Why even do the whole Mumbai socialite charade?" Just as Rajeev had asked me not long ago, I wanted to ask her, *Who are you, really?*

"You stand here wearing a necklace made out of rubies and ask me that?" She jabbed a finger in my direction. "C'mon now. Neither of us grew up rich. And if you're poor, you don't exist. Unless to be a laughingstock, exploited, or a scapegoat. I had enough of that from..." Her lips briefly slammed shut, but anger continued staining her face. "Anyway, it doesn't matter. But I wasn't going to be any of those things." I noted that Other Lata briefly placed both hands on the car's hood. She must have seen me notice, because she smoothly pulled out a handkerchief from her pocket.

"You can only be treated like you're invisible for so long until you realize you can use it to your advantage," she said, carefully wiping the areas she had touched. Other Lata bragged that she was easily able to infiltrate affluent circles as Mumbai Lata because of how much she learned from hostessing at private clubs like the Tellworth. "The same people who treated me like a nobody when I waited on them at the club slobbered all over me once they thought I was rich like them. I fooled them all. Because as you learned, they are so easy to fool. And unfortunately for you, none of them can tell two Indian women apart."

I bristled at not just her smugness, but the truth of her words. What the past year had made exceedingly clear was that the wealthy reveled in their ignorance toward those who did not look like them. This obtuseness is what Other Lata counted on to pull off her scam—and then have me be the one to take the fall for it.

"All right, little Lata, this has been fun. But it's time for me to go. Permanently." She stepped away from the car, then motioned toward it as if she were Vanna White presenting a new *Wheel of Fortune* game to solve. "Within this car are all the bells and whistles of your summer escapades with your fwennnds." She said this last word in a mocking, babyish tone. "Plus a few more goodies—think of them as parting gifts from me." Other Lata cocked her head to the side, her seething demeanor replaced by a giddy smile. "And here's a heads-up for your future court-appointed attorney: your fingerprints can be found on some of the items."

"What?" I wanted to lunge at her but steadied myself. "You're lying. That's impossible." When Other Lata continued simpering at me, I added, "But how?"

"That's for me to know and for you to be arrested for."

"Listen," I pleaded. "If you want to disappear, disappear. Why are you making me the fall guy for your crimes? All I ever did was attend a few parties. I never hurt anyone."

Another witch cackle. "Listen to yourself. You think you're better than me, but you've been lying to everyone here, pretending to be me. Including your new boyfriend. *If* he's your boyfriend. You two have the chemistry of a can of tuna fish."

I went cold all over at the mention of Rajeev. "Leave him out of this."

"I didn't bring him into this, you did. And I'm sure it's going to only improve his relationship with Marlena Santigold that his new girlfriend pledged a half million dollars she does not have. Except if she shoplifted it from Barneys. Right?"

She had me there. I watched helplessly as she meticulously refolded her handkerchief and placed it in her back pocket.

Then an idea flashed in my mind that had never occurred to me before and should have a long time before then.

"The difference between us is that I'm going to make amends for my actions. Not run away from what I did." I briefly touched the Mars Marble, which was starting to feel heavy around my neck. "I can accept what I did wrong and answer for it. But there's no way I'm going to answer for your crimes."

"Good for you, little Lata, good for you." There was that infuriating slow clap again. "The only problem is that someone has passed along an anonymous tip to the police about all the missing items in this car, and that you're the guilty party. So you might want to hustle if you're going to start making amends to all those rich white people back there. Because once they see you hauled away in handcuffs, they won't care what you will have to say. Trust me on that."

Everything that happened in the next few seconds I experienced both lightning fast and in excruciating slow motion. Other Lata leaped at me, her hand clutching the Mars Marble. Startled, I pulled away, which caused the necklace to fall apart in her hands. The jewels rippled and bounced off the ground like the glass marbles they were. But still attached to my neck was a thin wire with a recording device. Other Lata noticed it, and a look passed between us.

And then she bolted, whipping up a storm of dust as she went.

"Please tell me you got that," I said out loud, my body vibrating so much I longed to lean against the cursed Mercedes that allegedly bore evidence of my guilt.

Charmaine's voice quickly sounded in my ear. "I did."

As soon as Charmaine answered, I hotfooted in the direction I saw Other Lata head in, toward a sea of cars that lined the road and pooled in the center of a field. I scanned the horizon from all sides. But she was gone, as if she had never existed at all. The only remaining evidence that I had spent the last ten minutes speaking to someone was a black vest on the side of the road. Gingerly, I picked it up between my thumb and forefinger. The vest had the lingering scent of petunias and body odor.

"DeLuxe Outfitters," read the gold label affixed to the inside. Underneath, in smaller print: "Always Trust Our Finest with Yours."

21

Tom Ford

BECAUSE CHARMAINE'S PARTY INCLUDED A live band, he had employed a state-of-the-art sound system that included several speakers the size of refrigerators. I didn't know much about how sound systems worked, but for my purposes all I needed to know was that everyone who was gathered under the tent had heard the conversation between Other Lata and myself.

Charmaine waited for me at the Louise Bardot sculpture, our agreed-upon meeting place because it was far from the party while still in view of it. I quickly filled him in on Other Lata's description, as well as the direction she had fled.

"I hired someone to have eyes on you two in case she took off," he said, adjusting his glasses with a jittery hand. "But it's so dark once you leave the estate, I'm not sure how much luck he'll have. You okay?" Charmaine placed a hand on my shoulder, then briefly touched the wire still wound around my neck. "I'll go ahead and switch this off now."

I thanked him, my adrenaline turning me into a volcano of twitchiness and nerves. "Did they all hear?"

"They did. Everyone did. The stereo was so powerful I'm sure half of East Hampton heard."

"That's a relief. She said she called the police. But I don't know if she really did. Although I wouldn't put it past her. But the stolen goods, plus she said my fingerprints—"

"Okay, sit and breathe for a second. You got a confession out of her. Which is what all this was about."

Charmaine led me to a nearby bench, the same one where I had donned the Dior sunglasses one year earlier. We sat in silence for a few moments, our elbows touching, as if we both had to reassure ourselves the other person was still there. When I had first come up with the plan to ensnare Other Lata, I'd immediately contacted Charmaine and asked if he could throw a party with the goal of luring her to secretly record her confession. But Charmaine didn't think a taped confession was enough, and thought it had to happen in real time for an audience of people "designed to think the worst of you, especially when it directly impacted them."

When I had left Rajeev in the tent to go meet Other Lata, my pit stop inside the house was to meet with Charmaine and exchange the necklaces. After I let the security detail know that I was no longer comfortable wearing the Mars Marble, and they whisked it away in a velvet box, Charmaine gave me an imitation necklace made from pieces of red glass that shone and bounced in the light, similar to the rubies. Then, feeling like I was in a spy movie, I was also fitted with a microphone and small earpiece. The fake Mars Marble was my idea, but the fact that Charmaine was able to commission a credible facsimile in three weeks still stunned me. The sight of the rubies was what allowed Other Lata to let her guard down, because she could see that I had followed her directions and, in her estimation, was as guileless and pliable as I had been all summer. If I had tried to confront her without guaranteeing the one thing she wanted, she wouldn't have bothered to speak to me and would've simply walked away. Leaving me holding the proverbial bag.

Even though I was still weak-kneed, I stood up. "I have to find Rajeev."

Charmaine looked at me dubiously. "Are you sure you want to go back out there? It's kind of...a scene. Lots of people on their phones. You might get mobbed."

A couple of partygoers walked by us, and since they were only a few feet away, I could hear parts of their conversation. "So this Lata is the Lata who stole? Or she ran away? This is so confusing. There are two Latas?"

Hearing those words, I sat down again. A cool wind swirled around us, and goose bumps rose up on my skin. In response to my shivering, Charmaine took off his tuxedo jacket and placed it on my shoulders. The softness of the fabric actually helped soothe my nerves. To wear Charmaine's jacket was like wearing his protection against prying eyes and their assumptions and their gossip.

"This is nice," I said, pulling it closer over my shoulders, even as my dress once again sagged halfway down my bustline. Rather than hoist it up, I just let it be. If I flashed everyone, maybe that could be the hot topic of conversation instead.

"Tom Ford always makes me feel like James Bond. Especially tonight," Charmaine chuckled. "You were great with her, by the way. You handled her well. You could be James Bond too."

"Ha, doubtful but thanks. It all happened so fast, I'm not even sure I can remember everything that happened."

"How was it to confront her?"

"Weird." I shivered again. "It was like playing chess with a grand master. I always worried she was a few steps ahead of me." I kicked a pebble and watched it roll into the darkness. "She has a lot of anger."

"That was clear." Charmaine puffed out his cheeks and sighed. "To be honest, you guys sounded pretty alike to my ears. The only way to differentiate between the two of you is that she actually sounded like a Bond villain. Vicious and smug."

"That captures her essence in a nutshell." I stood up again, then handed Charmaine his jacket back before giving my dress several good tugs upward.

"Do you really want to walk into that maelstrom?" he asked gently.

"Not at all. But I need to check on Rajeev. I think I might have blown his mind seven ways to Sunday."

"Okay, then. Let's go." He stood and held out his arm.

"Stay close, if you don't mind."

"I'll whisk you there and whisk you back."

I imagine we looked somewhat shell-shocked as we approached the party, resembling a fairy-tale couple whose happily ever after came true, but at an absurd cost we hadn't seen coming. In the darkness outside of the tent, most people didn't notice or recognize me. Yet somehow within that crowd, I spotted Keiko and Rajeev walking in our direction up the hill, their faces lit up by the glow of cell phones. My heart thrummed when I saw them together, the two people dearest to me in this whole saga.

"There." I pointed them out to Charmaine.

He whistled. "Good eyes." Feeling my hand tense up on his arm, he added, "Want me to go with you?" I nodded.

Our meeting was brief, but spiky with strong feelings. It's actually heart-wrenching to think about, because their faces were so pained just by the mere sight of me.

"Hey," I called out. "Guys, hey."

They looked at me, dumbstruck. I didn't know how well they could see me, but they definitely recognized my voice. Keiko's face was better lit by the phone still held up near her face, and she gave me a weary look.

"Are you okay, Lata?"

"I am. Are you . . . both? Listen, I'm sure you have a lot of questions, and—"

The phone in Keiko's hand shifted and cast light on Rajeev. Though most of his face was in shadow, his eyes were visible. Rajeev was in distress, and when he looked directly at me, he was downright appalled. My heart panged to know that I was the cause of his anguish.

"We're going to go. We're leaving." Keiko pocketed her phone and took Rajeev by the hand and led him up the hill, as if she were a hyper little sister dragging her exhausted big brother around an amusement park.

Maybe Keiko I could win back over time. But I had lost Rajeev's trust, as simple as that. Honestly, I had never once earned it. And so with the clarity of a police siren wailing in the distance, I knew I had lost him forever.

By the way, that police siren was not a figurative one: we could all hear the sound of the police cars approaching Sea Cove.

"Shit." I stopped in my tracks. "What do I do?"

"Well, we have one hundred or so witnesses to a public confession of guilt that wasn't yours. Which was the whole point. And it might be easier to clear this up with them now anyway."

"Can we head back inside the house?" I felt so exposed and needed all the walls and doors to put a barrier between me and the fate Other Lata had arranged for me. Because even though I knew the party guests had heard us, what would prevent them from thinking it was all a ruse? Or that I was the true mastermind, who had plotted this to entrap Other Lata? Rich white people could use magical thinking any which way to suit their needs. They might still decide I was the one who had stolen from them or pledged donations in glittery envelopes. I needed more than just the fact that they bore witness to Other Lata's confession.

I needed to share the whole story. My story. And as quickly as possible.

Back up the hill we went, although we entered the house through a side door rather than the high-ceiling ones that the partygoers were using. Charmaine ushered me into the same guest room where we had made the necklace switch.

"I'll be right back." He gave me a wry smile. "The host's job is never done until every guest is welcome, even the ones wearing badges. You'll be okay here?"

I nodded, and then as soon as he shut the door, I got to work. I took my phone out of my purse and opened Twitter. And then created a new account called @TheOtherLata.

I'm not sure how much time passed between when I began tweeting and when Charmaine reopened the door, two officers following him. But it was enough to grant me the space to send out fifty-three tweets, including eight screenshots, in which I outlined the last year of my life, starting with the first Saturday of August in 2013 and ending with the second Saturday of August in 2014. Before I put my phone away to rise up to speak, the Twitter account already had one hundred followers. By early afternoon the next day, when Charmaine, his attorney, and I left the East Hampton Police Department, my new Twitter account had gained over 350,000 followers.

Twenty-four hours later, that number had exploded to 1.2 million.

22

One Week Later

A DAY AFTER CHARMAINE'S PARTY, I moved out of Anita's apartment, transporting myself and my belongings back to New Canaan via my parents' Subaru. Most of my things remain in suitcases and boxes in the garage. To be back in my childhood bedroom reminds me of my dreamy teenage self, gazing out the window, wondering what the future would hold for me.

But right now all I can do is lie in bed on a Saturday afternoon and stew about the past. Thinking *If only, if only.* If only I hadn't opened that email from Elephantine. If only I hadn't attended the Galaxy Unknown party or the first one at Sea Cove. If only I had stayed with my fifth-floor walk-up and easy, thankless job. At least then I was still a person. Now all I am is a pariah.

Here's what I don't recommend: becoming the white-hot center of attention for even one second of your life. In my case, it lasted for two days and twenty-one hours. My existence veered into the surreal as my name became a trending topic on Twitter and celebs as varied as Cher, Al Roker, and Kris Jenner became some of my million-plus followers. I even came up as a Hot Topic on *The View*, and my story was splashed over the front pages of both the *New York Post* and *New York Daily News*.

When I created the @TheOtherLata Twitter account, all I wanted was to get as many eyeballs on my story as possible, the words "evidence" and "proof" ringing through my head with every tweet I sent. But I didn't really think it through: if I were successful, then a side effect would be this kind of intense, tabloidy interest in every aspect of my life.

Thankfully a costumed Elmo brawled with a major movie star in front of an agog group of Girl Scouts in Times Square, displacing me as lead story in the New York papers, at least for now. Hopefully this means that Other Lata and I will stop being lumped together more than we already are. Despite my posting the Twitter thread to ensure the public would understand we are two very different people, our shared name has made us confusing to tell apart. And unfortunately, only one of us has a wealth of photos to be included in every single story. Other Lata has only a blurry pic from her Tellworth photo ID. But me? Too many to count. My smiling face stares out obliviously from MSN and Yahoo! News articles as words like "Fraud" and "Con Woman" hover over my head. It's no wonder that before I could ask for a leave of absence, Initiate PR's human resources department requested a "mutual parting of ways." At least I get to claim unemployment.

Even more hurtful than the conflation of myself with Other Lata are all the anonymous sources that ran to the media, giving their "insider info" about what I'm really like. The worst was a *Page Six* story titled "Lata the Liar," in which someone said about me, "She wore expensive clothes without any style. She was no better than a Real Housewife of New Jersey in that way." That's the moment I finally stop reading the news coverage. (On my laptop, that is. I turned off my phone as soon as I arrived at my parents' doorstep.)

A knock at the door. By the three sharp raps, I know it's my mother.

I don't have to be here. Charmaine offered to let me stay at one of his family's properties, but it's a condo on 79th and Madison, and that would mean hiding out among the very people who are most fascinated and appalled by both Latas. Also, how much can I ask of him? Not only did he help me with the Mars Marble scheme out of his own pocket, but he also retained an attorney to represent me. I can't keep depending on his generosity. And for maybe the first time ever, I don't want to be in New York City. Not while knowing that the number of followers of the @TheOtherLata Twitter account will only increase while the number of actual friends I have in the city dwindles down to single digits, if that.

Enter Ashok and Diya, opening the door without waiting for me to say "Come in." A panicked glance at my alarm clock tells me it's 1:20 p.m. I scramble out of bed and plop down at my desk, nearly knocking over a squat pile of old issues of the *New Yorker* as I land in my seat. My parents are in their weekend wear, matching sweat suits—hers in yellow, his in gray—that she purchased on sale from Marshalls. I'm in my pajamas, a J.Crew pink flannel set that I usually wear when I come here for Christmas. It's basically been my uniform since arriving, because that's how committed I am to not unpacking and making my stop here permanent. Even my toiletries are still in their zip-up plastic cases; I'm using the discount toothpaste, soap, and facial cleanser in the guest bathroom.

"Lata, we need to talk," my father says as he walks in.

At last, we're finally having the "what the hell is happening" conversation, which I assumed would have happened as soon as I parked the Subaru in the garage. But all week, my parents have left me alone. Except for calling me to come down for meals, but even then I would have upma or rice and sambar or microwave pizza by myself in the kitchen. Caught up in the vortex of the drama I created in the city, this suited me fine. But now that my mom and dad are in my room, seated on the edge of my mattress with tightly crossed legs and puckered mouths, I can step outside of my worries and wonder what the heck is going on with them.

"Okay," I tell the poster of the cast of *Friends* that hangs in the corner near my bed. Perhaps this conversation will be easier if I just stare at Jennifer Aniston's hair the entire time.

"Leave her, Ashok," my mom says, squirming so much that the mattress keeps shifting side to side. "Let's not do this now." Why is my mother acting like she's the one in trouble? As if she has to answer to me?

"We can't put this off, Diya. It's on the news, friends are asking, we have got to talk."

Finally, a confirmation. My parents know about the Other

Lata saga, even though I haven't said a word about it since arriving home. I'm not sure if they got wind before my arrival or after, but it's mind boggling that my name and face have been plastered all over Twitter and *Gawker* and *Page Six* and who knows where else, and they were able to go a whole week without saying anything. To hear my father say that "friends are asking" deepens my crater of regret and self-loathing, which widens with every passing day. I had been clinging to the fantasy that my parents had no idea what I had been up to and, foolishly, that they would never find out.

"Sure, let's talk." To have my father interrogating me in my childhood bedroom provokes me to respond like a scolded teenager. "I've shamed you forever, right?"

"We just want to know what happened." My mom sounds nearly as sullen as me and seems to be hypnotized by a spot on the pink carpet. She points her big toes together, creating an arrow shape with her feet.

"From you, and no one else." My dad says this sternly, but he seems to have also absorbed my mother's nervousness, his eyes flitting beyond me to the dresser that sits between my desk and closet.

"What have you heard?" I wheel my chair a few inches backward. Anything to put some space between me and them, and this moment I've been dreading for so long.

"Don't be smart, Lata." My dad briefly raises his hand as if to grab the armrest to pull me back, then stops himself.

"I'm not trying to be." I mean this. To know what they've heard would help me figure out the best way to spin this story to not agitate them more than necessary. Unable to sit still, I continue wheeling backward. My mom finally raises her gaze from the oh-so-fascinating carpet, and she stiffens. Whereas before she couldn't tear her eyes off the carpet, now she is staring past me, as if there were a boogeyman standing in the corner.

What is going on? My parents are acting as if being in a bedroom with a magenta bedspread and walls marked with posters of my teenage obsessions (*Friends*, Sylvia Plath, Spice Girls) gives them hives. When not trading anxious gazes with my mom, my dad can't stop staring past me either. Right at my dresser.

My antenna goes up. What if they weren't avoiding me because of my actions, but because of theirs?

As someone living in her pajamas and out of her duffel bag, I hadn't bothered opening my dresser until two days ago. While rummaging for some clean socks, I came across my pink plastic Jem lunch box in the bottom drawer. This was weird for two reasons. One, the lunch box had been banished to the attic long ago, along with everything else I had treasured between the ages of one and ten. And two, my dresser, like my bedroom, has remained frozen in time since the day I left for college. Seeing Jem squeezed in between balls of socks, scarves, and winter hats was strange, but not strange enough to warrant further investigation.

Until now. Slowly I stand, watching my parents' faces register confusion, then alarm, as I push the chair aside and kneel down beside the dresser. My dad lurches up, but before he can stop me, I open the drawer and take out the Jem lunch box.

"Wait—" my mom calls out.

I pop it open, revealing four joints, rolling papers, baggies of weed, several lighters, and a few tins marked in an undecipherable hand. After my initial shock, I laugh so hard I double over.

"Are you two stoners?"

———

Never in my life did I imagine I would be seated at my parents' dining room table, the three of us chatting like we were old pals catching up at a high school reunion as we filled each other in about the past year.

And it was my mom who initiated this surprising denouement, taking the Jem lunch box from me and gently shutting it. "Let's have a talk. A real talk." My mother's usual clipped way of talking, her perennially hunched shoulders as if walking into a heavy wind, had dissipated from the moment I revealed Jem's secret stash.

I went first, of course. I owed them that much. It was a relief for me to disabuse them of the notion that I was in trouble with the law, which was what they had feared when their friends sent them stories with headlines such as "This Indian Con Woman Has the Upper East Side Shook" and "Lata on the Lam." With those kinds of news articles, I'm thankful that no reporters ended up knocking on my parents' front door. And maybe because they had become late-in-life stoners, they took my whole story in stride. Dare I say, even with admiration?

"If those rich people-sheeple believed you, that's their

problem," my dad says, sipping a Scotch on the rocks. Oh, did I not mention we were all drinking at two thirty p.m. on a Saturday?

"I agree," my mom says while refilling our glasses of merlot, which we're drinking out of matching "I Heart Connecticut" coffee mugs.

"Who are you guys?" I look back and forth between my mother and father, awed. "Is this like *Invasion of the Body Snatchers*?"

"Don't be silly." My mom gently swats my hand. "What you did wasn't right, but you didn't hurt anyone. And thank god that stupid woman didn't hurt you."

"That's true," I say, shifting on my chair's plastic covering. In sharing the story of my stint as Downtown Lata, I didn't include my credit card debt and shoplifting. Right now, they don't need to know how much of a shit pickle I'm in that's solely my fault.

"And she's gone?" My dad snaps his fingers. "Just like that?"

"Gone with the wind," I chuckle uneasily. "No one even knows if Lata Murthy was her real name."

"No charges? You sure they're not going to come after you?" I had been worried about this very thing after Other Lata alleged that my fingerprints were on the stolen items. But it ended up being an empty threat since no prints had been found, not even hers.

"I spoke with the police, and my friend corroborated everything I said. No one believes I'm responsible for her crimes."

"Wow. Wow, wow, wow," Dad repeats. "You got lucky."

"I know, Dad, I know."

The dining room gets the least light of the entire house, especially with the curtains drawn. Outside it's a sunny afternoon, but this room has a cozy dimness that seems to relax all of us. Besides the flowing alcohol, the fact that we can't see each other clearly contributes to our ability to shed our roles of parent and child and, for the first time ever, address each other as peers.

I let a few moments pass in companionable silence, glad to have answered all their questions. Then, in a cartoonishly disapproving tone, I ask, "And what's been happening with the two of you?"

They exchange sly smiles.

"We're having...fun," Dad says. "We're being free."

"What does that mean?"

My parents look at each other again, and now they are full-on cackling, their bodies heaving, my dad slapping the table repeatedly.

"What? What? Tell me!" I have never seen them this carefree—even youthful!—in my entire life.

The story comes out in fits and starts, as each parent interrupts the other to fill in their side. But the gist is that my parents' troubles began eight years ago, when a couple named Pinky and Benny Bhudiya moved to nearby Westport. (Think of it as the Beverly Hills of Connecticut.) The two joined my parents' social circle, a loosely connected group of immigrant desis who all attend the same temple and cultural functions. As owners of a super-successful chain of high-end jewelry stores, not only were Pinky and Benny filthy rich, they were also intensely charismatic. An otherwise harmonious group of pharmacists and physicians and bankers and engineers quickly splintered into those Pinky and Benny chose to befriend and those they ignored, like my parents. All of my mom's closest friends eventually drifted over to Team Pinky, seduced by her showy gifts and elaborate parties. As pharmacists, my parents found themselves among the lowest on the totem pole. They weren't shunned, exactly. But what was once a friendly community had become split into *Survivor*-style alliances, with nearly everyone vying to stay in the Bhudiyas' good graces.

The worst part was that even though they didn't have kids, Pinky and Benny loved to pass judgment on everyone else's children. It would be "Did you hear that he got rejected by Harvard?" or "Of course they're getting divorced, he met her at a bar" or, in my case, "I hear she earns peanuts at her little computer job. Who will want her? She will never get married, no matter how much Diya and Ashok pray for it." My parents stopped going to temple after that.

I wasn't imagining the distance that had settled over my parents with every passing year, but when I was growing up, at least they were on speaking terms. I had always figured their estrangement occurred once I left for college—since they were done raising me, they no longer had something in common. Now I think they could have weathered their empty nest and powered through, but the Bhudiyas' arrival had curdled their social life and friendships. Rather than finding comfort in one another, my parents shut each other out. For my dad, that meant resuming a vice from his graduate school days.

He tried to keep this secret by making after-dinner visits to the attic, but of course my mom noticed the odor floating down to the second floor. They had so many fights about my dad's marijuana use that my dad moved into the guest bedroom. And that's the dynamic I had noticed during my visits over the past few years, their misery making it difficult for them to even pretend to be united in front of me. Their whole marriage could have remained this way, a churning storm of resentful silence.

Except that six months ago, Pinky and Benny were arrested for embezzlement. Not only that, but when the cops arrived at the Bhudiya residence, Benny was in flagrante with someone who was not his wife, but their married next-door neighbor Susie. And the hypocrisy of these two Judgy Judgintons lording over them all those years, damaging their friendships and talking shit about their daughter, broke something in my mother.

Once the Bhudiyas made the local evening news, their McMansion overrun with federal agents and yellow tape, Mom turned off the television and asked for a "pot cigarette." Dad, surprised, led her to my bedroom—my bedroom!—and instructed her on how to smoke a joint. And they have been blunt buddies ever since.

"You are blowing my mind. You wouldn't even let me have soda until I was fourteen, and now you go to my room each night and get high?" I shake my head in amazement. "Why couldn't I have you as my parents twenty years ago?"

Mom laughs. "You were never supposed to know. Sometimes I still get heart palpitations that someone will find out, that a police car will pull up in the driveway—"

"I tell her no one cares. We're in our own home. No one

will report us. But she takes an hour-long shower each night to make sure the smell doesn't cling to her."

"Ashok, shush." Mom pushes her mug aside. "I just...It's been nice to break a rule. Do something that feels good."

How I could relate. "No doubt seeing Pinky and Benny go down in a blaze of shame helped with that."

Mom titters, and Dad lets out one merry "ha." The expectations that always ruled over me, not to do one thing that stepped over the line for fear of "What will people say? What will people think?" had always originated from my parents. It never occurred to me that this way of thinking, passed down generationally, had started to chafe at them too.

I place both my hands on the table, spreading my fingers outward as far as they can go. I have never had such an open and honest conversation with my parents before. I might never again. So I have to ask.

"Do you two...love each other? Are you happy together?"

A long pause. Next door, a lawn mower grunts and belches before kicking into a low hum.

"Why do you ask?" Mom finally responds. She holds her coffee mug close, running her hands over it as if it were a genie's lamp. "Do we not seem happy?"

I take a breath, then dive in. "As long as I can remember, you always seemed to be like roommates assigned to the same living space. And then you had the joint responsibility of taking care of me. Once I was out of the house, you had even less in common. It was like we were all playing roles for one another. You were the strict parents. I was the child, slightly rebellious but not too much." This is cathartic to say out loud.

From age twelve to two years ago, I filled pages of journals with anger and despair over why the Murthy household was so inert, as if even loving each other was just us going through the motions of what was expected of us.

"That sounds right," Dad says, and Mom looks at him with surprise. "Doesn't it? We were so young when we met, our early twenties, married a few weeks after, and then found ourselves in this country. And we were both only children, just like you. Our parents depended on us to send back whatever we could. No time to think, only to keep going."

"We did the best we could," Mom adds. "Were you unhappy?"

"I just only wished I had sensed more affection between you back then, like I do now. No regrets. I never wanted for anything. I had a good childhood," I rush to add. "It's just really nice to see you in this place now." The dimness is too intense as we pass into late afternoon. I switch on a lamp but on its softest setting, so that we can still take refuge in the shadows.

"More wine?" Dad asks while refilling our mugs. As he does, I give the past six months some thought. I was so busy with my Downtown Lata existence that it didn't register that my mother's weekly check-ins asking "See you on Sunday?" became biweekly, then even more infrequent than that.

"Would you have never told me about this?"

"We didn't want to embarrass you." Mom picked at a loose thread on her sweatshirt. "This is not how parents are supposed to be, acting like they're fifteen." Despite their forehead creases and spikes of gray hair invading their hairlines, my parents really do exude the giddiness of teenagers. For once, Mom and Dad have a bond over something that gives them pleasure. The fact that it was a secret to the world must have made it more thrilling. "We thought you would think we were being silly. How could you take us seriously as your parents?"

"You wouldn't have embarrassed me. If anything, it would have hurt me to know you had this secret life outside of me. That there was a pocket of happiness you two shared that only existed when I'm not here."

"We hadn't thought of it that way," Dad admits. "We only wanted to protect you."

"Well, just so you know, I'm glad I know. I like seeing you this way, looser and more, like, connected. It's nice." My parents exchange relieved looks. How sweet that they would ever feel worried about shaming me when I had done exponentially more to bring shame to them. Now that Mom and Dad have a nightly "pot cigarette" ritual, getting high while pointing proverbial middle fingers in the direction of the Pinkys and Bennys of the world, I can ask them the question that took root in my brain the moment I emerged from the East Hampton Police Department. Dazed and blinking in the sunlight, my phone buzzing with hundreds of notifications, a silver lining presented itself to me, and I desperately wanted to take it.

"So, I have this opportunity. A couple of magazines have reached out, wanting to interview me about what happened. But I don't want to trust my story to anyone else; I'd rather write it myself. Same as the tweets." With nothing to lose, I responded to the inquiries by proposing I tell my own story.

Of all the publications, only one said yes. And it happened to be my favorite one, *Gotham*. "I really want to do this—I've never had anything like this happen before. I'm not sure if I will ever again. It would give me a chance to really give my side of the story in a definitive way. Also maybe be the start of a real writing career." My dad scratches his forehead and seems perturbed. "I've been holding back because I didn't want to cause you any more humiliation."

"Joan Didioff," Dad says. "Isn't that who you said you wanted to be?"

"Joan Didion. And you remember that?" For Career Day in tenth grade, I gave a presentation on what I wanted to do one day, and I said that I wanted to have a career like Joan Didion's.

"Is this your chance to be her?" Dad asks, looking sideways at Mom.

"It would be. But it would mean a lot of scrutiny, on all of us. The Pinkys and Bennys will have their pitchforks out. I will be the cautionary tale for a lot of desi families."

To my astonishment, my mom reaches for my hand. "If this is what you want, then do it. You'll have to live with the story over your head, regardless. Why not tell it yourself?"

"Really?" Tears spring to my eyes. "Thanks, Mom."

"We've seen these Richie Riches all our life, Lata. Thinking they're better than us. I only thought it bothered me..." My mom wipes away a tear of her own. "I never actually thought how you would be impacted too. Which is my mistake. I—"

"Mom, no!" I cry out, leaping from my chair to give her a hug. "We're not going to look backward anymore. All I could ever want, you both gave me. Especially right now." I feel my Dad beside me, his arms surrounding me as I embrace Mom. We are not a hugging family—we've said "I love you" less than five times—so this physical closeness is alien to all of us. We grit through and stay awkwardly pretzeled together, my dad's warm breath smothering my ear, my chin hovering on my mother's bony shoulder. My stomach rumbles, and of course that sets Diya off in mom mode, hurrying to warm up dinner while asking me to set the table. This could have been any other weekend night at home while growing up, and for once this is a comforting thought.

As we have dinner, I make a request—which they immediately reject.

"Can I watch you guys toke up?"

"Toke? What is this toke?" my dad responds at the same time my mom says, "No! That would be too—" She stops midsentence and her eyes go wide. "Wait, do you? Have you?"

"Never mind, guys." I smile deeply. For the first time in my entire life, I am happy to be New Canaan Lata, having dinner with her parents, and have it feel not like a chore but like a regular practice I can look forward to. "We don't have to do everything together as a family."

23

One Month Later

A YEAR AND A MONTH after opening the Elephantine email, it's me and my inbox again, facing another monumental decision. But this time, rather than debating whether or not to open an email, I debate whether or not to send one.

> From: Lata Murthy
> Date: Thu, Sep 18, 2014 at 12:31 PM
> Subject: Re: Lata Article
> To: Erin Harper
>
> Hi Erin—
> Attached is a draft of my article. I look forward to your feedback.
>
> Thanks,
> Lata

Would you believe I struggled with those seventeen words more than the article draft? According to Forbes.com, there are fifty-seven ways to sign off an email, and I tried every single one of them ("Warm regards," "Sincerely," "Best," "All Best") before going with the simple "Thanks." I'm just delaying because I'm seeing the demarcation of a new Before and After in my life. Once this article goes out to *Gotham*, this is officially who I want New York City, and the rest of the world, to know me as. Not just the actions of my hot-dog-juggling, shoplifting self, but how I choose to share my story. My actual writing. I've never had this many people potentially read my words.

Terrifying. Scary. Unnerving. Bone chilling. (Merriam-Webster has an endless supply of synonyms for "frightening.")

I'm clicking "Send." I just clicked "Send."

This is the first time I've submitted my writing to an authority figure since college. I'm more than just a bundle of nerves. Quadruple the bundle and then multiply it by a thousand—that's a more accurate description of my mental state as I await her feedback. Hopefully, Erin the Editor won't regret taking a chance on the prose stylings of a former trivia writer turned half-hearted PR flack. While I've submitted a few short stories to literary journals, they all were greeted with form rejections. So I'm going to need all the guidance I can get before the piece runs in the January issue. Potentially as the cover story, Erin told me casually during our first and, so far, only phone call. Which is why I'm terrified that my writing won't measure up.

At least composing the draft was easier than expected. My

@TheOtherLata tweets proved helpful in giving me a chronology of events to use as a starting point for recording my life over the past year. But to retell my story in detail also meant cataloging each of my deceptions, and the people I deceived. Rajeev, Keiko, and to a lesser extent, Anita, Zaila, David Jay, and the rest of the gang. None of them have reached out, nor have I tried to contact them.

For the past four weeks, the person I've spent the most time with is Other Lata. Not just in recounting how our paths crossed, but also in trying to dig up anything new about my nemesis. Besides going down internet rabbit holes that took me nowhere, I ventured into the city a few times. I made these trips with my copy of the police sketch that was made in the hours after Charmaine's party, a rendering based on my description of Other Lata. The drawing was an eerie match for her steely eyes and hard mouth, surprising me with its accuracy, as if the sketch artist had photocopied my memories. I also had the Facebook video saved to my phone, but that wasn't nearly as clear an image as the sketch. A sketch that led me to my biggest, and ultimately only, lead.

Which, if you can believe it, I shared with Marlena Santigold.

———

"Shuba? That's her real name?" Marlena studied the drawing, then looked at me, then back to the drawing. Her tiny porcelain cup of espresso sent curls of heat toward the ceiling.

"Shuba Shetty." Marlena's Park Avenue office was all light and glass, seemingly designed to transform sunrays into sparkling works of art. When I had sent her an apologetic email about ten days after Charmaine's party, taking full responsibility and pleading to not have my actions harm her relationship with Rajeev, she had surprised me by inviting me to her office. With her busy schedule, we didn't have a chance to meet until after Labor Day. In the weeks leading up to my visit with Marlena, I had visited every storefront within a three-mile radius of the Tellworth. And a few hours before our three p.m. appointment, I had struck gold. I was still buzzing from this breakthrough when I arrived at Marlena's, and it all came tumbling out not long after she ushered me inside.

"How did you find out?"

"There's a coffee cart on the corner of Worth Street and West Broadway, a few blocks from the Tellworth." While I had visited the area quite frequently, this had been my first time coming by during the morning rush, which was why I had finally spotted it. "I asked the coffee guy if he recognized the drawing, and he said, 'You know her? She owes me fifty dollars.'"

"Wow! You're quite the detective, Lata." Marlena beamed at me, more than I deserved.

"I don't know about that."

"What else did you learn?" Marlena's landline rang, and she pressed a button and silenced it.

"That she was a big flirt, and her flirting skills helped when she wanted a coffee but didn't have any money on her. Which seemed to be quite a lot. But one time the coffee guy was adamant and said 'No money, no coffee.' So Lata—I mean Shuba— went to fish her wallet out of her purse, but the strap broke and the purse fell to the ground, with all her belongings flying out. He helped her pick it all up." The coffee guy noted that Other Lata / Shuba had acted indignant, as if by asking her to pay for the coffee, he had caused her purse to break. She had snatched her things up in a huff, cursing him out as she left. As he closed up his cart later that day, the coffee guy saw a green-and-white card sticking out from under his tire. "It was an entry card for a building of some kind. And it had said her name was Shuba Shetty. He thought she would come back for it, but she never did. He never saw her again."

Marlena whistled. "That's a big lead, Lata. I'm impressed." I responded with a chagrined smile, not feeling worthy of any kind of praise, but lapping it up anyway. Her phone rang again, and this time she picked up and murmured into the receiver. I tried not to stare at her while she took the call, entranced by how she made a simple charcoal blouse seem extravagantly chic just by the mere act of wearing it. Not knowing why Marlena had summoned me to her office, I'd dressed as if going to a job interview, the same cream blazer, black silk top, and pencil skirt I had worn to my interview at Initiate PR. This was the ensemble that finally got me to unpack my suitcases in New Canaan, though wearing these clothes in front of Marlena made me feel foolish, as if I were playing the part of "Woman Who Has Her Shit Together." I kept my head low and picked at my cuticles as I listened to her speak, her voice soft and musical. When I heard the phone returned to its cradle, I looked up to see Marlena taking me in thoughtfully.

"Interesting you two don't share the same name."

"I'm sorry?"

"Lata now seems likely to be an alias. You might be the real Lata after all." Even though she said this warmly, I absorbed her words with a pang, as if I'd spotted a friend on the street and waved to say hello, but she hadn't noticed and had kept on walking. Why this would register as a small disappointment is something I'm still trying to figure out.

Even as her phone rang again, Marlena ignored it to tell me that the Tellworth was under fire for employing someone that had conned its elite clientele and evaded notice despite its stringent security and background checks for members and employees alike. As a result, she and many of her friends had canceled their memberships. Though I wasn't the Lata responsible, a wave of guilt swept through me anyway. It brought me back to the fact that I had no idea why Marlena wanted to meet with me. But I did have a specific reason for seeing her.

"I don't want to take up too much of your time. I know how busy you are." A triangle of light hit her desk, tracing a rainbow along its smooth surface. "I really want to apologize in person for my actions, Mrs. Santigold. I really admire all you stand for, and what MoonRose stands for." With a mixture of pride and embarrassment, I handed her a cashier's check for $7,000. The money came from selling most of my wardrobe, including all my shoplifted items, on Poshmark and Facebook Marketplace. "It's of course not what I had originally said I wanted to give to MoonRose, but I wanted to give *something*."

She opened her mouth to speak, but I hurried on, wanting to deliver the speech I had practiced in my head for the past few days. "I obviously can't follow through on the amount I initially pledged, as much as I'd like to. But if you'll allow me, I'd like to still make good on it by donating my time. Five thousand hours, five hundred thousand hours. Whatever you need, I want to help."

Marlena glanced at me, then picked up the check I had slid over. She had the most beautiful hands I'd ever seen, with the slim and elegant fingers of a classical pianist, and her pale white manicure flecked with shimmers of gold. Meanwhile, my nails had been bitten down to the quick. Writing made me a literal nail-biter, and all my self-doubt was channeled into my ragged cuticles.

"Thank you, Lata. I appreciate you would want to make things right with me." I nodded, not knowing what to say next. I wanted to ask about Rajeev and his runway show. But just thinking of Rajeev was a slap to my heart, because the runway show at the Lincoln Center tents hadn't materialized. Right before Labor Day weekend, he announced that rather than showing in the tents, he would instead have a private showing at the Santigold home. I couldn't bear to read any fashion blogs after that, too sick with regret that my actions had impacted the most important moment in his career. He had already been so stressed out, and then I had taken a bowling ball to all his anxieties and knocked him over with a strike. As I was about to excuse myself and thank her for her time, Marlena said my name again.

"But if you're really serious about making amends with MoonRose, then I'd like to discuss something with you."

Now that I've turned in the first draft of my Other Lata article to *Gotham*, I can focus on another email, this time from the employment office of the Santigold Foundation. It is the onboarding link to join the organization as a communications officer. The salary is only a bit more than what I earned at TriviaIQ. But I've never been happier to reenter the ranks of the employed, especially if it means that eventually I'll be able to move back to New York City.

What Marlena sees in me, I still can't even fathom. Despite the lies and the trouble my actions had inadvertently caused, the fact that an accomplished woman like her wants to hire me—it's honestly a little mind boggling. My parents have become obsessed with Marlena, going down their own internet rabbit holes, researching her and her foundation to better understand why one of the "Richie Riches" would be so generous. But really all I can do is prove to Marlena that her instincts were right.

Actually, Marlena's belief in me is the reason why there is a burgundy Salvatore Ferragamo shoebox on my desk, sealed with masking tape, an inscrutable word scrawled on the lid in black ink. Because when I told Marlena about how the coffee cart guy had found Shuba Shetty's entry card, I didn't mention that he had held on to it and sold it to me in exchange for the same amount Other Lata owed him. And after my appointment with Marlena, our meeting emboldened me to take the 7 train to Long Island City and visit the mysterious building, which turned out to be a dilapidated brick storage facility operating out of the dreary warehouse district. A storage facility where Shuba Shetty had rented a unit for several years before she abruptly stopped payment in August without claiming her belongings. Company policy instructed that the facility keep the contents of her unit for three months before disposal, but using a good chunk of my weekly unemployment benefits, I persuaded them to sell the items to me.

And weirdly, all that was in the storage unit were several empty cardboard boxes and this shoebox. Perhaps Other Lata took off with her things after hours and accidentally left it behind. And of course I should hand it over to the authorities.

Yet so far I've not been able to part with it. Or open it.

I've been staring at the shoebox for days, not sure if I want to know what I don't yet know about her.

24

Two Months Later

FOR A BRIEF MOMENT OR two, November in New York City really does feel like *When Harry Met Sally*. The weather is cool but not cold, perfect for scarves and tweed jackets and coffees held with leather gloves, with bright oranges and yellows crowding out the greenery. The fact that New York can't remain frozen in this moment but must eventually give way to the bare, leafless trees of January, all gray skies and twenty-degree temps that last from New Year's Day until the end of March, is a travesty that no one has ever tried to solve.

"New York needs to have Autumnland," I tell Zaila on a call while walking back from the Midtown DMV during my lunch break. "Like if Rye can have Playland, this city needs an amusement park permanently dedicated to the fall season. Could you imagine?"

Zaila gasps. "Like a year-round Stars Hollow! With pumpkin spice and hay bale mazes."

"Right?" I laugh. "I think we really have something here."

We had moved in together two weeks ago. She had broken it off with Nika for good in early October. Nika's brother Dan had been arrested in an undercover drug bust, and their powerful parents had leaned on the judge to get him off with just a few hours of community service. Zaila objected to how his privilege always guarded him from the consequences of his actions, Nika responded defensively, and what followed was a pained, prolonged discussion in which they realized their love was not strong enough to bridge the differences in how they viewed the world. Seeking a complete break from Nika and what she represented, Zaila decided it was time to stop depending on her mother and stepfather financially and fully strike out on her own. And so she moved out of Nika's modernist DUMBO penthouse and found a two-bedroom in Washington Heights. The only reason Zaila had even gotten in touch when the rest of our friend group went ice cold on me was that she was desperate for a roommate she could trust. Someone who wouldn't mind living way uptown and would thereby allow Zaila to bypass having to resort to the wilds of Craigslist to find someone to share a small but cozy apartment in the basement of a brownstone.

"At least I already know all the skeletons in your closet," Zaila had said to me at the time, after I greeted her phone call with a mixture of surprise and gratitude. "The fact you have a job and can afford to pay your half of the rent is even better." While I had been bounced from behind the velvet rope, Zaila had walked away willingly. Yet we were equally relieved to find that we could carve out a place for ourselves

outside of our former gilt-edged lives and have each other as
company.

Zaila and I chat a few more moments about what we
should make for dinner tonight, before collapsing into gig-
gles and just saying, "Eff it, we'll do takeout ramen again."
Our phone call has lasted long enough for me to traverse
ten congested city blocks uptown and arrive in Bryant Park.
Desperate for coffee, I'm thankful to notice the Starbucks
that sits kitty-corner from the park. It's rare that I go below
42nd Street these days, with my home in uptown Manhattan
and the MoonRose offices located at 76th and Madison. But
the need to renew my driver's license in person brought me
to Midtown Manhattan, where another lifetime ago I spent
nearly all my time. Ordering takeout ramen then too, but
with a different roommate. I haven't talked to Mimi in nearly
a year, and I keep putting off checking in with her. Deep
down I know she likely never wants to talk to me again, and
I don't begrudge her for it. I threw over our friendship to live,
in her words, like a *Gossip Girl* character, and there are some
betrayals you just don't move past.

During my walk uptown, the wind became ornery, causing
pedestrians to pull their jacket collars up and tug their hats
closer over their ears. So entering a busy Starbucks during
lunch hour, even though it is crowded and stuffy, feels welcome in comparison. As always whenever it comes time to
give my name to someone at a coffee shop or restaurant, I get
self-conscious. Will people hear me say "Lata" and think it's
the woman from the viral Twitter thread, an account that at
its peak amassed 2.3 million followers? Likely not. My story

is barely zeitgeisty anymore, since there have been no new developments to keep interest going. For now, everyone has moved on. But for how long?

The *Gotham* article is officially scheduled for the January issue, although whether it will be a cover story is still undecided. And since the article includes more details about the saga than I could share 140 characters at a time, and names some people while protecting the identities of others, I worry about the spotlight seeking me out again. Sometimes I want to email my editor and tell her, "Never mind, don't publish." Because after Erin the Editor returned my first draft with dozens of questions in the vein of "Can you give more details?" and "Why should we care?" I finally opened up Shuba Shetty's shoebox. And I quickly determined that while its contents wouldn't help the police track her down, they would help me finally write an article that Erin would approve of. (And I was right: she sent back a thx. looks good, which I received as giddily as if being showered in rose petals.)

I offer my name to the cashier, who of course barely registers a reaction to it. More people file inside, bringing the wind with them, and now this Starbucks is getting too crowded, and the air here is getting not just stuffier but also odd and unpleasant, like coffee beans mixed with unwashed socks. So I squeeze past muttering customers gathered around the pickup area so that I can claim a place at the picture window. But unfortunately the only free spot is right next to the door, which keeps ushering in shivering customers and cool blasts of air. A quick glimpse at my phone tells me that even if I take a cab, there is no way I'll make it back to work on time. Why can't I click my heels three times à la Dorothy and be instantly transported to the warm confines of the office? Or better yet, join Harry, Sally, and the Gilmore Girls in Autumnland?

The door keeps opening, and I tighten my light gray scarf closer to my neck, but it is too dismal and flimsy to protect me against the razor-sharp gusts. Note to self: it's time to upgrade to warmer accessor—

Wait. Is that Rajeev?

I can see, reflected in the window, the unmistakable silhouette of a man with his height and build, standing at the back of the cashier's line. I slowly wheel around, and there is Rajeev, cupping his hands over his mouth to warm them up. My whole body is startled. What do I do? Should I say hello? Do I have any right to?

The Starbucks is playing a mix of pop songs, old and new. At this very moment, it segues from Taylor Swift's "Red" to the Bangles' "Eternal Flame." Way too on the nose, Starbucks. But hearing this eighties pop song reminds me of another one I heard with Rajeev present, and how Belinda Carlisle's "Mad About You" inspired me to go for it and kiss him. The memory of that moment, the dazzling elation of feeling his lips on mine, the dark night sky populated with tiny bursts of fireworks as if celebrating with us, overwhelms me. As Susanna Hoffs sing-asks if you can hear her heart beating, I can hear mine, urging me forward. If I don't talk to him now, who knows if I'll ever get the chance again.

Before another person can stand behind Rajeev, I rush to the line and tap him on the shoulder. He spins around, and his eyes go wide. So wide, as if seeing a ghost. Well, this is going to be the chattiest, most profusely apologetic ghost he's ever met.

"Hi, yes, it's me. Please don't walk away. Just two minutes of your time, okay? And then you'll never have to see me again." I wind my hands in my thin, useless scarf. Rajeev has his collar up on his camel jacket and slowly nods as he folds it down.

"I was already here. I didn't follow you in." What a terrible way to start this conversation I've been rehearsing in my head since that August night at Sea Cove. "I never expected to run into you. I'm never even here! I work uptown. Maybe you know that already? With Marlena?"

He nods. His face is impassive. The line moves, and now he's only five people away from the cashier. The seconds are impatient. Susanna Hoffs is winding up her impassioned plea about her burning feeling.

So much of what I say comes out in a rush, spanning the entirety of the next song. I tell him about my conversation with Marlena and my donation to MoonRose, which, thanks to the magazine commission, now totals $10,000. That even though I can never honor my initial pledge to her, I am committed to volunteering the equivalent time and energy, in addition to the fact that I now had a job with the organization. But even with all of this, I realize that nothing will ever rectify how I personally hurt Rajeev with my lies, not just breaking his trust but also causing harm to his career. If he knows of any way I can make it right with him, I'll happily do it, with the understanding that I lost out on something special with the most incredible person I have ever known.

"The last thing I want to say," I add as the line inches

closer to the front, with only one person between him and the cashier, "is that you changed me for the better. There was more of that other Lata in me than I wanted to believe." I say this last part while finally making direct eye contact with him. His brown eyes are creased and sad, but at least he doesn't look away. "I never really thought that I was a bad person. But I was definitely a selfish one. Someone who wanted desperately to be liked and accepted and did some not good things just so I could fit into this idea of who I wanted to be. I could have justified all of it to myself forever, but being in the company of someone as principled as you . . ."

Rajeev is next in line. The person ordering ahead of him is asking about soy versus oat versus almond milk. I have a few more precious seconds.

I also have attracted the attention of nearly everyone in Starbucks.

Declaring yourself to the person you wronged means speaking as if trying to be heard over the roar of a hundred airplanes. At least it does for me. Which means some customers are whispering to each other while others are just downright staring, enjoying the spectacle of someone putting their heart on the line. As for Rajeev, his face is unreadable. Even if he never forgives me, I just want him to know this one thing.

"Seeing myself through your eyes changed me, Rajeev. And every day I'm working on being someone who can look at her reflection and like who she sees. Thank you for that. I couldn't imagine a greater gift. And it's my pledge to you, and myself, to make that count. To be someone who makes things better for others, just as you did for me."

"Next?" The cashier eyes us, and Rajeev hesitates. I totally sandbagged him. All he wanted was an espresso, and instead he got the weepy, mad declarations of an ex.

The Starbucks is filled with an expectant air, with the other customers watching us as if we were the climactic scene of a movie. The whole room goes absolutely still. Oh shit—there's no way I can embarrass Rajeev in such a public way again. I nod stupidly at him, give him a wave, ready to flee back into the windy, bustling streets.

And then a barista sharply calls out, "Latte for Lata?" Except the way she pronounces it, it comes out as "Lah-tah?" Observing everyone staring at us, she looks our way. "Is there a Lata here?"

I freeze. Rajeev freezes too. My gaze skitters past him to the scuffed floor. If only it would open up with a giant crack and swallow me whole, anything to spare him and me from this humil—

"Yes, she is." To my surprise, Rajeev steps out of line to pick up my coffee. As he hands it to me, he flashes me his sweet grin, the one that could halt world wars just from its sheer, pure goodness. I can't help it—I rush into his arms, and he embraces me back. Someone standing behind us asks, "Wait, is that the Lata girl from Twitter?"

No one responds to her question. Instead, still in Rajeev's arms, I blush as I hear everyone break out in applause.

25

Three More Months Later

THE LINCOLN CENTER TENTS ARE a madhouse of activity from the moment you step inside. I've seen several seasons of *Project Runway*, but even that show can't capture how frenzied the atmosphere feels within. The anticipation is wildly high for Rajeev's show, and I can't help but feel that I'm about 30 to 50 percent responsible.

My article was chosen as the *Gotham* cover story after all. The cover shows my face artfully obscured in shadow alongside an insert of Shuba Shetty from her police sketch. "THE TWO LATAS," the headline proclaims over our faces. I have fifteen copies, my parents have forty, and I always carry one issue with me wherever I go. Not to show it off, but to remind myself that after a lifetime of doubting my writing abilities, I had my work published by a high-profile publication. We all need touchstones to remind us *this is it, it's all happening.* And so even though this might scream that I'm an egomaniac who needs validation, I can't help needing to have it in my possession at all times. But it doesn't mean I want to talk about it or be recognized in public, especially right now. Not when today, finally, Rajeev G is showing his collection in an official Mercedes-Benz Fashion Week tent. Where he was always meant to be.

With five minutes before the show starts, I take my seat in the first row, near the model entrance, wearing a Zara black dress with gold chain detailing at the waist, paired with my beloved Sergio Rossi boots, the only item I didn't sell from my Mumbai socialite era. Across the runway and closer to the center is Marlena, and we wave at each other before several women converge on her to give air kisses. And just a few seats down from her are several fashion editors and celebrities who have decided to use the halo of their fame to illuminate Rajeev. In my immediate vicinity are a former Disney star turned in-demand cable TV actress, a daytime talk show host, and a pop star with the number two hit on the Billboard charts. My gratitude at seeing each one take their place as the cameras *pop, pop, pop* with flashes, their images soon to be disseminated worldwide, forever associated with this moment, is immense. And the weird thing is that a few cameras flash my way too. The article has officially been out for one month and eight days. To my mortification and my parents' strange delight, the story was briefly discussed on *The View* (again), *The Tonight Show*, and *Howard Stern*. The word "doppelganger" was thrown out liberally in these conversations, but that doesn't quite describe what Other Lata was to me, or me to her.

"Wow, they're taking your picture!" squeals Shalini, Rajeev's younger sister, who has just arrived along with her older sister, Malini.

I shake my head, embarrassed. "They take everyone's picture, we're in the front row." This is only my fourth time meeting Rajeev's sisters, but they are so playful and nosy in the way I imagine sisters are that I am delighted they've basically adopted me into their party of two.

"No, on the way I heard people talking about you!" Shalini replies cheerily. "That's the girl who wrote the article about going to rich-people parties and pretended to be rich too."

"Oh god." I mean, that is my story, but there's a lot more to it. Three thousand words, to be precise. But perhaps I'm naive to think everyone will read the whole thing. Two people who definitely did are the G Sisters, my nickname for the pair when chatting about them with Rajeev and Zaila. After the article came out, Shalini sent me a flurry of texts at odd hours with comments and questions overrun with exclamation points, while Malini wrote me a very sweet email saying how happy she was that "this Shuba character (if that's even her real name!?!) brought you and my brother together."

The lights dim right after the two take their seats, a golden light illuminating the runway as the tent thrums with jazzy techno beats. My excitement at seeing Rajeev's show has me nearly bouncing out of my chair. I've purposely avoided knowing a single thing about what he's been working on, wanting my first time seeing the collection to happen in the tent. Yet my bubbly anticipation is undercut with dark currents of anxiety and remorse. Because during his private showing hosted by Marlena in September, he had only fifteen looks on view. Some he simply hadn't completed on time, while others didn't meet his standards. And then there were the ones he excluded because they had been inspired by me and my "free-spirited" behavior.

He confessed this as we were lying together in his bed in an echo of our Fourth of July sleepover. But this time, we were naked. Ten days after our Starbucks reunion, we had decided to start dating again. And for us, dating meant that we needed to finally have sex. After all, we met in September 2013 and had our first date in July 2014. We had been long overdue. (And it was definitely worth the wait.)

"I'm sorry about that, Lata." We were big spooning and little spooning, and so his words were soft and low against my ear, while his body satisfactorily subsumed mine. "I was being childish, trying to erase you in that way."

"You had every right." My voice went high pitched and teary, my throat burning with self-recrimination. "I'm the one who's sorr—"

"Beep." He briefly lifted his arm off of me and glanced at his watch. "You've hit the number of times you can say the word 'sorry' in twenty-four hours." Rajeev chuckled, then pulled me in closer to him. "Seriously, no more sorries. I'm just happy to have this second shot to show at the tents in February. And that is what I'm focusing on."

Rajeev's forgiveness of my transgressions hadn't eased my conscience, but it did make it easier to reconnect with some of our original friend group. Keiko had moved to London in January after receiving a promotion, but we texted daily, if not hourly. I met with Micheline for dinner a few times and remained Facebook friends with Anita, David Jay, and Kingsley. Yet the festering guilt remained.

"It's just that I know how hard you've worked. To know I was the reason it didn't happen..."

"You have to let it go." Rajeev tenderly kissed my shoulder, and I turned my small spoon self to face him.

"Really?" I wanted to, so badly.

"Really. The past can't be changed. All you can do is go forward." I now knew he was thinking about his family. His father was a rageful alcoholic, and his mother perpetually enabled her husband, even to the detriment of Rajeev and his siblings. As adults, the three of them cut off their parents and formed their own family unit, not caring how this estrangement looked to those in their tight-knit Indian community. They saved themselves, with no regrets.

It showed an impressive amount of strength on all their parts, but their situation wasn't comparable to mine. Not when I was the transgressor.

Rajeev must have seen this dark cloud of thought settling over me, because he hooked his arm around my waist and drew me close so that our hearts were aligned, then arrayed a line of kisses along my neck. Our bodies took over then, and we gave into each other for a second time. (This was when he noticed my tristate tattoo—"Oh ho, what's this?"—and outlined its borders with his tongue.) But afterward, wrapped up in his arms, I still couldn't settle into the bliss of finally being with him. It felt like standing on a rug and sensing there were invisible hands ready to rip it out from underneath you at any moment.

"I'm sorry. I just don't get how you can get over what I did." I broke away from him and rose up from bed into a kneeling position, hugging a pillow to my chest. "Aren't relationships built on trust? And I broke ours from the get-go." I wasn't just trying to protect his heart anymore, but mine too. If we failed a second time, I wouldn't be able to take it.

With a sigh, he sat up too. "To be honest, knowing the whole story helps. I mean, the Other Lata part of it all. Now I feel like I'm finally getting to know you." He leaned over and brushed a lock of hair from my forehead. "Out of everything that happened, our connection has always been real. So think of it as starting over from scratch. We're a blank page, and we're going to write our future together." After a beat, he groaned. "Too cheesy, right?"

"On a scale from cheddar to brie, I'd say that was pretty gouda." I playfully tapped him with the pillow.

He laugh-snorted, then tackled me to the bed . . . and, well, you get the rest.

But as Rajeev's preparations for the February show accelerated, so did my self-flagellation. Because no matter how Zen Rajeev was about this, it didn't erase the fact that my actions had knocked him over so badly that he had canceled his first tent show. What if there had been no Marlena, who believed in him and continued underwriting him? Would Rajeev be so forgiving then?

These are the unrelenting thoughts that keep me grounded

in the quicksand, not completely ready to let myself off the hook.

———

Rajeev's collection is as dazzling as I expected. The initial looks are slouchy and comfortable, slacks and jersey skirts and cozy knitwear, but as the music transitions from lo-fi to harder edged, the clothes take on more structure and intricate design work and include several gowns that seem destined for the red carpet. I spy one actress take a photo of an elegant swath of aubergine silk and mouth to her seatmate, "Oscars."

Midway through the show a model struts down the runway in a stylish blazer-esque minidress, which seems to be a lush chestnut faux fur. And unlike the rest of the models, who sport strappy black stilettos, the faux-fur model wears pink heels! I don't think it's possible to stop smiling.

The G Sisters are oohing and aahing over each look, and I spontaneously grab Shalini's hand because I am just so happy watching them take delight and pride in their beloved brother's work. So I don't immediately notice how each model's hair has a little more oomph and volume, but when I do, I take it as another example of Rajeev injecting whimsy into his work. Once I see the final model sporting a giant beehive and Saira Banu–esque eyeliner, I finally register this one last personal tribute to my summer of Other Lata. I stand up and applaud, hollering and laughing and not caring about the cascade of camera phone flashes that burst around me. As the model with the beehive sashays down the runway and exits the stage, I have this thought and decide I must believe it.

Our story started with Other Lata, but where it goes from here is up to us.

The lights come up, and all the models walk out one by one, with Rajeev appearing at the end to take a shy bow. The G Sisters and I whoop even louder, and there are wet marks on their faces and I'm crying too. How often do you get front row seats to a loved one's absolute triumph?

Yet even in the midst of Rajeev's triumph and the lingering glory of mine, I do not forget how much is owed to Marlena, beaming on the opposite side of the runway, raising her bejeweled arms in rhythmic applause. She offered me a job when I was a pariah; she was the major financial backer of Rajeev's fashion line. We both worked hard and deserved our due, especially Rajeev. But still, it's hard not to feel conflicted about her role in our professional lives. She is not a fairy godmother in couture, but a powerful woman who belongs to one of the richest families in New York City.

Same with Charmaine. He showed me a huge kindness throughout the saga, and I said as much in my *Gotham* article. But I also mentioned the circumstances of how Charmaine and I had become entangled: the stolen Rolex Prince, which I had forgotten Charmaine had never told his family about. Once the article came out, I received a letter from Charmaine's lawyer notifying me legal action would be taken if I spoke about him again in the media or came within five hundred feet of Charmaine or any member of the Von Bon family. Perhaps Charmaine had become embarrassed that it was now public knowledge he lost a family heirloom to Other Lata. Equally likely is that he cannot even risk sending me so much as a text message without incurring his family's wrath—and potentially losing his share of the enormous family fortune.

After being at Other Lata's mercy last year, I am leery of any puppet strings. Having been inside the circles of wealth and power has me wanting to construct a moat around me and raise the drawbridge. Because in this world, pure benevolence is a fairy tale.

Rajeev should, and likely will, continue his professional relationship with Marlena. My gratitude for Marlena will always be immense, but I'm at work on a five-year plan that does not include staying employed by the Santigold Foundation. I can't pursue a future while looking over my shoulder, awaiting the moment the string is yanked and I must do what is asked. Other Lata taught me that.

I will need the reminder, though. So I'm going to get a new tattoo, on my right forefinger, of the number five. Five as in five-year plan—the future is not promised and goals are not yet reached, and I need to keep thinking ahead and reevaluate what I want every five years. My fairy godmother must always be myself.

"I'm not sure who I'm happier for, Rajeev or you two!" I say to both sisters once the show officially ends. The audience leaps up, and just as there was a mad dash to enter the tent, now there is a race to exit as soon as possible. "Thanks for letting me sit with you."

"Sit with us? You're the celebrity!" Shalini says, motioning toward the people taking my picture. A ponytailed brunette holding a mini-recorder is pushing her way through the scrum toward me, her eyes locking with mine.

"Do you find all this weird?" Malini says, linking her arm through mine.

"The weirdest."

When first arriving at the tent, I was able to avoid the press because I skipped the step-and-repeat to shelter backstage, sitting in a corner, trying my best not to get a sneak peek at any of the looks. Instead I scrolled through my emails, rereading each one sent by production companies who were eager to turn "The Two Latas" into a feature film. All seventeen of them.

And I've said no to each and every one.

Rajeev and Zaila and even my parents said I should have given these offers more thought. And the pragmatic part of me, the one who is still worried about her sizable debt and doesn't want to live with a roommate for the rest of her life, is the one who revisits these emails, bursting with praise for my article and how they would love to discuss taking my story to the screen. I could have flown out to Los Angeles, let them invite me to executive boardrooms and fancy restaurants, and then asked them the only question that mattered to me. But I thought I would save us all some time by putting it in an email instead.

"Can we cast Indian American actresses to play both Latas?"

The responses were the same. "We see this movie as an awards play," or "We want this to be a major crowd pleaser," or "We would love to cast a movie star like Jennifer Lawrence or Emma Stone."

"Is that a no?"

No. No no no no no no no.

And so my answer to each of them is always no in return.

I'm holding out for the day that someone sees the story of myself and Other Lata not as something that can so easily be transposed onto the shoulders of glamorous white actresses. But as a story worth telling onscreen because it is *our* story and should be told by people that look like us. It's what I owe Other Lata and myself.

Her name might be Shuba Shetty (or not—she might have multiple aliases), but to me she will always be Other Lata. And my relationship to her changed once I finally opened her shoebox, one week before my article deadline. Inside was a random assortment of objects that I surmised were childhood treasures: a Ring Pop, still in its packaging. A two-dollar bill. A Hello Kitty pencil box that contained three unused pencils and a green eraser in the shape of Keroppi's head. A 14-karat gold necklace with a locket that showed a baby photo, bountiful cheeks and blond ringlets. A silver ring blackened by age, a dusty garnet at the center.

And a photograph. It showed a bearded man and a little girl standing in front of a station wagon with suitcases strapped onto the roof. The man was dressed in a handyman uniform, and the girl was in pigtails and sneakers. The girl's grimace, downturned and defensive, matched my memory of the woman in the valet uniform. The photograph was also creased in the corners, as if it was held often, and not carefully with pinched fingers, but cradled in a palm.

At the bottom of the box was a diary whose cover showed a

unicorn floating lazily in a pink-purple sky. Each diary entry was a list, all written in the bubble-type lettering of a young girl on the verge of tweenhood. There were twenty-three lists in total, each starting with an underlined name and then an inventory of sorts: movies and song titles, nail polish colors and street addresses. And also, observations. Angela smiles every time a certain boy's name is mentioned, Lola only wears clothes from Hollister and Tommy Hilfiger, Swapna's family spends every Christmas in Hawaii, CJ's most prized possession is her grandmother's locket. The final name was scratched out venomously with a black marker, only the tail of a *y* visible through all the scratches. The last entry on that girl's list wasn't a checklist item, but a denunciation in red marker: *IDIOT BITCH.*

I no longer have the shoebox, since I handed it over to the detectives investigating her case. They weren't happy with me for opening it, even though I had worn gloves while handling its contents. But after dusting it all for fingerprints, they found none. That's how careful and scrupulous she was with even her most private possessions.

"I think our lives collided because we were both trying to find escape routes from our shame," I wrote in my article after noting my discovery of Other Lata's belongings. "Never feeling accepted, never feeling good enough. We bought into the idea that luxury and wealth would paper over our wounds. But her pain was far greater than mine. And so it drove her to do more extreme things."

What I didn't write in my article, but what I think of often, is how much Other Lata must have hated me. Because we had both put on the Lata Murthy as Mumbai socialite persona to infiltrate a world that wouldn't otherwise accept us. But by virtue of her scheme, Other Lata kept herself on the outside, because she was constantly studying and judging people so she could con them. And she created Lata the Mumbai social-ite out of spite for those she was trying to deceive, mocking their ignorance by creating such a ridiculously fake persona. But I sought only belonging and was surprisingly welcomed in among them. So Other Lata must have despised that I took that persona and made it real, real enough to gain friends, real enough to even win someone's heart.

Yes, she tried to ruin my life. Despite that, all I feel is com-passion for her.

This is what is on my mind when the ponytailed brunette and two other reporters approach me to ask questions that will appear in Fashion Week roundups on websites and blogs the following day.

"Where do you think the other Lata is now?" asks Ponytail.

"I tried my best to find her, but I have no idea." The G Sis-ters are on their phones, each emanating a slight impatience, and I almost tell them to go see their brother without me. But I don't want to be left alone with these women and their matching harried expressions.

"Do you think she's read your article?" asks the second one, her iPhone hovering just under my nose.

"I hope so." Not that I would ever say so while being interviewed, but I do often wonder if Other Lata will read my article and reach out. I don't know what I'd expect her to say. Probably that I got the story all wrong. Perhaps she's somewhere across the country, working on her own version of what happened, in which I'm the incompetent villain and she's the charismatic hero. "But I doubt it."

"If you could talk to her now, what would you want her to know?" The third one is squeezed so close to me that I can see the sweat collecting at her temples. She seems the least experienced of the three, the one who desperately needs a good quote for her editor.

"She was an interesting person to experience. I don't condone what she did, but I'm glad she exists in the world. She was always unapologetically true to herself. In that way, we should all be more like her."

I hadn't planned on saying this final thing out loud, but I saw myself in the young reporter, and so I gave her the one true sentiment I could communicate that hadn't already been said in my article. Based on the reporter's beaming face, I gave her something to work with. Although it might blow back on me—"Lata Murthy Praises Lata the Con Woman: 'We Should All Be More Like Her'" is a likely headline to greet me in tomorrow's newspapers—I don't really care. One thing the whole saga has taught me is that the Other Lata story will forever be associated with me, for better or worse. I told my story, and other people will decide how to tell mine based on whatever purposes they have. To try to control or worry about that would be crazy making, especially since I'm the kind of public figure destined to be in "Where Are They Now?" articles ten years from now.

I'm a blip in the news. But my story continues.

As Malini, Shalini, and I move through the masses to go

backstage and congratulate the man of the hour, there's some movement in my peripheral vision that catches my eye. A shadow, or something hazy I can't quite pin down. I keep trying to turn my head to see what is moving just beyond me, but it's too hectic and loud, and so I finally just focus on getting backstage so I can finally see Rajeev.

His sisters run up to congratulate him first, and I take photos of them hugging him and festooning him with bouquets. Stupidly, I haven't brought him anything congratulatory. When it is my time to throw my arms around him, the first words out of my mouth are an apology.

"The fact that you're here is all that matters to me," he says as he gives me a tight squeeze. "Did you like the show?"

"Rajeev, I loved it! The beehive, everything! You're so amazing."

He squeezes tighter, and as he does, it is like the volume in the room decreases, and it's just the two of us listening to each other breathe. In his arms, with his sisters close by, and all of us giddy over his huge achievement, there is little else I could want in the world that would give me this kind of infinite happiness.

I peck Rajeev on the cheek, then we part as more people come up to congratulate him. It's a mob scene back here, but in the most pleasant way. Models are chatting while undressing and returning to their street clothes, hair stylists and makeup artists are packing up their gear, friends and friends of friends are milling about, exchanging pleasantries and air kisses. And I'm on the lookout for Zaila and Keiko. Keiko decided to fly in at the last minute from London to make the show, and Rajeev snagged them the last two tickets that were left, in the last row. I can't wait to see them both, so I'm hopping up and down, trying to look past the heads and through the bodies of those congregated back here, glancing at my phone all the while to see if my friends are going to text me their location.

And that's when I see her.

Other Lata.

She stares back at me, slightly startled, looking more rumpled than I have ever seen her. But unmistakably her. And I surprise myself by waving at her. She waves back. My head jerks back at seeing this, and so does hers.

Then the crowd briefly parts, and where I expect to see Other Lata is only a full-length mirror.

I am looking at my own reflection.

"Who are you waving at?" Rajeev asks, appearing at my side. "Are Zaila and Keiko here yet?"

Before I can respond, he bends down and picks something off the ground. It's my magazine cover story, which fell out of my purse when we embraced earlier.

"I think you dropped this." He holds it up and looks at the cover with pride. "Look at what you did."

I spin around, pointing at the RAJEEV G / NYFW 2015 sign hanging over my shoulder. "And look at what you did!" We laugh, and it's a weepy joyous laughter, the exhalation of something we wanted actually coming true. And amid the noise and heat and Zaila and Keiko calling our names, just steps away from reaching us, a wave of euphoria overwhelms me. I envelop him in a hug, and he responds by wrapping his arms around my waist, the copy of my magazine still rolled up in his grasp.

"Our story begins now." I look at him expectantly, hoping he can read into those words all I'm ready to let go of, so we can move forward together.

Rajeev's eyes widen and he nods. "Now," he repeats with a smile.

I know I said I had experienced an infinite happiness before, but this moment, the two of us surrounded by his work while he holds mine, and the people we love close by, this is it. This is that feeling.

I think of all the other Latas, the past versions of me, the anxious child and the restless teenager and the despairing one who lived in Hell's Kitchen and the one from three months ago, all their individual anxieties and dreams. And I picture them all raising their heads in unison for the briefest of moments, as if they could sense my overwhelming love and gratitude for each of them. *Keep going*, I urge. There is a slight nod, echoing across ages and decades. And then I snap back into the present. But by standing here and knowing my future awaits me with every breath I take, I know they all heard me.

Acknowledgments

To be an author is to always be awed by and appreciative of how much work it takes to transform words on a page into the book you're holding now. This is my third time with the wonderful team at Grand Central, and it's been a true pleasure to work with them again: Danielle Thomas, Andy Dodds, Lauren Sum, Theresa DeLucci, Leena Oropez, Liz Connor, Rebecca Holland, Luria Rittenberg, Janice Lee, Xian Lee, Amy Quinn, Maisa Nammari, plus Sarah Kellogg for yet another remarkable cover design. The fact that my books are easily identifiable because of her work is an unexpected gift. And, of course, my incredible editor, Karen Kosztolnyik, who always brings out the absolute best in me and my writing.

I'm beyond fortunate to have Andrea Somberg as my literary agent. I truly think it is every author's dream to have someone as generous and thoughtful as her. My sincere thanks to Andrea as well as my wonderful TV/film agent Rich Green, and everyone at Harvey Klinger Literary Agency and The Gotham Group.

If a book exists in the world, it's likely the author had some very supportive people in her orbit. My thanks to all my friends, whether we've known each other for ages or had the pleasure to meet recently. And my utmost gratitude to Mayuri Amuluru Chandra, Juhea Kim, Sailaja Suresh, and Qian Julie Wang, who responded immediately, and with tremendously helpful feedback, when I put out a call for readers with very short notice; Ash Davidson, Adele Myers, Coco Mellors, Caroline Frost Szymanski, and Karen Winn for our restorative Zoom calls, and Juhea for introducing me to such a lovely group; Julia Bartz, Saumya Dave, and Stephanie Wrobel for monthly meetups that always include excellent advice, even better gossip, and of course, breakfast burritos; my fellow pop culture "ministers" Jennifer Armstrong, Erin Carlson, Saul Austerlitz, and Thea Glassman, proud of us for taking a leap together to try something new; Daphne Palasi Andreades, Annika Sharma, and Swati Teerdhala for their invaluable camaraderie in matters of writing and in life; and Jessica Wells-Hasan, for being a constant source of optimism, encouragement, and strength.

Books exist for readers, and my deepest appreciation to those who read this novel or my previous ones, and to librarians and booksellers who champion books and provide community. I also want to thank Anna Dragon and Erin Harper for their generous donations to the We Need Diverse Books and Worcester Public Library fundraisers, both of whom won the opportunity to have characters named after them in this novel. (In the case of Anna, she asked that a character be given the name Alissa Carroll.)

I truly lucked out in the family department and am so thankful to my parents, Dattatreya Kumar and Shuba; my siblings, Pavan and Anjali; and my niece and grandmother, both named Leela. (And because I'm amused this continues to come up in conversation, even as recently as a few weeks ago, here is my official thank-you to Mom, Dad, Pav, and Anj for each taking turns picking me up at five a.m. when I hosted a late-night college radio show. My four listeners appreciated it, as did I.)

And to Corey: Twenty years ago I fell in love twice. The first time was when I moved to New York City, and the second time was when I met you. And after all this time, I'm more in love than ever. Marriage and romance are not concepts often thought of in the same sentence, but they are for me, because of you.

About the Author

Kirthana Ramisetti is the author of *Advika and the Hollywood Wives* and *Dava Shastri's Last Day*, a *Good Morning America* Book Club selection optioned for television by Max. Her novels have received acclaim from *TIME*, *Cosmopolitan*, the *Washington Post*, *BuzzFeed*, Associated Press, and more. Besides cofounding the newsletter Ministry of Pop Culture, her writing has appeared in many publications including the *New York Times*, the *Wall Street Journal*, *The Atlantic*, *Elle*, and *Salon*. She lives in New York City.